Essex*Works.*

· quality of life

D0297481

Please return this book on or before the date shown above. To renew go to www.essex.gov.uk/libraries, ring 0845 603 7628 or go to any Essex library.

Essex County Council

I AM
HALF-SICK
of SHADOWS

...

I AM
HALF-SICK
of SHADOWS

A Flavia de Luce Novel

ALAN BRADLEY

◆ ◆ ◆

First published in Great Britain in 2011 by Orion Books,
an imprint of The Orion Publishing Group Ltd
Orion House, 5 Upper Saint Martin's Lane
London WC2H 9EA

An Hachette UK Company

1 3 5 7 9 10 8 6 4 2

A CIP catalogue record for this book is
available from the British Library.

ISBN (Hardback) 978 1 4091 1420 8
ISBN (Export Trade Paperback) 978 1 4091 1421 5

Printed in Great Britain by CPI Group (UK) Ltd, Croydon, CR0 4YY

The Orion Publishing Group's policy is to use papers that are natural,
renewable and recyclable products and made from wood grown in sustainable
forests. The logging and manufacturing processes are expected to
conform to the environmental regulations of the country of origin.

www.orionbooks.co.uk

For Shirley

. . . She hath no loyal knight and true,
  The Lady of Shalott.

But in her web she still delights
To weave the mirrored magic sights,
For often through the silent nights
A funeral, with plumes and lights,
  And music, went to Camelot;
Or, when the moon was overhead,
Came two young lovers lately wed.
"I am half-sick of shadows," said
  The Lady of Shalott.

ALFRED TENNYSON
"The Lady of Shalott"

·ONE·

TENDRILS OF RAW FOG floated up from the ice like ago-
nized spirits departing their bodies. The cold air was a
hazy, writhing mist.

Up and down the long gallery I flew, the silver blades
of my skates making the sad scraping sound of a butcher's
knife being sharpened energetically on stone. Beneath
the icy surface, the intricately patterned parquet of the
hardwood floor was still clearly visible—even though its
colours *were* somewhat dulled by diffraction.

Overhead, the twelve dozen candles I had pinched
from the butler's pantry and stuffed into the ancient
chandeliers flickered madly in the wind of my swift passage. Round and round the room I went—round and
round and up and down. I drew in great lungfuls of the
biting air, blowing it out again in little silver trumpets of
condensation.

When at last I came skidding to a stop, chips of ice flew up in a breaking wave of tiny coloured diamonds.

It had been easy enough to flood the portrait gallery: An India-rubber garden hose snaked in through an open window from the terrace and left running all night had done the trick—that, and the bitter cold which, for the past fortnight, had held the countryside in its freezing grip.

Since nobody ever came to the unheated east wing of Buckshaw anyway, no one would notice my improvised skating rink—not, at least, until springtime, when it melted. No one, perhaps, but my oil-painted ancestors, row upon row of them, who were at this moment glaring sourly down at me from their heavy frames in icy disapproval of what I had done.

I blew them a loud, echoing raspberry tart and pushed off again into the chill mist, now doubled over at the waist like a speed skater, my right arm digging at the air, my pigtails flying, my left hand tucked behind my back as casually as if I were out for a Sunday stroll in the country.

How lovely it would be, I thought, *if some fashionable photographer such as Cecil Beaton should happen by with his camera to immortalize the moment.*

"Carry on just as you were, dear girl," he would say. "Pretend I'm not here." And I would fly again like the wind round the vastness of the ancient panelled portrait gallery, my passage frozen now and again by the pop of a discreet flashbulb.

Then, in a week or two, there I would be, in the pages

of *Country Life* or *The Illustrated London News*, caught in mid-stride—frozen forever in a determined and forward-looking slouch.

"*Dazzling . . . delightful . . . de Luce,*" the caption would read. "*Eleven-year-old skater is poetry in motion.*"

"Good lord!" Father would exclaim. "It's Flavia!

"Ophelia! Daphne!" he would call, flapping the page in the air like a paper flag, then glancing at it again, just to be sure. "Come quickly. It's Flavia—your sister."

At the thought of my sisters I let out a groan. Until then I hadn't much been bothered by the cold, but now it gripped me with the sudden force of an Atlantic gale: the bitter, biting, paralysing cold of a winter convoy—the cold of the grave.

I shivered from shoulders to toes and opened my eyes.

The hands of my brass alarm clock stood at a quarter past six.

Swinging my legs out of bed, I fished for my slippers with my toes, then, bundling myself in my bedding—sheets, quilt, and all—heaved out of bed and, hunched over like a corpulent cockroach, waddled towards the windows.

It was still dark outside, of course. At this time of year the sun wouldn't be up for another two hours.

The bedrooms at Buckshaw were as vast as parade squares—cold, drafty spaces with distant walls and shadowy perimeters, and of them all, mine, in the far south corner of the east wing, was the most distant and the most desolate.

Because of a long and rancorous dispute between two of my ancestors, Antony and William de Luce, about the sportsmanship of certain military tactics during the Crimean War, they had divided Buckshaw into two camps by means of a black line painted across the middle of the foyer: a line which each of them had forbidden the other to cross. And so, for various reasons—some quite boring, others downright bizarre—at the time when other parts of the house were being renovated during the reign of King George V, the east wing had been left largely un-heated and wholly abandoned.

The superb chemical laboratory built by his father for my great-uncle Tarquin, or "Tar," de Luce had stood forgotten and neglected until I had discovered its treasures and made it my own. With the help of Uncle Tar's meticulously detailed notebooks and a savage passion for chemistry that must have been born in my blood, I had managed to become quite good at rearranging what I liked to think of as the building blocks of the universe.

"Quite good?" a part of me is saying. "Merely 'quite good'? Come off it, Flavia, old chum! You're a bloody marvel, and you know it!"

Most chemists, whether they admit it or not, have a favourite corner of their craft in which they are forever tinkering, and mine is poisons.

While I could still become quite excited by recalling how I had dyed my sister Feely's knickers a distinctive Malay yellow by boiling them in a solution of lead acetate, followed by a jolly good stewing in a solution of potassium chromate, what really made my heart leap up with joy was my ability to produce a makeshift but handy poison by scraping the vivid green verdigris from the copper float-ball of one of Buckshaw's Victorian toilet tanks.

I bowed to myself in the looking glass, laughing aloud at the sight of the fat white slug-in-a-quilt that bowed back at me.

I leapt into my cold clothing, shrugging on at the last minute, on top of everything else, a baggy grey cardigan I had nicked from the bottom drawer of Father's dresser. This lumpy monstrosity—swarming with khaki and maroon diamonds, like an overbaked rattlesnake—had been knitted for him the previous Christmas by his sister, Aunt Felicity.

"Most thoughtful of you, Lissy," Father had said, deftly dodging any outright praise of the ghastly garment itself. When I noticed in August that he still hadn't worn the thing, I considered it fair game and it had, since the onset of cold weather, become my favourite.

The sweater didn't fit me, of course. Even with the sleeves rolled up I looked like a baggy monkey picking bananas. But to my way of thinking, at least in winter, woolly warmth trumps freezing fashion any day of the week.

I have always made it a point never to ask for clothing for Christmas. Since it's a dead cert that you'll get it anyway, why waste a wish?

Last year I had asked Father Christmas for some badly needed bits of laboratory glassware—had even gone to the trouble of preparing an itemized list of flasks, beakers, and graduated test tubes, which I tucked carefully under my pillow and, by the Lord Harry! he had brought them!

Feely and Daffy didn't believe in Father Christmas, which, I suppose, is precisely the reason he always brought them such dud gifts: scented soap, generally, and dressing gowns and slipper sets that looked and felt as if they had been cut from Turkey carpet.

Father Christmas, they had told me, again and again, was for children.

"He's no more than a cruel hoax perpetrated by parents who wish to shower gifts upon their icky offspring without having to actually touch them," Daffy had insisted last year. "He's a myth. Take my word for it. I am, after all, older than you, and I know about these things."

Did I believe her? I wasn't sure. When I was able to get away on my own and think about it without tears springing to my eyes, I had applied my rather considerable deductive skills to the problem, and come to the conclusion that my sisters were lying. *Someone*, after all, had brought the glassware, hadn't they?

There were only five possible human candidates. My father, Colonel Haviland de Luce, was penniless, and was therefore out of the question, as was my mother, Harriet, who had died in a mountaineering accident when I was no more than a baby.

Dogger, who was Father's general roustabout and jack-of-all-trades, simply hadn't the resources of mind, body, or finances to lug round lavish gifts secretly by night in a drafty and decaying country house. Dogger had been a prisoner of war in the Far East, where he had suffered so awfully that his brain had remained connected to those horrors by an invisible elastic cord—a cord that was sometimes still given a jerk by cruel Fate, usually at the most inopportune moments.

"'E 'ad to eat rats!" Mrs. Mullet had told me, wide-eyed in the kitchen. "Rats, fancy! They 'ad to fry 'em!"

With everyone in the household disqualified for one reason or another as the Bringer of Gifts, that left only Father Christmas.

He would be coming again in less than a week and, in order to settle the question for once and for all, I had long ago laid plans to trap him.

Scientifically.

Birdlime, as any practical chemist will tell you, can be easily manufactured by boiling the middle bark of holly for eight or nine hours, burying it under a stone for a fort-night, and then, when it is disinterred, washing and pul-verizing it in running river water and leaving it to ferment. The stuff had been used for centuries by bird-sellers, who had smeared it on branches to trap the songbirds they sold in the city streets.

The great Sir Francis Galton had described a method of manufacturing the stuff in his book *The Art of Travel; or, Shifts and Contrivances Available in Wild Countries*, a signed copy of which I had found among a heavily under-lined set of his works in Uncle Tar's library. I had followed Sir Francis's instructions to the letter, lugging home in midsummer armloads of holly from the great oaks that grew in Gibbet Wood, and boiling the broken branches over a laboratory Bunsen burner in a stew pot borrowed—

without her knowledge—from Mrs. Mullet. During the final stages, I had added a few chemical twists of my own to make the pulverized resin a hundred times more sticky than the original recipe. Now, after six months of preparation, my concoction was powerful enough to stop a Gabon gorilla in its tracks, and Father Christmas—if he existed—wouldn't stand a chance. Unless the jolly old gentleman just happened to be travelling with a handy bottle of sulphuric ether, $(C_2H_5)2O$, to dissolve the birdlime, he was going to stay stuck to our chimney pot forever—or until I decided to set him free.

It was a brilliant plan. I wondered why no one had thought of it before.

Peering out through the curtains, I saw that it had snowed in the night. Driven by the north wind, white flakes were still swirling madly in the light of the downstairs kitchen window.

Who could be up at such an hour? It was too early for Mrs. Mullet to have walked from Bishop's Lacey.

And then I remembered!

Today was the day the intruders were arriving from London. How could I ever have forgotten such a thing?

It had been more than a month ago—on November 11, in fact, that grey and subdued autumn day upon which everyone in Bishop's Lacey had mourned in silence all those whom they had lost in the wars—that Father had summoned us to the drawing room to break the grim news.

"I'm afraid I have to tell you that the inevitable has

happened," he said at last, turning away from the window, out of which he had been staring morosely for a quarter of an hour.

"I needn't remind you of our precarious financial prospects . . ."

He said this forgetting the fact that he reminded us daily—sometimes twice in an hour—of our dwindling reserves. Buckshaw had belonged to Harriet, and when she had died without leaving a will (Who, after all, could even imagine that someone so brimming over with life could meet her end on a mountain in far-off Tibet?) the troubles had begun. For ten years now, Father had been going through the courtly steps of the "Dance of Death," as he called it, with the grey men from His Majesty's Board of Inland Revenue.

Yet in spite of the mounting pile of bills on the foyer table, and in spite of the increasing telephonic demands from coarse-voiced callers from London, Father had somehow managed to muddle through.

Once, because of his phobia about "the instrument," as he called the telephone, I had answered one of these brash calls myself, bringing it to rather an amusing end by pretending to speak no English.

When the telephone had jangled again a minute later, I picked up the receiver at once, then jiggled my finger rapidly up and down on the cradle.

"Hello?" I had shouted. "Hello? Hello? I'm sorry—Can't hear you. Frightful connection. Call back some other day."

On the third ring, I had taken the receiver off the hook and spat into the mouthpiece, which began at once to give off an alarming crackling noise.

"Fire," I had said in a dazed and vaguely monotonous voice. "The house is in flames . . . the walls and the floor. I'm afraid I must ring off now. I'm sorry, but the firemen are hacking at the window."

The bill collector had not called back.

"My meetings with the Estate Duty Office," Father was saying, "have come to nothing. It is all up with us now."

"But Aunt Felicity!" Daffy protested. "Surely Aunt Felicity—"

"Your aunt Felicity has neither the means nor the inclination to alleviate the situation. I'm afraid she's—"

"Coming down for Christmas," Daffy interrupted. "You could ask her while she's here!"

"No," Father said sadly, shaking his head. "All means have failed. The dance is over. I have been forced at last to give up Buckshaw—"

I let out a gasp.

Feely leaned forward, her brow furrowed. She was chewing at one of her fingernails: unheard of in someone as vain as she.

Daffy looked on through half-shut eyes, inscrutable as ever.

"—to a film studio," Father went on. "They will arrive in the week before Christmas, and will remain in full possession until their work is complete."

"But what about us?" Daffy asked. "What's to become of us?"

"We shall be allowed to remain on the premises," Father replied, "provided we keep to our quarters and don't interfere in any way with the company's work at hand. I'm sorry, but those were the best terms I could manage. In return, we shall receive, in the end, sufficient remuneration to keep our noses above water—at least until next Lady Day."

I should have suspected something of the kind. It was only a couple of months since we had received a visitation from a pair of young men in scarves and flannels who had spent two days photographing Buckshaw from every conceivable angle, inside and out. Neville and Charlie, they were called, and Father had been exceedingly vague about their intentions. Supposing it to be just another photo visit from *Country Life*, I had put it out of my mind.

Now Father had been drawn again to the window, where he stood gazing out upon his troubled estate.

Feely got to her feet and strolled casually to the looking glass. She leaned in, peering closely at her own reflection.

I knew already what was on her mind.

"Any idea what it's about?" she asked in a voice that wasn't quite her own. "The film, I mean."

"Another one of those blasted country house things, I believe," Father replied, without turning round. "I didn't bother to ask."

"Any big names?"

"None that I recognize," Father said. "The agent rattled on and on about someone named Wyvern, but it meant nothing to me."

"*Phyllis* Wyvern?" Daffy was all agog. "Not *Phyllis* Wyvern?"

"Yes, that's it," Father said, brightening, but only a little. "Phyllis. The name rang a bell. Same name as the chairwoman of the Hampshire Philatelic Society.

"Except that *her* name is Phyllis *Bramble*," he added, "not Wyvern."

"But Phyllis Wyvern is the biggest film star in the world," Feely said, openmouthed. "In the *galaxy!*"

"In the universe," Daffy added solemnly. "*The Crossing Keeper's Daughter*—she played Minah Kilgore, remember? *Anna of the Steppes* . . . *Love and Blood* . . . *Dressed for Dying* . . . *The Secret Summer*. She was supposed to have played Scarlett O'Hara in *Gone With the Wind*, but she choked on a peach stone the night before her screen test and couldn't speak a word."

Daffy kept up to date on all the latest cinema gossip by speed-reading magazines at the village newsagent's shop.

"She's coming here to Buckshaw?" Feely asked. "Phyllis Wyvern?"

Father had given the ghost of a shrug and returned to staring glumly out of the window.

I hurried down the east staircase. The dining room was in darkness. As I walked into the kitchen, Daffy and Feely looked up sourly from their porridge troughs.

"Oh, there you are, dear," said Mrs. Mullet. "We was just talkin' about sendin' up a search party to see if you was still alive. 'Urry along now. Them fillum people will be 'ere before you can say 'Jack Robertson.' "

I bolted my breakfast (clumpy porridge and burnt toast with lemon curd) and was about to make my escape when the kitchen door opened and in came Dogger on a rush of cold, fresh air.

"Good morning, Dogger," I said. "Are we picking out a tree today?"

For as long as I could remember, it had been a tradition for my sisters and me, in the week before Christmas, to accompany Dogger into the wood on Buckshaw's eastern outskirts, where we would gravely consider this tree and that, awarding each one points for height, shape, fullness, and general all-round character before finally selecting a champion.

Next morning, as if by magic, the chosen tree would appear in the drawing room, set up securely in a coal scuttle and ready for our attentions. All of us—except Father—would spend the day in a blizzard of antique tinsel, silver and gold garlands, coloured glass balls, and little angels tooting pasteboard trumpets, hovering as long as we could over our small tasks until late in the darkening afternoon when, reluctantly, the thing was done.

Because it was the single day of the year upon which my sisters were a little less beastly to me than usual, I looked forward to it with barely suppressed excitement. For a single day—or for a few hours at least—we would be carefully civil to one another, teasing and joking and sometimes even laughing together, as if we were one of those poor but cheerful families from Dickens.

I was already smiling in anticipation.

"I'm afraid not, Miss Flavia," Dogger said. "The Colonel has given orders for the house to be left as is. Those are the wishes of the film people."

"Oh, bother the film people!" I said, perhaps too loudly. "They can't keep us from having Christmas."

But I saw at once by the sad look on Dogger's face that they could.

"I shall put up a little tree in the greenhouse," he said. "It will keep longer in the cool air."

"But it won't be the same!" I protested.

"No, it won't," Dogger agreed, "but we shall have done our best."

Before I could think of a reply, Father came into the kitchen, scowling at us as if he were a bank manager and we a group of renegade depositors who had somehow managed to breach the barriers before opening time.

We all of us sat with eyes downcast as he opened his *London Philatelist* and turned his attention to spreading his charred toast with pallid white margarine.

"Nice fresh snow overnight," Mrs. Mullet remarked cheerily, but I could see by her worried glance towards the window that her heart was not in it. If the wind kept blowing as it was, she would have to wade home through the drifts when her day's work was done.

Of course, if the weather were too severe, Father would have Dogger ring up for Clarence Mundy's taxicab—but with a stiff winter crosswind, it was always touch and go whether Clarence could plough through the deep piles that invariably drifted in between the gaps in the hedge-rows. As all of us knew, there were times when Buckshaw was accessible only on foot.

When Harriet was alive, there had been a sleigh with bells and blankets—in fact, the sleigh itself still stood in a shadowy corner of the coach house, behind Harriet's Rolls-Royce Phantom II, each of them a monument to its departed owner. The horses, alas, were long gone: sold at auction in the wake of Harriet's death.

Something rumbled in the distance.

"Listen!" I said. "What was that?"

"Wind," Daffy replied. "Do you want that last piece of toast, or shall I have it?"

I grabbed the slice and gobbled it down dry as I dashed for the foyer.

·TWO·

A BLAST OF COLD air blew a flurry of freezing flakes into my face as I tugged open the heavy front door. I wrapped my arms around myself, shivering, and squinted out at the winter world.

In the first bleak light of day, the landscape was a black-and-white photograph, the vast expanses of the snowy lawn broken only by the ink-black silhouettes of the stark, leafless chestnut trees that lined the avenue. Here and there on the lawns, white-capped bushes bent towards the earth, cringing under their heavy loads.

Because of the blowing snow, it was impossible to see as far as the Mulford Gates, but something out there was moving.

I wiped the condensation from my eyes and looked again.

Yes! A small spot of pale colour—and then another—

had appeared upon the landscape! In the lead was an immense pantechnicon, its scarlet colour growing ever more vivid as it came growling towards me through the falling snow. Lumbering along in its wake like a procession of clockwork elephants was a string of lesser vans . . . two . . . three . . . four . . . five . . . no, six of them!

As the pantechnicon made its slow, stiff-jointed final turn into the forecourt, I could clearly make out the name on the side: *Ilium Films,* it said, in bold cream and yellow letters, painted as if in three dimensions. The lesser lorries were similarly marked, but still impressive as they pulled up in a herd around their leader.

The door of the pantechnicon swung open and a massive sandy-haired man climbed down. He was dressed in overalls, with a flat cap on his head and a red handkerchief wrapped round his neck.

As he crunched towards me through the snow, I was suddenly aware of Dogger at my side.

"S'truth," the man said, wincing at the wind.

With a disbelieving shake of his head, he approached Dogger, sticking out a raw, meaty hand.

"McNulty," he said. "Ilium Films. Transport Department. Jack-of-all-trades and master of 'em all."

Dogger shook the huge hand but said nothing.

"Need to get this circus round the back of the house and out of the north wind. Fred's generator cuts up something fierce when it gets too cold. Needs coddling, Fred's generator does.

"What's *your* name, little girl?" he asked suddenly, turning to me and crouching down. "Margaret Rose, I'll

bet. Yes, that's it . . . Margaret Rose. You're a Margaret
Rose if I ever saw one."

I had half a mind to march upstairs to my laboratory,
fetch down a jar of cyanide, seize this boob's nose, tilt his
head back, pour the stuff down his throat, and hang the
consequences.

Fortunately, good breeding kept me from doing so.

Margaret Rose, indeed!

"Yes, that's right, Mr. McNulty," I said, forcing a smile
of amazement. "Margaret Rose *is* my name. However did
you guess?"

"It's the sixth sense I'm gifted with," he said, with what
looked like a practised shrug. "Me Irish blood," he added,
putting on a bit of the old brogue, and giving me a saucy
tip of his cloth cap as he stood up.

"Now, then," he said, turning to Dogger, "their lord-
ships and ladyships will be along at noon in their motorcars. They'll be hungry as hounds after the drive down
from London, so look sharp and see that you've got buckets of caviar laid on."

Dogger's face was a total blank.

"Here, I'm only joking, mate!" McNulty said, and for a
horrible moment I thought he was going to dig Dogger in
the ribs.

"Joking, see? We travel with our own canteen."

He gave a jerk of his thumb to indicate one of the vans
that sat patiently waiting in the forecourt.

"Joking," Dogger said. "I understand. If you'll be so
good as to remove your boots and follow me . . ."

As Dogger closed the door behind him, McNulty

stopped and gaped at his surroundings. He seemed particularly in awe of the two grand staircases that led up to
the first floor.

"S'truth!" he said. "Do people actually live like this?"

"So I am given to believe," Dogger said. "This way,
please."

I tagged along as Dogger gave McNulty a whirlwind
tour: dining room, firearms museum, Rose Room, Blue
Room, morning room . . .

"The drawing room and the Colonel's study are off
limits," Dogger said, "as has been previously agreed upon.
I have affixed a small white circle to each of those doors
as a reminder, so that there will be no breach of—their
privacy."

He had almost said "our privacy." I was sure of it.

"I'll pass the word," McNulty said. "Should be no
sweat. Our lot's pretty clannish, as well."

We made our way through to the east wing and into
the portrait gallery. I was half expecting to find it as it
had been in my dream: an icy, flooded wasteland. But
the room remained as it had been since time immemo-
rial: a long dim train shed of glowering ancestors who,
with just a few exceptions (Countess Daisy, for instance,
who was said to have greeted visitors to Buckshaw by
turning handsprings on the roof in a Chinese silk smock)
seemed to have subsided, one and all, into a collective
and perpetual sulk that did not exactly gladden one's
heart.

"Use of the portrait gallery has been negotiated—"
Dogger was saying.

"But none of yer 'obnail boots on the floor, mind!" a voice cut in. It was Mrs. Mullet.

Hands on hips, she gave McNulty her proprietary glare, then in a softer voice said: "Beggin' your pardon, Dogger, but the Colonel's off now to London for 'is stamp meet. 'E wishes to see you about the tinned beef, an' that, before 'e goes."

"Tinned beef" was a code word meaning that Father needed to borrow money for train and taxi fare. I had discovered this by listening at the door of Father's study. It was a fact I wished I didn't know.

"Of course," Dogger said. "Excuse me for a moment."

And he vanished in the way he does.

"You'll have to lay down some tarpaulings on that floor," Mrs. Mullet told McNulty. "'Par-key,' they calls it: cherry wood, mahogany, walnut, birch—six different kinds of oak is in it. Can't 'ave workmen tramplin' all over the likes of that, can I?"

"Believe you me, Mrs. . . ."

"Mullet," said Mrs. Mullet. "With an 'M.'"

"Mrs. Mullet. My name's McNulty—also with an 'M,' by the way. Patrick McNulty. I can assure you that our crew at Ilium Films are hired for their fussy natures. In fact, I can confide in you—knowing it will go no further—that we've just come from shooting a scene in-side a certain royal residence without one word of com-plaint from You-Know-Who."

Mrs. M's eyes widened.

"You mean—"

"Exactly," McNulty said, putting a forefinger to his

lips. "You're a very shrewd woman, Mrs. Mullet. I can see that."

She gave a flimsy smile, like the Mona Lisa, and I knew that her loyalty was bought. Whatever else he was, Patrick McNulty was as slick as nose oil.

Now Dogger was back, his face bland and capable, giving away nothing. I followed as he led the way upstairs and into the west wing.

"The room at the south end of the corridor is Miss Harriet's boudoir. It is strictly private, and is not to be entered upon any account."

He said this as if Harriet had just stepped out for a couple of hours to pay a social call in the county, or to ride with the Halstead-Thicket Hounds. He did not tell McNulty that my mother had been dead for ten years, and that her rooms had been preserved by Father as a shrine where no one, or so he thought, could hear him weeping.

"Understood," McNulty said. "Over and out. I'll pass it along."

"The two bedrooms on the left belong to Miss Ophelia and Miss Daphne, who will share a room for the duration. Choose the one you wish to use as a setting and they'll settle for the other."

"Sporting of them," McNulty said. "Val Lampman will be seeing to that. He's our director."

"All other bedrooms, sitting rooms, and dressing rooms, including those along the north front, may be assigned as you see fit," Dogger went on, not batting an eye at the mention of England's most celebrated cinema director.

Even *I* knew who Val Lampman was.

"I'd best be getting back to my crew," McNulty said, with a glance at his wristwatch. "We'll organize the lorries, then see to the unloading."

"As you wish," Dogger told him, and it seemed to me there was a touch of sadness in his voice.

We descended the stairs, McNulty openly running his fingers over the carved banister ends, craning his neck to gawk at the carved panelling.

"S'truth," he muttered under his breath.

"You'll never guess who's directing this film!" I said, bursting into the drawing room.

"Val Lampman," Daffy said in a bored voice, without looking up from her book. "Phyllis Wyvern doesn't work with anyone else nowadays. Not since—"

"Since what?"

"You're too young to understand."

"No, I'm not. What about Boccaccio?"

Daffy had recently been reading aloud to us at tea, selected tales from Boccaccio's *Decameron*.

"That's fiction," she said. "Val Lampman is real life."

"Says who?" I countered.

"Says *Cinema World*. It was all over the front page."

"What was?"

"Oh, for God's sake, Flavia," Daffy said, throwing down her book, "you grow more like a parrot every day: '*Since what? Says who? What was?*' "

She mimicked my voice cruelly.

"We ought to teach you to say 'Who's a pretty bird, then?' or 'Polly wants a biscuit.' We've already ordered you a cage: lovely gold bars, a perch, and a water dish to splash about in—not that you'll ever use it."

"Sucks to you!"

"I deflect it back unto you," Daffy said, holding out an invisible shield at arm's length.

"And back to you again," I said, duplicating her gesture.

"Ha! Yours is a brass shield. Brass doesn't bounce sucks. You know that as well as I do."

"Does!"

"Doesn't!"

It was at this point that Feely intervened in what had been, until then, a perfectly civilized discussion.

"Speaking of parrots," she said, "Harriet had a lovely parrot before you were born—a beautiful bird, an African Grey, called Sinbad. I remember him perfectly well. He could conjugate the Latin verb '*amare*' and sing parts of 'The Lorelei.' "

"You're making this up," I told her.

"Remember Sinbad, Daffy?" Feely said, laughing.

" '*The boy stood on the burning deck,*' " Daffy said. "Poor old Sinby used to scramble up onto his perch as he squawked the words. Hilarious."

"Then where is he now?" I demanded. "He should be still alive. Parrots can live more than a hundred years."

"He flew away," Daffy said, with a little hitch in her voice. "Harriet had spread a blanket on the terrace, taken you out for some fresh air. Somehow you managed to work loose the catch on the door of the cage, and Sinbad flew away. Don't you remember?"

"I didn't!"

Feely was looking at me with eyes which were no longer those of a sister.

"Oh, but you did. She often said afterwards that she wished it had been you who had flown away, and Sinbad who had stayed."

I could feel the pressure rising in my chest, as if I were a steam boiler.

I said a forbidden word and walked stiffly from the room, vowing revenge.

There were times when a touch of the old strychnine was just the ticket.

I would go upstairs straight away to my chemical kitchen and prepare a delicacy that would have my hateful sisters begging for mercy. Yes, that was it! I would spice their egg salad sandwiches with a couple of grains of *nux vomica*. It would keep them out of decent company for a week.

I was halfway up the stairs when the doorbell rang.

"Dash it all!" I said. There was nothing I hated more than being interrupted when I was about to do something gratifying with chemicals.

I trudged down from the landing and flung open the door angrily.

There, looking down his nose at me, stood a chauffeur in livery: light chocolate coat with corded trim, flared breeches tucked into tall tan leather boots, a peaked cap, and a pair of limp brown leather gloves held a little too casually in his perfectly manicured hands.

I didn't like his attitude, and, come to think of it, he probably didn't like mine.

"De Luce?" he asked.

I stood motionless, waiting for decency.

"Miss de Luce?"

"Yes," I said grudgingly, peering round his body as if there might be others like him hiding in the bushes.

The pantechnicon and vans had gone from the fore-court. A maze of snowy tracks told me that they had been moved round to the back of the house. In their place, idling silently in little gusts of snow, was a black Daimler limousine, polished, like a funeral coach, to an unearthly shine.

"Come in and close the door," I said. "Father's not aw-fully keen on snowdrifts in the foyer."

"Miss Wyvern has arrived," he announced, drawing himself to attention.

"But—" I managed, "they weren't supposed to be here until noon . . ."

Phyllis Wyvern! My mind was spinning. With Father away, surely I couldn't be expected to . . .

I'd seen her on the silver screen, of course, not just at the Gaumont, but also at the little backstreet cinema in Hinley. And once, also, when the vicar had hired Mr. Mitchell, who operated Bishop's Lacey's photo studio, to run *The Rector's Wife* in St. Tancred's parish hall, hoping, I suppose, that the story would arouse a feeling of sympathy in our parish bosoms for his rat-faced—and rat-hearted—wife, Cynthia.

Of course, it had no such effect. Despite the fact that the film was so old and scratched and full of splices that it sometimes made the picture leap about on the screen like a jumping jack, Phyllis Wyvern had been magnificent in the role of the brave and noble Mrs. Willington. At the end, when the lights came up, even the projectionist was in tears, although he'd seen the thing a hundred times before.

Nobody gave Cynthia Richardson a second look, though, and I had seen her afterwards, in the darkness, slinking home alone through the graveyard.

But how does one talk, face-to-face, with a goddess? What does one say?

"I'll ring for Dogger," I said.

"I'll see to it, Miss Flavia," said Dogger, already at my elbow.

I don't know how he does it, but Dogger always appears at precisely the right instant, like one of those figures that pops out of the door on a Swiss clock.

And suddenly he was walking towards the Daimler, the chauffeur slipping and sliding in front of him, trying to be the first to take hold of the car's door handle.

Dogger won.

"Miss Wyvern," he said, his voice coming clearly to my ears on the cold air. "On behalf of Colonel de Luce, may I welcome you to Buckshaw? It's a pleasure to have you with us. The Colonel has asked me to express his regrets that he is not here to greet you."

Phyllis Wyvern took Dogger's extended hand and stepped out of the car.

"Watch your step, miss. The footing is treacherous this morning."

I could see her every breath distinctly on the cold air as she took Dogger's arm and floated towards the front door. Floated! There was no other word for it. In spite of the slick walkway, Phyllis Wyvern floated towards me as if she were a ghost.

"We weren't expecting you until noon," Dogger was saying. "I regret that the walkways have not yet been fully shovelled and ashes put down."

"Think nothing of it, Mr.—"

"Dogger," Dogger said.

"Mr. Dogger, I'm just a girl from Golders Green. I've managed in snow before and I expect I shall manage again.

"Oops!" She giggled, pretending to slip and smiling up at him as she clung to his arm.

I couldn't believe how tiny she was, her head barely level with his chest.

She wore a tight-fitting black suit with a white blouse with a black and yellow Liberty scarf, and, despite the greyness of the day, her complexion was like cream in a summer kitchen.

"Hullo!" she said, stopping in front of me. "I've seen this face before. You're Flavia de Luce, if I'm not mistaken. I was hoping you'd be here."

I stopped breathing and I didn't care.

"Your photo was in the *Daily Mirror*, you know. That

dreadful business about Stonepenny, or Bonepenny, or whatever he was called."

"Bonepenny," I said. "Horace Bonepenny."

I had given my assistance to the police in that case when they were completely stymied.

"That's it," she said, sticking out a hand and seizing mine as if we were sisters. "Bonepenny. I keep up paid subscriptions to the *Police Gazette* and *True Crime*, and I never miss so much as a single issue of the *News of the World*. I simply adore reading about all the great murderers: the Brides in the Bath . . . the Islington Mumbler . . . Major Armstrong . . . Dr. Crippen . . . the stuff of great drama. Makes you think, doesn't it? What, after all, would life be without puzzling death?"

Exactly! I thought.

"And now I think we should go inside and not keep poor Mr. Dogger standing out here in the cold."

I glanced quickly at Dogger, but his face was as reflective as a millpond.

As she brushed past me, I couldn't help thinking: *I'm breathing the same air as Phyllis Wyvern!*

My nostrils were suddenly filled with her scent: the odour of jasmine.

It had probably been concocted in some perfumery, I thought, from phenol and acetic acid. Phenol, or "benzanol," I recalled, had been discovered in the midseventeenth century by a German chemist named Johann Rudolf Glauber, although it was not actually isolated until nearly two hundred years later by one of his countrymen, Friedlieb Ferdinand Runge, who extracted it from coal tar and christened it "carbolic acid." I had synthesized the extremely poisonous stuff myself by a process which involved the incomplete oxidation of benzene, and I remembered with pleasure that it was the most powerful embalming agent known to mankind: the stuff that is used whenever a body is required to last, and last, and last.

It was also to be found in certain of the Scotch whiskies.

Phyllis Wyvern had swept past me into the foyer and was now spinning round in a delighted circle.

"What a gloomy old place!" she said, clapping her hands together. "It's perfect! Absolutely perfect!"

By now, the chauffeur had brought the luggage and was piling it inside the door.

"Just leave it there, Anthony," she said. "Someone will see to it."

"Yes, Miss Wyvern," he replied, making a great show of coming to attention. He almost clicked his heels.

There was something vaguely familiar about him, but I couldn't, for the life of me, think what.

He stood there for a long moment, perfectly still, as if he were expecting a tip—or was he waiting to be asked in for a drink and a cigar?

"You may go," she announced rather abruptly and the spell was broken. In an instant he was no more than a member of the chorus in *The Chocolate Soldier*.

"Yes, Miss Wyvern," he said, and as he turned away from her towards the door, I saw on his face a look of—what was it?—contempt?

·THREE·

"THIS ONE IS SUNNIER, miss," Dogger was saying. "If you don't mind, we shall put you in here until your assigned bedroom has been made ready."

We had been looking at bedrooms, and had arrived at last at Feely's.

Since we didn't get much sun at this time of year, I guessed that Dogger could only be thinking of former days.

"It will do admirably," Phyllis Wyvern said, drifting to the window. "View of a little lake—check . . . a romantic ruin—check . . . glimpses of the wardrobe van. What more could a leading lady ask?"

"May I unpack?" Dogger asked.

"No, thank you. Bun will take care of it. She'll be along directly."

"It's no trouble, I assure you," Dogger said.

"Most kind of you, Dogger, but no—I must insist. Bun

is very possessive. She'd swear like blue lightning if she thought anyone else had laid hands on my belongings."

"I understand," Dogger said. "Will there be anything else? May I ask Mrs. Mullet to bring you a pot of tea?"

"Dogger, you are a treasure beyond rubies. I'd love nothing better. I'm going to slip into something more comfy and immerse myself in Val's abominable script. It's as much as your life is worth if one isn't word perfect by the time the lights are set up."

"Thank you, miss," Dogger said, and was gone.

"Funny old stick," she said. "He's been with you forever, of course?"

"Father and Dogger were in the army together," I said, bristling slightly.

"Ah, yes, companions-in-arms. Quite common nowadays, I understand. Tit for tat. You save my life now and I'll save yours later. Perhaps you saw me in *The Trench in the Drawing Room*? Much the same plot."

I shook my head.

At that instant the door flew open and Feely came rushing in.

"What the *hell* do you think you're *doing*?" she shouted. "I told you before what would happen if I caught you in my room again."

She had not noticed Phyllis Wyvern standing at the window.

She made a grab for me.

"No!"

Feely spun round to see who had spoken. Her raised hand fell to her side, where it hung limply.

For a moment they stood there staring at each other, Feely as if she had been confronted by some ghastly spectre, Phyllis Wyvern as she looked when she'd clung defiantly to the rain-lashed spire of the cathedral in the final moments of *The Glass Heart*.

Then Feely's lower lip began to quiver, her eyes suddenly brimming with tears.

She turned and fled.

"So," said Phyllis Wyvern after a long silence, "you have an older sister, too."

"That was Feely," I said. "She—"

"No need to explain. Older sisters are much alike the world over: half a cup of love and half one of contempt."

I couldn't have put it better myself!

"My sister's the same," she said. "Six years older?"

I nodded.

"Mine, too. I see we have a great deal more in common than a taste for horrific murder, Flavia de Luce."

She came across the room and, putting a finger under my chin, raised my eyes to hers. And then she hugged me.

She actually hugged me, and I breathed in her jasmine—synthetic or not.

"Let's go down to the kitchen for tea. It will save Mrs. Mullet a trip upstairs."

I beamed at her. I almost took her hand.

"It will also," she added, "give us a chance to pick up the latest gossip. Kitchens are hotbeds of scandal, you know."

*   *   *

"Ohhhhh!" Mrs. Mullet said as we walked into the kitchen. Aside from that, and gaping a bit, she handled it quite well.

"We decided to come down to the Command Centre," Phyllis Wyvern said. "Is there anything I can do to help?"

I could see that she had won Mrs. Mullet over—just like that.

"No, no, no," she said breathlessly, "sit yourself down, miss. The water's almost at the boil, and I've got a nice lardy cake comin' out the oven."

"Lardy cake!" Phyllis Wyvern exclaimed, putting her hands in front of her eyes and peeking out through her fingers. "Good lord! I haven't had lardy cake since I was in pigtails!"

Mrs. Mullet beamed.

"I makes 'em for Christmas, as did my mother before me, and 'er mother before 'er. Lardy cake runs in the family, so to speak."

And so it did, but I wasn't going to let the cat out of the bag.

"'Ere now," she said, pulling the cake from the oven with a pair of pot holders and placing it on a wire rack. "Look at that. Almost good enough to eat!"

It was an old joke, and although I'd heard it a hundred times before, I laughed dutifully. There was more truth in it than Phyllis Wyvern knew, but I wasn't going to spoil her treat. Who knew? She might even find the stuff edible.

If cooking were a game of darts, most of Mrs. Mullet's concoctions would be barely on the board.

Mrs. Mullet sliced the cake into twelve pieces.

"Two for each soul in the 'ouse'old," she proclaimed, with a glance at Dogger as he came into the kitchen. "That's what they taught us up at Lady Rex-Wells's place: 'Two slices a soul, keeps you out of the 'ole.' Meanin' the grave, of course. The old lady said it meant everyone from 'erself right on down to the gardener's boy. A reg'lar tartar she was, but she lived to be ninety-nine and a half, so there must be somethin' in it."

"What do you think, Dogger?" Phyllis Wyvern asked Dogger, who was taking his tea unobtrusively, standing in the corner.

"Good lard makes good bile. Good bile makes good digestion, which results in great longevity," Dogger said rather tentatively, looking into his cup. "Or so I have heard."

"And all because of a double helping of lardy cake!" Phyllis Wyvern said, clapping her hands together in delight. "Well, here's to the second hundred years."

She picked up her fork and lifted a morsel to her mouth, pausing halfway to give Mrs. Mullet a smile that must have cost someone a thousand guineas.

She chewed reflectively.

"Oh, my goodness!" she said, putting the fork down on her plate. "Oh, my goodness!"

Even her magnificent acting ability couldn't suppress the little gag reflex I saw at her throat.

"I knew you'd like it," Mrs. Mullet crowed.

"But I must be brutal and rein myself in," Phyllis Wyvern said, pushing the plate roughly away and getting to her feet. "I tend to make a swine of myself when there's cake to be had, and with lardy cake, it's no more than a day from lips to hips. I'm sure you'll understand."

Mrs. Mullet lifted the plate away and placed it a little too carefully behind the sink.

I knew without a doubt that she would take the slice of cake home, wrap it in gift paper, and put it in her china cabinet between the china-dog salt and peppers marked "A Present From Blackpool" and the slender glass bird that bobbed up and down as it sipped water from a tube.

When her friend Mrs. Waller came to visit, Mrs. Mullet would reverently unwrap the mouldy relic. "You'll never guess 'oo ate the missin' bit of this," she would say in a hushed voice. "Phyllis Wyvern! Look—you can still see 'er teeth marks. Just a peek, mind—quick, so's it doesn't go stale."

The doorbell rang and Dogger put down his tea.

"That will be Bun," Phyllis Wyvern said, with a wry grin. "She'll claim to have missed her connection from Paddington. She always does."

"I'll fix 'er a nice cup of tea," Mrs. Mullet said. "The train always makes your stomach go all skew-gee—at least it does mine.

"Gives me the dire-rear," she whispered in my ear.

In a moment, Dogger was back, followed by a round little woman with iron-rimmed spectacles, her hair tied back in a large tight ball like the tail of the horse, Ajax, that had once been owned by one of my ancestors, Florizel de Luce. Both of them, Florizel and Ajax, immortalized in oils, now hung side by side in the portrait gallery.

"I'm sorry I'm late, Miss Wyvern," the little woman said. "The taxicab took a wrong turning and I missed my connection at Paddington."

Phyllis Wyvern looked round triumphantly at each of us, but she said nothing.

I felt rather sorry for the little creature, who, now that I thought about it, looked like a flustered cannonball.

"I'm Bun Keats, by the way," the woman said, giving a jerk of the head to each of us in the room. "Miss Wyvern's personal assistant."

"Bun's my dresser—but she has even greater aspirations," Phyllis Wyvern said in a haughty, theatrical voice, and I could not tell if she was teasing.

"Hurry along now, Bun," she added. "Spit-spot! My wardrobe wants unpacking. And if my pink dress is wrinkled again, I'll cheerfully strangle you."

She said this pleasantly enough but Bun Keats did not smile.

"Are you related to the poet, Miss Keats?" I blurted, anxious to lighten the moment.

Daffy had once read me "Ode to a Nightingale," and I'd never forgotten the part about drinking hemlock.

"Distantly," she said, and then she was gone.

"Poor Bun," Phyllis Wyvern said. "The more she tries—the more she tries."

"I'll give her a hand," Dogger said, moving towards the door.

"No!"

For an instant—but only for an instant—Phyllis Wyvern's face was a Greek mask: her eyes wide and her mouth twisted. And then, almost at once, her features subsided into a carefree smile, as if the moment hadn't happened.

"No," she repeated quietly. "Don't do that. Bun must have her little lesson."

I tried to catch Dogger's eye, but he had moved away and begun rearranging tins in the butler's pantry.

Mrs. Mullet turned busily to polishing the covers on the Aga.

As I trudged upstairs, the house seemed somehow colder than before. From the tall, uncurtained windows of my laboratory, I looked down upon the vans of Ilium Films, which were clustered, like elephants at a watering hole, round the red brick walls of the kitchen garden.

The crew members were going about their work in a well-rehearsed ballet, lifting, shifting, unloading rope-handled shipping boxes: always a pair of hands in the right place at the right time. It was easy to see that they had done this many times before.

I warmed my hands over the welcoming flame of a Bunsen burner, then brought a beaker of milk to a bubbling boil and stirred in a good dollop of Ovaltine. At this time of year, no refrigerator was required to keep milk chilled: I simply kept the bottle on a shelf, alphabetically, between the manganese and the morphine, the latter bottle neatly labelled in Uncle Tarquin's spidery handwriting.

Uncle Tar had been shown the door under mysterious

circumstances just before taking a double first at Oxford. His father, by way of compensation, had built the remarkable chemistry laboratory at Buckshaw in which Uncle Tar had spent, by choice, the remainder of his days, conducting what was said to be top-secret research. Among his papers I had discovered several letters that suggested he had been both friend and advisor to the young Winston Churchill.

As I sipped at the Ovaltine, I shifted my gaze to the painting that hung above the mantelpiece: a beautiful young woman with two girls and a baby. The girls were my sisters, Ophelia and Daphne. I was the baby. The woman, of course, was my mother, Harriet.

Harriet had secretly commissioned the work as a gift for Father just before setting out on what was to become her final journey. The painting had lain for ten years, almost forgotten, in an artist's studio in Malden Fenwick, until I had discovered it there and brought it home.

I'd made happy plans to hang the portrait in the drawing room: to stage a surprise unveiling for Father and my sisters. But my scheme was thwarted. Father had caught me smuggling the bulky painting into the house, taken it away from me, and removed it to his study.

Next morning I had found it hanging in my laboratory.

Why? I wondered. Did Father find it too painful to look upon his blighted family?

There was no doubt that he had loved—and still loved—Harriet, but it sometimes seemed that my sisters and I were no more to him than ever-present reminders of what he had lost. To Father we were, Daffy had once said, a three-headed Hydra, each one of our faces a misty mirror of his past.

Daffy's a romantic, but I knew what she meant: We were fleeting images of Harriet.

Perhaps that was why Father spent his days and nights among his postage stamps: surrounded by thousands of companionable, comforting, unquestioning countenances, not one of which, like those of his daughters, mocked him from morning till night.

I had thought about these things until my brains were turning blue, but I still didn't know why my sisters hated me so much.

Was Buckshaw some grim training academy into which I had been dumped by Fate to learn the laws of survival? Or was my life a game, whose rules I was supposed to guess?

Was I required to deduce the secret ways in which they loved me?

I could think of no other reason for my sisters' cruelty. What had I ever done to them?

Well, I had poisoned them, of course, but only in minor ways—and only in retaliation. I had never, or at least hardly ever, begun a row. I had always been the innocent—

"No! Watch it! Watch it!"

A scream went up outside the window—harsh at first, and agonised, then quickly cut off. I flew to the window and looked out to see what was happening.

Workers were flocking round a figure that was pinned against the side of a lorry by an upended packing case.

I knew by the red handkerchief at his neck that it was Patrick McNulty.

Down the stairs I ran, through the empty kitchen and out onto the terrace, not even bothering to throw on a coat.

Help was needed. No one among the ciné crew would know where to turn for assistance.

"Keep back!" one of the drivers said, seizing me by the shoulders. "There's been an accident."

I twisted away from him and pressed in for a closer look.

McNulty was in a bad way. His face was the colour of wet dough. His eyes, brimming with water, met mine, and his lips moved.

"Help me," I think he whispered.

I put my first and fourth fingers into the corners of my mouth and blew a piercing whistle: a trick I had learned by watching Feely.

"Dogger!" I shouted, followed by another whistle. I put my heart and soul into it, praying that Dogger was within earshot.

Without taking his eyes from mine, McNulty let out a sickening gasp.

Two of the men were heaving at the crate.

"No!" I said, louder than I had intended. "Leave it."

I had heard on the wireless—or had I read it somewhere?—about an accident victim who had bled to death when a railway crane had been moved away too soon from his legs.

To my surprise, the larger of the men nodded his head. "Hold on," he said. "She's right."

And then Dogger was there, pushing through the gathering crowd.

The men fell back instinctively.

There was an aura about Dogger that brooked no nonsense. It was not always in evidence—in fact, most of the time, it was not.

But at this particular moment, I don't think I had ever felt this power of his—whatever it was—so strongly.

"Take my hand," Dogger told McNulty, reaching between the lorry and the packing case, which was now teetering precariously.

It seemed to me an odd—almost biblical—thing to do. Perhaps it was the calmness of his voice.

McNulty's bloodied fingers moved, and then entwined themselves with Dogger's.

"Not too hard," Dogger told him. "You'll crush my hand."

A sick, silly grin spread across McNulty's face.

Dogger unfastened the top half of McNulty's heavy jacket, then worked his hand slowly into the sleeve. His long arm slid along McNulty's arm, feeling its way, inch by inch along the space between the upended case and the lorry.

"You told me you were master of many trades, Mr. McNulty," Dogger said. "Which ones, in particular?"

It seemed rather an odd question to ask, but McNulty's eyes shifted slowly from mine to Dogger's.

"Carpentry," he said through gritted teeth. It was easy to see that the man was in terrible pain. "Electrical . . . plumbing . . . drafting . . ."

Cold sweat stood out in globules on his brow.

"Yes?" Dogger asked, his arm steadily at work between the heavy box and the lorry. "Any more?"

"Bit of tool making," McNulty went on, then added, almost apologetically, "I have a metal lathe at home . . ."

"Indeed!" Dogger said, looking surprised.

". . . to make model steam engines."

"Ah!" Dogger said. "Steam engines. Railway, agricultural, or stationary?"

"Stationary," McNulty said through gritted teeth. "I fit them up with . . . little brass whistles . . . and regulators."

Dogger removed the handkerchief from McNulty's neck, twisting it quickly and tightly about the upper part of the trapped arm.

"Now!" he said briskly, and a hundred willing hands, it seemed, were suddenly gripping the packing case.

"Easy, now! Easy! Steady on!" the men told one another—not because the words were needed, but as if they were simply part of the ritual of shifting a heavy object.

And then quite suddenly they had lifted the crate away with no more effort than if it had been a child's building block.

"Stretcher," Dogger called, and one was brought forward instantly. *They must carry these things with them wherever they go*, I thought.

"Bring him into the kitchen," Dogger said, and in less

time than it takes to tell, McNulty, wrapped in a heavy blanket, was raising himself on his good elbow from the kitchen floor, sipping at the cup of hot tea that was in Mrs. Mullet's hand.

"Chip-chip," he said, giving me a wink.

"And now, Miss Flavia," Dogger said, "if you wouldn't mind giving Dr. Darby a call . . ."

"Um," Dr. Darby said, fishing with two fingers for a crystal mint in the paper bag he always carried in his waistcoat pocket.

"Let's get you to the hospital where I can have a decent look at you. X-rays, and all that. I'll take you myself, since I'm going that way anyway."

McNulty was now getting up painfully from a chair at the kitchen table, his arm and hand in a sling, bandaged from shoulder to knuckles.

"I can manage," he growled, as many hands reached out to help him.

"Put your arm round my shoulder," Dr. Darby told him. "The good people here will understand there's nothing in it."

Crammed together in a corner of the kitchen, the men from the film studio laughed loudly at this, as if the doctor had made a capital joke.

I watched as McNulty and Dr. Darby moved cautiously through to the foyer.

"Now we're for it," one of the men grumbled when they had gone. "How're we to get on without Pat?"

"It'll be Latshaw, then, won't it?" said another.

"I suppose."

"God help us, then," said the first, and he actually spat on the kitchen floor.

Until that moment, I hadn't noticed how cold I was. I gave a belated shiver, which didn't escape the notice of Mrs. Mullet as she came bustling in from the pantry.

"Upstairs with you, dear, and into an 'ot bath. The Colonel'll be fair cobbled to come 'ome and find you been out gallivantin' in the snow nearly naked, so to speak. 'E'll 'ave Dogger's and my 'eads on a meat platter. Now off you go."

·FOUR·

AT THE BOTTOM OF the stairs, I was taken with a sudden but brilliant idea.

Even in summer, taking a bath in the east wing was like a major military campaign. Dogger would have to lug buckets of water from either the kitchen or the west wing to fill the tin hipbath in my bedroom, which would afterwards have to be bailed out, and the bathwater disposed of by dumping it down a WC in the west wing or one of the sinks in my laboratory. Either way, the whole thing was a pain in the porpoise.

Besides, I had never really liked the idea of dirty bath-water being brought into my *sanctum sanctorum*. It seemed somehow blasphemous.

The solution was simple enough: I would bathe in Harriet's boudoir.

Why hadn't I thought of it before?

Harriet's suite had an antique slipper bathtub, draped with a tall and gauzy white canopy. Like an elderly railway engine, the thing was equipped with any number of interesting taps, knobs, and valves with which one could adjust the velocity and the temperature of the water.

It would make bathing almost fun.

I smiled in anticipation as I walked along the corridor, happy in the thought that my chilled body would soon be immersed to the ears in hot suds.

I stopped and listened at the door—just in case.

Someone inside was singing!

"O for the wings, for the wings of a dove!
Far away, far away, would I rove!
In the wilderness build me a nest . . ."

I edged the door open and slipped inside.

"Is that you, Bun? Fetch me my robe, will you? It's on the back of the door. Oh, and while you're at it, a nice drinksie-winksie would be just what the doctor ordered."

I stood perfectly still and waited.

"Bun?"

There was a faint, yet detectable note of fear in her voice.

"It's me, Miss Wyvern . . . Flavia."

"For God's sake, girl, don't lurk like that. Are you trying to frighten me to death? Come in here where I can see you."

I showed myself around the half-open door.

Phyllis Wyvern was up to her shoulders in steaming

water. Her hair was piled on top of her head like a hay-
stack in the rain. I couldn't help noticing that she didn't
look at all like the woman I'd seen on the cinema screen.
For one thing, she was wearing no makeup. For another,
she had wrinkles.

I felt, to be perfectly honest, as if I'd just walked in on
a witch in mid-transformation.

"Put the lid down," she said, pointing to the toilet.
"Have a seat and keep me company."

I obeyed at once.

I hadn't the heart—the guts, actually—to tell her that
Harriet's boudoir was off-limits. But then, of course, she
had no way of knowing that. Dogger had explained the
ground rules to Patrick McNulty before she'd arrived.
McNulty was now on his way to the hospital in Hinley,
and probably hadn't had time to pass along the message.

Part of me watched the rest of me being in awe of the
most famous movie star in the world . . . the galaxy . . .
the universe!

"What are you staring at?" Phyllis Wyvern asked suddenly. "My puckers?"

For once, I couldn't think of a diplomatic answer.

I nodded.

"How old do you think I am?" she asked, picking up a
long cigarette holder from the edge of the tub. The smoke
had been invisible in the steam.

I thought carefully before answering. Too low a number would indicate flattery; too high could result in disas-
ter. The odds were against me. Unless I hit it dead-on, I
couldn't win.

"Thirty-seven," I said.

She blew out a jet of smoke like a dragon.

"Bless you, Flavia de Luce," she said. "You're bang on! Thirty-seven-year-old stuffing in a fifty-nine-year-old sausage casing. But I've still got some spice in me."

She laughed a throaty laugh, and I could see why the world was in love with her.

She plunged a pudding-sized bath sponge into the water, then squeezed it over her head. The water streamed down her face and dribbled off her chin.

"Look! I'm Niagara Falls!" she said, making a silly face.

I couldn't help myself: I laughed aloud.

And then she stood up.

At that very instant, as if in a scene from one of those two-act comedies the St. Tancred's Amateur Dramatic Society put on at the parish hall, a loud voice in the outer room said, "*What* in blue blazes do you think you're doing?"

It was Feely.

She came storming—there's no other way to express it—*storming* into the room.

"You know as well as I do, you, you filthy little swine, that no one is allowed—"

Naked, except for a few soap bubbles, Phyllis Wyvern stood staring at Feely through the swirling steam.

Time, for an instant, was frozen.

I was seized by the mad thought that I'd been suddenly thrust into Botticelli's painting *The Birth of Venus*, but I quickly rejected it: Even though Feely's expression *was* rather like the "I'll-huff-and-I'll-puff" look on the face of the wind god, Zephyrus, Phyllis Wyvern was no Venus—not by a long chalk.

Feely's face was turning the colour of water in which beets have been boiled.

"I . . . I . . .

"I beg your pardon," she said, and I could have cheered! Even in the rush of that bizarre moment, I couldn't help thinking that it was the first time in Feely's life she had ever uttered those words.

Like a courtier withdrawing from the Royal Presence, she backed slowly out of the room.

"Hand me my towel," commanded the bare-naked queen, and stepped out of the bath.

"Oh, *here* you are," Bun Keats said behind me. "The door was open, so I—"

She caught sight of me and shut her mouth abruptly.

"Well, well, well," said Phyllis Wyvern. "The delinquent Bun condescends at last to grace us with her presence."

"I'm sorry, Miss Wyvern. I've been seeing to the unpacking."

" 'I'm sorry, Miss Wyvern. I've been seeing to the unpacking.' God help us."

She mimicked her assistant's voice in the same cruel and cutting way that Daffy had mimicked mine, but in this case, though, the imitation was brilliant. Professional.

I realized at once that a great actress can never be greater than when she's starring in her own life.

Tears sprang to Bun Keats's eyes, but she bent over and began picking up soggy towels.

"I don't think these rooms are part of the agreement, Miss Wyvern," she said. "I'd already laid out your bath in the north wing."

"Mop up this mess," Phyllis Wyvern said, ignoring her. "Use the towels. There's nothing worse than a wet floor. Someone could slip and break their neck."

I took the opportunity to make myself scarce.

Outside, the weather had worsened. I watched from the drawing room window as the snow, driven by a merciless north wind, blurred the outlines of the vans and lorries. By late afternoon, the wind had lessened a little and the stuff was now coming straight down in the gathering dark.

I turned from the window to Daffy, who was sunk deep into an armchair, her legs dangling over the arms. She was reading *Bleak House* again.

"I love books where it's always raining," she had once told me. "So much like real life." I wasn't sure if this was one of her clever insults, so I did not reply.

"It's snowing like stink outside," I said.

"It always snows outside. Never inside," she said without looking up from her book. "And don't say 'stink.' It's common."

"Do you think Father will make it home from London?"

Daffy shrugged. "If he does, he does. If he doesn't, he can bunk over the night at Aunt Felicity's. She doesn't usually charge him more than a couple of quid for bed and breakfast."

She reversed herself in the chair, making it clear that the conversation was at an end.

"I met Phyllis Wyvern this morning," I said.

Daffy did not reply, but I saw that her eyes had stopped moving across the page. At least I had her attention.

"I talked to her while she was bathing," I confided. I did not mention that this had taken place in Harriet's boudoir. Whatever I was, I wasn't a rat.

There was no response.

"Aren't you interested, Daffy?"

"There's time enough to meet these thespians later. They always put on a dog and pony show before the actual filming begins. A grace and favour thing. They call it 'yakking up the yokels.' Someone will take us round and show us all the ciné gear and tell us what a bloody marvel it is. Then they'll introduce us to the actors, beginning with the boy who plays the hero as a child and falls through the ice, and ending with Phyllis Wyvern herself."

"You seem to know a lot about it."

Daffy preened a little.

"I try to keep myself well informed," she said. "Besides, they shot a couple of exteriors at Foster's last year, and Flossie dished the dirt."

"I wouldn't expect there was much dirt if they were only shooting exteriors," I said.

"You'd be surprised," Daffy said darkly, and went on with her reading.

* * *

At four-thirty, the doorbell rang. I had been sitting on the stairs watching the electricians as they snaked miles of black cable from the foyer to far-flung corners of the house.

Father had ordered us to keep to our quarters and not to interfere with the work at hand, and I was doing my best to obey. Since the eastern staircase led up to my bedroom and laboratory, it could be considered, technically at least, as part of my quarters, and I certainly had no intention of interfering with the ciné crew.

Several rows of chairs had been set up in the foyer as if a meeting were planned, and I threaded my way through them to see who was at the door.

With all the noise and bustle of the workmen, Dogger mustn't have heard the bell.

I opened the door and there, to my surprise, amid the whirling snow, stood the vicar, Denwyn Richardson.

"Ah, Flavia," he said, brushing the flakes from his heavy black coat and stamping his galoshes like a cart horse's feet, "how lovely to see you. May I come in?"

"Of course," I said, and as I stepped back from the door, a certain foreboding came over me. "It's not bad news about Father, is it?"

Even as one of Father's oldest and dearest friends, he seldom paid a visit to Buckshaw, and I knew that an unexpected vicar at the door could sometimes be an ominous sign. Perhaps there had been an accident in London. Perhaps the train had run off the tracks and overturned in a snowy field. If so, I wasn't sure that I wanted to be the first to hear it.

"Good lord, no!" the vicar said. "Your father's gone up to London today, hasn't he? Stamp meeting, or some such thing?"

Another thing about vicars was that they knew everyone's business.

"Will you come in?" I asked, not knowing what else to say.

As he stepped inside, the vicar must have seen me looking past him in astonishment at his tired old Morris Oxford, which sat in the forecourt looking remarkably spruce for its age, a layer of snow on the roof and bonnet giving it the appearance of an overly iced wedding cake.

"Winter tyres *plus* snow chains," he said in a confidential tone. "The secret of any truly successful ministry. The bishop tipped me off, but don't tell anyone. He picked it up from the American soldiers."

I grinned and slammed the door.

"Good lord!" he said, staring at the maze of cables and the forest of lighting fixtures. "I didn't expect it to be anything like this."

"You knew about it? The filming, I mean?"

"Oh, of course. Your father mentioned it quite some time ago . . . asked me to keep mum, though, and so, of course, I have. But now that the vast convoy has rolled through Bishop's Lacey, and the caravanserai set up within the very grounds of Buckshaw, it can be a secret no longer, can it?

"I must admit to you, Flavia, that ever since I heard Phyllis Wyvern was to be here, in the flesh, so to speak, at Buckshaw, I've been making plans of my own. It's not

often that we're gifted with so august . . . so lumi-
nous . . . a visitor and, well, after all, one must grind with
whatever grist one is given—not that Phyllis Wyvern
may be said to be grist in any sense of the word, dear me,
no, but—"

"I met her this morning," I volunteered.

"Did you indeed! Cynthia will be quite jealous to hear
of it. Well, perhaps not jealous, but possibly just a tiny bit
envious."

"Is Mrs. Richardson one of Phyllis Wyvern's fans?"

"No, I don't believe so. Cynthia is, however, the cousin
of Stella Ferrars, who, of course, wrote the novel *Cry of
the Raven*, upon which the film is to be based. Third
cousin, to be sure, but a cousin nonetheless."

"Cynthia?" I could scarcely believe my ears.

"Yes, hard to believe, isn't it? I can scarcely credit it
myself. Stella was always the black sheep of the family,
you know, until she married a laird, settled down in the
heathered Highlands, and began cranking out an endless
procession of potboilers, of which *Cry of the Raven* is
merely the latest. Cynthia had been hoping to pop by and
give Miss Wyvern a few pointers on how the role of the
heroine should be played."

I almost went "*Phhfft!*" but I didn't.

"And that's why you're here? To see Miss Wyvern?"

"Well, yes," the vicar said, "but not on that particular
topic. Christmas, as you've no doubt heard me say on
more than one occasion, is always one of the greatest op-
portunities not only to receive but also to give, and I have
been hoping that Miss Wyvern would see her way clear to

re-create for us just a few scenes from her greatest triumphs—all in a good cause, of course. The Roofing Fund, for instance—dear me—"

"Would you like me to introduce you to her?" I asked.

I thought the dear man was going to break down completely. He bit his lip and pulled out a handkerchief to wipe his glasses. When he realized he had forgotten to bring them with him, he blew his nose instead.

"If you please," he said.

"I hope we won't be intruding," he added as we made our way up the stairs. "I hate to be a beggar but sometimes there's really no choice."

He meant Cynthia.

"Our last little venture was something of a bust, wasn't it? So there's all that much more to make up this time."

Now he was referring, of course, to Rupert Porson, the late puppeteer, whose performance in the parish hall just a few months ago had been brought to an abrupt end by tragedy and a woman scorned.

Bun Keats was sitting in a chair at the top of the stairs, her head in her hands.

"Oh dear," she said as I introduced her to the vicar. "I'm terribly sorry, I'm afraid I have the most awful migraine."

Her face was as white as the crusted snow.

"How dreadful for you," the vicar said, putting a hand on her shoulder. "I can sympathize wholeheartedly. My wife suffers horribly from the same malady."

Cynthia? I thought. *Migraines?* That would certainly explain a lot.

"She sometimes finds," he went on, "that a warm compress helps. I'm sure the good Mrs. Mullet would be happy to prepare one."

"I'll be all right . . ." Bun Keats began, but the vicar was already halfway down the stairs.

"Oh!" she said, with a little cry. "I should have stopped him. I don't mean to be any trouble, but when I'm like this I can hardly think straight."

"The vicar won't mind," I told her. "He's a jolly good sort. Always thinking of others. Actually, he came round to see if Miss Wyvern could be persuaded to put on a show to raise funds for the church."

Her face, if it were possible, went even whiter.

"Oh, no!" she said. "He mustn't ask her that. She has a bee in her bonnet about charities—dead set against them. Something from her childhood, I think. You'd best tell him that before he brings it up. Otherwise, there's sure to be a most god-awful scene!"

The vicar was coming back up the stairs, surprisingly, taking them two at a time.

"Sit back, dear lady, and close your eyes," he said in a soothing voice I hadn't heard before.

"Miss Keats says Miss Wyvern is indisposed," I told him, as he applied the compress to her brow. "So perhaps we'd better not mention—"

"Of course. Of course," the vicar said.

I would invent some harmless excuse later.

A voice behind me said, "Bun? What on earth . . . ?"

I spun round.

Phyllis Wyvern, dressed in an orchid-coloured lounging

outfit and looking as fit as all the fiddles in the London Philharmonic, was wafting along the corridor towards us.

"She's suffering a migraine, Miss Wyvern," the vicar said. "I've just fetched a compress . . ."

"Bun? Oh, my poor Bun!"

Bun gave a little moan.

Phyllis Wyvern snatched the compress away from the vicar and reapplied it with her own hands to Bun's temples.

"Oh, my poor, dearest Bun. Tell Philly where it hurts."

Bun rolled her eyes.

"Marion!" Phyllis Wyvern called, snapping her fingers, and a tall, striking woman in horn-rimmed glasses, who must once have been a great beauty, appeared as if from nowhere.

"Take Bun to her room. Tell Dogger to summon a doctor at once."

As Bun Keats was led away, Phyllis Wyvern stuck out her hand.

"I'm Phyllis Wyvern, Vicar," she said, clasping his hand in both of hers and giving it a little caress. "Thank you for your prompt attention. This has been a trying day all round: first poor Patrick McNulty, and now my dearest Bun. It's most distressing—we're all such a large, happy family, you know."

I had a quick flash of déjà vu: Somewhere I'd seen this moment before.

Of course I had! It could have been a scene from any one of Phyllis Wyvern's films.

"I am in your debt, Vicar," she was saying. "If you

hadn't happened along, she might have taken a bad tumble on the stairs."

She was dramatizing the situation: That wasn't the way it had happened at all.

"If ever there's anything I can do to show my gratitude, you've only to ask."

And then it all came tumbling out of the vicar's mouth—at least most of it. Fortunately he didn't mention Cynthia's coaching lessons.

"So you see, Miss Wyvern," he finished up, "the roof has been more or less at risk since George the Fourth, and time is now of the essence. The verger tells me he's been finding water in the font, of late, that wasn't placed there for ecclesiastical purposes, and—"

Phyllis Wyvern touched his arm.

"Not another word, Vicar. I'd be happy to roll up my sleeves and pitch in. I'll tell you what; I've just had the most marvellous idea. My co-star, Desmond Duncan, will be arriving this evening. You may recall that Desmond and I had some small success both in the West End and on film with our *Romeo and Juliet*. If Desmond's game—and I'm sure he will be . . ."

She said this with a naughty wink and a twinkle.

". . . then surely we shall be able to cobble something together to keep St. Tancred's roof from caving in."

·FIVE·

I'D BEEN SPENDING SO much time sitting halfway down the stairs that I was beginning to feel like Christopher Robin.

That's where I was now, looking out across the crowded foyer, where several dozen of the film crew were gathered in little knots, talking. The only one I recognized was the woman called Marion, who had led Bun Keats away in the afternoon. Since Bun was nowhere in sight, I guessed she was still resting in her room.

"Ladies and gentlemen!" someone called out, clapping their hands for attention. "Ladies and gentlemen!"

The buzz of conversation stopped as abruptly as if it had been cut off with scissors.

A pale young man with sandy hair had made his way to the bottom of the staircase, climbed up a couple of steps, and turned to face the others.

"Mr. Lampman will address you now."

A few discreet lights were brought up to compensate for Buckshaw's antiquated electrical system.

From somewhere in the shadows behind them, a tiny middle-aged man made his appearance and, like a boy on a country road, strolled slowly and casually across the foyer as if he had all the time in the world. He was dressed, from the top down, in a rather battered olive-green fedora hat, a black roll-neck sweater, and black slacks.

In a different costume, Val Lampman might have passed for a leprechaun.

He turned and faced the others. I noticed that he didn't ascend even one of the stairs.

"It's nice to see so many of the old familiar faces—and a few new ones as well," he said. "Among the latter is Tom Christie, our assistant director—"

He stopped to put his hand on the shoulder of a curly-haired man who had now come over to join him.

"—who will be seeing that everyone is zipped up and that none of you walk into walls."

A small but polite laugh went up.

"As most of you know by now, we're embarking under a bit of a handicap. Pat McNulty has suffered an unfortunate injury, and although I'm assured that he's going to be all right, we're just going to have to get on without his benevolent mother hen tactics, at least for the time being.

"Ben Latshaw will be in charge of technical crew until further notice, and I know you'll extend him every courtesy."

Heads swivelled, but I couldn't see who they were looking at.

"I'd hoped to have a read-through of the first scene with Miss Wyvern and Mr. Duncan, but as he's not arrived yet, we'll substitute scene forty-two with the maid and the postman. Where are the maid and the postman? Ah! Jeannette and Clifford—good show. See Miss Trodd, and we'll meet upstairs as soon as we're finished here."

Jeannette and Clifford made their way across the foyer towards the horn-rimmed Marion, who waved a clipboard in the air to guide them through the throng.

Marion Trodd—so that was her name.

"Val, darling! Sorry I'm late."

The voice rang out like a crystal trumpet, bouncing from the polished panelling of the foyer.

Everyone turned to watch Phyllis Wyvern begin her descent from the landing of the west staircase. And what a descent it was. She had changed into a Mexican dancer's costume: white frilled blouse and a skirt like the canopy of a seaside roundabout.

The only thing missing was a banana in her hair.

There was a smattering of light applause and a single wolf whistle at which she pretended to blush, fanning her cheeks with her hand.

She must be freezing in those short sleeves, I thought. Perhaps working under hot lights had made her immune to the English winter.

She paused once, to give a helpless little shrug and point her chin to the upper reaches of the house.

"Poor, dear Bun," she said, in a suddenly solemn

voice—a voice meant to carry. "I tried to get some soup into her, but she couldn't keep it down. I've given her something to help her sleep."

Arriving at the bottom of the stairs, she floated across the foyer, seized Val Lampman's forearms, as if to keep him from touching her, and pecked at his cheek.

Even from where I sat, I could see that she missed him by a mile. She looked a little peeved, I thought, that he had stolen her thunder.

As they held each other at arm's length, the front door opened and Desmond Duncan made his entry.

"Sorry, all," he said in that voice of his that was known round the world. "Last matinée at the panto. Command performance. Simply couldn't bear to tear myself away from the poor dears."

He was bundled up in some kind of heavy fur coat—buffalo or yak, I thought. On his head was a wide-brimmed floppy hat of the sort worn by artists on the Continent.

"Ted!" he said, patting one of the electricians on the back. "How's the missus? Still collecting matchbooks? I've got one she might like to have—straight from the Savoy.

"Only two matches missing," he added with a broad pantomime wink.

I had seen Desmond Duncan in a film whose name I have forgotten: the one about the little girl who hires a failed barrister to force her estranged parents to reconcile. I had also seen pictures of him in some of the fan magazines Daffy kept hidden at the bottom of her undies drawer.

He had a sharp, beaked nose, and a projecting chin,

which gave him the profile of a thunderbolt: a profile that was probably instantly recognizable from Greenland to New Guinea.

A sudden gasp from above and behind me caused me to crane my neck and look up. I should have known! Daffy and Feely were peering through the balusters. They must be flat on their bellies on the floor.

Feely made shooing motions with her hands, indicating that I wasn't to give away their presence by staring at them.

I bounded up the stairs and lay down on the floor between them. Daffy tried to pinch me, but I rolled away.

"Do that again and I'll scream your name and your brassiere size," I hissed, and she shot me a villainous look. Daffy had only recently begun to develop and was still shy about trumpeting the details.

"Look at them!" Feely whispered. "Phyllis Wyvern and Desmond Duncan—actually together here—at Buckshaw!"

I peered down through the railings just in time to see them touch fingertips—like God and Adam on the ceiling of the Sistine Chapel, except that their respective clothing gave them the appearance, from above, of something more like a large bison coming face-to-face with a small pinwheel whirligig.

Desmond Duncan was now removing the bulky coat, which was taken instantly away by a little man who had been trailing him.

"Val!" he said loudly, looking round to take in the whole of the foyer. "You've done it again!"

By way of reply, Val Lampman smiled a tight smile and glanced almost too casually at his watch.

"Right, then," he said. "All present and accounted for. Jeannette and Clifford, as you were. You may stand down. We'll be taking the principals this evening, after all. First read-through tomorrow morning at seven-thirty, costumes at nine-fifteen. Miss Trodd will hand out the sheets in two hours' time."

"Now's your chance," Daffy whispered, nudging Feely. "Go ask him!"

In the foyer, the actors and crew were beginning to drift away, leaving Val Lampman alone at the bottom of the stairs jotting something in a notebook.

"No! I've changed my mind," Feely said.

"Silly camel!" Daffy told her. "Do you want me to ask him? I will, you know.

"She's going to be one of the extras," Daffy whispered. "She's got her heart set on it."

"No!" Feely said. "Shush!"

"Oh, Mr. Lampman," Daffy said, in quite a loud voice, "my sister—"

Val Lampman looked up into the shadows.

Feely punched Daffy on the upper arm. "Stop it!" she hissed.

I got up from the floor, gave my face a rub with the palm of my hand, adjusted my clothing, and walked down the stairs in a way that would have made Father proud.

"Mr. Lampman?" I said at the landing. "I'm Flavia de Luce, of the Buckshaw de Luces. My sister Ophelia is seventeen. She was hoping you'd be able to give her a small walk-on part." I pointed. "That's her up there peeking through the banister."

Val Lampman shaded his eyes and looked up into the dim woodwork.

"Please show yourself, Miss de Luce," he said.

Upstairs, Feely got to her knees, then to her feet, dusted herself off, and peered foolishly down over the railings.

There was an awkward silence. Val Lampman lifted his fedora and scratched his thin flaxen hair.

"You'll do," he said at last. "See Miss Trodd in the morning."

The telephone rang in its cubicle beneath the stairs, and, although I couldn't see him, I heard Dogger's measured footsteps coming through from the kitchen to answer it. After a muffled conversation, he came out into view and spotted me on the stairs.

"That was the vicar," he said. "Miss Felicity rang him to say that Colonel de Luce will be staying the night in London."

It must be snowing like stink! I thought, rather uncharitably.

"Odd that Aunt Felicity didn't telephone *here*," I said.

"She's been trying for more than an hour, but the line was engaged. She rang up the vicar instead. As it happens, he's driving over to Doddingsley in the morning to pick up some extra holly for the church decorations. He's kindly offered to meet Colonel de Luce and Miss Felicity at the railway station there and bring them to Buckshaw."

*　*　*

"*The holly and the ivy,*" I carolled loudly, not caring that I was a little off-key.

> "*When they are both full grown,*
> *Of all the poisons that are in the wood,*
> *The holly wears the crown.*"

Probably, I thought, because it contained theobromine, the bitter alkaloid that is also to be found in coffee, tea, and cocoa, and was first synthesized by the immortal German chemist Hermann Emil Fischer from human waste. The theobromine in the berries and leaves of the holly was just one of the cyanogenic glycosides, which, when chewed, release hydrogen cyanide. In what quantities, I had yet to determine, but just the thought of such a delicious experiment made the hairs on my forearms stand up in pleasure!

"You're thinking of the ilicin," Dogger said.

"Yes, I'm thinking of the ilicin. It's an alkaloid in the holly leaves, and it causes diarrhoea."

"So I believe I have read somewhere," Dogger said.

I could use the same batch of holly I'd dragged home to make the birdlime!

"*You'd better watch out . . .*" I sang, as I skipped upstairs with more than just the capture of Father Christmas in mind.

Wet, heavy flakes were falling straight down towards the earth, no two alike as they plummeted past the lighted window of my laboratory—yet all of them members of the same family.

In the case of snowflakes, the family's name is H_2O, known to the uninitiated as water.

Like all matter, water can exist in three states: At normal temperatures it's a liquid. Heated to 212 degrees Fahrenheit, it becomes a gas; cooled below 32 degrees, it crystallizes and becomes ice.

Of the three, ice was my favourite state: Water, when frozen, was classified as a mineral—a mineral whose crystalline form, in an iceberg, for instance, was capable of mimicking a diamond as big as the *Queen Elizabeth*.

But add a bit of heat and *poof!*—you're a liquid again, able to run easily, with only the assistance of gravity, into the most secret of places. Just thinking of some of the subterranean spots in which water has been makes my stomach tickle!

Then, raise the temperature enough, and *Ali-kazam!* you're a gas—and suddenly you can fly.

If that's not magic, I don't know what is!

Hyponitric acid, for instance, is absolutely fascinating: At –4 degrees Fahrenheit, it takes the form of colourless prismatic crystals; warm it up to just 7 degrees and it becomes a clear liquid. At 30 degrees the liquid turns yellow and then orange, until at 82 degrees, it boils and becomes a brownish-red vapour: all within a range of no more than 86 degrees!

Stupendous, when you stop to think about it.

But getting back to my old friend water, the thing of it is this: No matter how hot or how cold, no matter its state, its form, its qualities, or its colour, each molecule of water still consists of no more than a single oxygen atom bonded to two sister atoms of hydrogen. It takes all three of them to make a blinding blizzard—or a thunderstorm, for that matter . . . or a puffy white cloud in a summer sky.

O Lord, how manifold are thy works!

Later, in bed, I turned out the light and listened for a while to the distant sounds of people moving about, making last-minute preparations for the morning. Somewhere in the west wing they would still be adjusting their spotlights; somewhere Phyllis Wyvern would be boning up on her script.

But at last, after what seemed like a very long time, the day's work was done and, with a last few reluctant creaks and groans, Buckshaw slept in the silence of the falling snow.

·SIX·

I AWAKENED TO THE sound of shovelling. Crikers! I must
have overslept!

Leaping out from under the eiderdown, I struggled into
my clothing before my flesh could freeze.

The world outside my bedroom windows was the sickly
shade of an underdeveloped snapshot: a bruised black and
white, under which lay an ever so slightly menacing tinge
of purple, as if the sky were muttering, "Just you wait!"

A few taunting flakes were still sifting down slowly like
little white warning notes from the gods, shaking their
tiny frozen fists as they fell past the window.

Half the film crew, it seemed, were at work clearing a
maze of pathways between the vans and lorries.

I dug quickly through a pile of gramophone records
(Daffy told me I had pronounced it "grampaphone" when

I was younger) and, picking out the one I was looking for, dusted it on my skirt.

It was "Morning," by Edvard Grieg, from his *Peer Gynt* suite: the same piece of music that Rupert Porson (deceased) had used at the parish hall last September to open his puppet performance of *Jack and the Beanstalk.*

It wasn't my favourite piece of morning music, but it was infinitely better than "Let's All Sing Like the Birdies Sing." Besides, the disk had that lovely picture of the dog, his head tilted quizzically as he listens to his master's voice coming out of a horn, not realizing that his master is behind him painting his picture.

I gave the gramophone a jolly good cranking and dropped the needle onto the surface of the spinning disk.

"La-la-la-LAH, la-la la-la, LAH-la-la-la," I sang along, even putting the little hitches in the right places, until the end of the main melody.

Then, because it seemed to suit the bleakness of the day, I adjusted the control to reduce the speed, which made the music sound as if the entire orchestra had suddenly been overcome with nausea: as if someone had poisoned the players.

Oh, how I adore music!

I flopped limply round the room, sagging with the slowing music like a doll whose sawdust stuffing is pouring out, until the gramophone's spring ran all the way down and I collapsed on the floor in a boneless heap.

*   *   *

"I hope you haven't been getting underfoot," Feely said. "Remember what Father told us."

I let my tongue crawl slowly out of my mouth like an earthworm emerging after a rain, but it was a wasted effort. Feely didn't take her eyes from the sheet of paper she was studying.

"Is that your part?" I asked.

"As a matter of fact, it is."

"Let's have a dekko."

"No. It's none of your business."

"Come on, Feely! I arranged it. If you get paid, I want half."

Daffy inserted a finger in *Bleak House* to mark her place.

" 'In BG, OOF, a maid places a letter on the table,' " she said in a matter-of-fact tone.

"That's all?" I asked.

"That's it."

"But what does it mean?"

"It means that in the background, out of focus, a maid places a letter on the table. Just as it says."

Feely was pretending to be preoccupied, but I could tell by the rising colour of her throat that she was listening. My sister Ophelia is like one of those exotic frogs whose skin changes colour involuntarily as a warning. In the frog, it's trying to make you think that it's poisonous. It's much the same in Feely.

"*Caramba!*" I said. "You'll be famous, Feely!"

"Don't say '*Caramba*,' " she snapped. "You know Father doesn't like it."

"He'll be home this morning," I reminded her. "With Aunt Felicity."

At that, a general glumness fell over the table and we finished our breakfasts in stony silence.

The down train from London was due at Doddingsley at five past ten. If Clarence Mundy had been picking them up in his taxicab, Father and Aunt Felicity would be at Buckshaw within half an hour. But today, allowing for the snow and the practised funereal pace at which the vicar usually drove, it seemed likely to be well past eleven before they arrived.

It was, in fact, not until a quarter past one that the vicar's Morris pulled up exhausted at the front door, piled like a refugee's cart with various peculiarly shaped objects projecting from the windows and lashed to the roof. As soon as they climbed out of the car, I could tell that Father and Aunt Felicity had been quarrelling.

"For heaven's sake, Haviland," she was saying, "anyone who can't tell a chaffinch from a brambling ought not to be allowed to look out the window of a railway carriage."

"I'm quite sure it *was* a brambling, Lissy. It had the distinctive—"

"Nonsense. Bring my bag, Denwyn. The one with the large brass padlock."

The vicar seemed a bit surprised to be ordered about in such an offhanded manner, but he pulled the carpetbag from the backseat of the car and handed it to Dogger.

"Clever of you to think of winter tyres and chains,"

Aunt Felicity said. "Most ecclesiastics are dead washouts when it comes to motorcars."

I wanted to tell her about the bishop, but I kept quiet.

Aunt Felicity bore down on the front door in her usual bulldog manner. Beneath her full-length motoring coat, I knew, she would be wearing her complete Victorian explorer's regalia: two-piece Norfolk jacket and skirt, with extra pockets sewn in for scissors, pens, pins, knife, and fork (she travelled with her own: "You never know who's eaten what with strange cutlery," she was fond of telling us); several lengths of string, assorted elastics, a gadget for cutting the ends off cigars, and a small glass travelling container of Gentleman's Relish: "You can't find it since the war."

"You see?" she said, stepping into the foyer and taking in the jungle of motion picture equipment at a glance. "It's just as I told you. The ciné moguls have their hearts set on laying waste to every noble home in England. They're Communists to the last man Jack. Who do they make their pictures for? 'The People.' As if the people are the only ones who need entertaining. Pfagh! It's enough to make the heavenly hosts bring up their manna."

I was glad she hadn't said God, as that would have been blasphemous.

"Mornin', Lissy!" someone called out. "Tryin' to go straight, are you?" It was Ted, the same electrician Desmond Duncan had spoken to. He was occupied on a scaffold with an enormous light.

Aunt Felicity stifled an enormous sneeze, rummaging in her purse for a handkerchief.

"Aunt Felicity," I asked incredulously, "do you know that man?"

"Ran into him somewhere during the war. Some people never forget a name or a face, you know. Quite remarkable. In the blackout, I daresay."

Father pretended he hadn't heard, and made straight for his study.

"If it was in the blackout," I asked, "how could he see your face?"

"Impertinent children ought to be given six coats of shellac and set up in public places as a warning to others." Aunt Felicity sniffed. "Dogger, you may take my luggage up to my room."

But he had already done so.

"I hope they haven't put me in the same wing of the house as those Communists," she muttered.

But they had.

They'd given her the room next to Phyllis Wyvern's.

Aunt Felicity had no sooner stumped off to her quarters than Phyllis Wyvern herself strolled casually into the foyer, script in hand, mouthing words as if she were memorizing some particularly difficult lines.

"My dear vicar." She smiled as she spotted him lurking just inside the door. "How lovely to see you again."

"The pleasure belongs to Bishop's Lacey," the vicar said. "It is not often that our sequestered little village is honoured with a visitation of someone of . . . ah . . . such stellar magnitude. I believe the first Queen Elizabeth, in

1578, was the last such. There's a brass plaque in the church, you know . . ."

It was easy to see that he'd said precisely the right thing. Phyllis Wyvern fairly purred as she replied.

"I've been giving some thought to your proposal . . ." she said, leaving a long pause, as if to suggest the vicar had asked her hand in marriage.

He went a little pink and smiled like a happy saint.

". . . and decided that sooner is better than later. Poor Val is facing a couple of unforeseen difficulties: an injured wrangler, a missing camera, and now, I'm told, a frozen generator. We're not likely to expose any film for a couple of days yet. I know it's terribly short notice, but do you think you could arrange something for tomorrow?"

A shadow crossed the vicar's face.

"Dear me," he said, "I shouldn't wish to seem ungrateful, but there *are* certain difficulties of a . . . ah . . . practical nature."

"Such as?" she asked charmingly.

"Well, to be perfectly frank, the WC in the parish hall has gone for a burton. Which means, of course, that any public function is simply not on. Poor Dick Plews, our plumber, has been laid up with influenza for days now, and not likely to be up and about for quite some time. The poor dear man's eighty-two, you know, and though he's usually as chipper as a sparrow, this bitter cold . . ."

"Perhaps one of our technical people could—"

"Most kind of you, I'm sure, but I'm afraid that's not the worst of it. Our furnace, too, has been baring its fangs. The Monster in the Basement, we call it. It's a Deacon and Bromwell, made in 1851, and shown at the Great Exhibition—a great steel octopus of a thing with the temperament of a scorpion. Dick has been having an affair of the heart with the brute since he was no more than a lad at his father's knee. He coddles it outrageously, but in recent years he's been reduced to casting replacement parts by hand, and, well, you see . . ."

I hadn't noticed him yet, but Father had come from his study and was standing quietly beside a pile of packing cases.

"Perhaps a solution is more closely at hand," he said, coming forward. "Miss Wyvern, welcome to Buckshaw. I'm Haviland de Luce."

"Colonel de Luce! What a pleasure to meet you at last! I've heard so much about you. I'm greatly indebted to you for so graciously opening your lovely home to us."

Lovely home? Was she being facetious? I couldn't tell.

"Not at all," Father was saying. "We are all of us debtors in one way or another."

There was an uneasy silence.

"I, for instance," he went on, "am in the debt of my friend the vicar for fetching my sister and me from the train at Doddingsley. A most hazardous mission over treacherous roads, brought to a happy conclusion by his remarkable driving skills."

The vicar muttered something about winter tyres augmented with snow chains and then subsided to allow Father his time in the spotlight with Phyllis Wyvern.

They were still holding hands and Father was saying: "Perhaps I may be allowed to offer the use of Buckshaw for your performance? It is, after all, only for an evening, and I'm sure it wouldn't infringe upon our agreement if the foyer were cleared and set up with chairs for a few hours."

"Splendid!" the vicar chimed in. "There's room enough here for every soul in Bishop's Lacey, man, woman, and child, with room left over for elbows. Come to think of it, it's even more spacious than the parish hall. How odd that I didn't think of it before! It's too late for posters and handbills, but I'll ask Cynthia to produce some tickets on the hectograph. But first things first. She'll need to get the ladies of the Calling Circle organized to ring round the village and sign everyone up."

"And I'll have a word with our director," Phyllis Wyvern said, letting go of Father's hand at last. "I'm sure it will be all right. Val can't say no to me in certain spheres, and I'll see to it that this is one of them."

She smiled charmingly but I noticed that both Father and the vicar looked away.

"Good morning, Flavia," she said at last, but her acknowledgment of my presence came too late for my liking.

"Good morning, Miss Wyvern," I said, and walked off coolly towards the drawing room with a kiss-my-nelly look on my face. I'd show her a thing or two about acting!

My eyes must have bugged out of their sockets. Dressed in the green silks she had worn when she played the part of Becky Sharp in the Dramatic Society's production of

Vanity Fair, Feely was standing in front of a small round table, putting down a letter, picking it up, and putting it down again.

She would do this most delicately, then with a jerk of hesitation—and then with a sudden thrust, as if she couldn't stand the sight of the thing. She was rehearsing her appearance—or at least the appearance of one of her hands—in *Cry of the Raven*.

"I was chatting with Phyllis," I said casually, stretching the facts a little. "She and Desmond Duncan are doing a scene from *Romeo and Juliet* on Saturday night, here in the foyer. For charity."

"No one will come," Daffy said sourly. "In the first place, it's too close to Christmas. In the second, it's too short notice. In the third, in case they haven't thought of it, no one's going anywhere in this weather without snow-shoes and a Saint Bernard."

"Bet you're wrong," I said. "I'll bet you sixpence the whole village turns out."

"Done!" Daffy said, spitting on her palm and shaking my hand.

It was the first physical contact I'd had with my sister since the day, months before, that she and Feely had trussed me up and dragged me into the cellars for a candle-light inquisition.

I shrugged and walked to the door. A quick glance before leaving showed me that the hand of Becky Sharp was still mechanically picking up and putting down the letter like a clockwork wraith.

Although there was something pathetic about her actions, I couldn't, for the life of me, think what it was.

Halfway along the corridor, I became aware of angry voices in the foyer. Naturally, I stopped to listen. I am both blessed and cursed with Harriet's acute sense of hearing: an almost supernatural sensitivity to sound for which I have sometimes given thanks and sometimes despaired, never knowing until later which it was to be.

I recognized at once that the voices were those of Val Lampman and Phyllis Wyvern.

"I don't give a tinker's damn what you've promised," he was saying. "You'll simply have to tell them that it's off."

"And look like a bloody fool? Think about it, Val. What's it going to cost?—a couple of hours at a time of day when we're not working anyway. I'm doing it on my own time, and so is Desmond."

"That isn't the point. We're already behind schedule and things are only going to get worse. Patrick . . . Bun . . . and we've only been here a day. I simply don't have the resources to keep shoving shipping crates around so that you can do your Faerie Queene impression."

"You heartless brute," she said. Her voice was cold as ice.

Val Lampman laughed.

"*The Glass Heart.* Page ninety-three, if I'm not mistaken. You never forget a line, do you, old girl?"

Incredibly, she laughed.

"Come on, Val, be a sport. Show them you've got more in your heart than meat."

"Sorry, old love," he said. "No can do this time."

There was a silence, and I wished I could see their faces, but I couldn't move without giving away my presence.

"Supposing," Phyllis Wyvern said in little more than a whisper, "that I told Desmond about that interesting adventure of yours in Buckinghamshire?"

"You wouldn't dare!" he hissed. "Come off it, Phyllis—you wouldn't *dare!*"

"Would I not?"

I could tell that she'd got on her high horse again.

"Damn you," he said. "Damn you and damn you and damn you!"

There was another silence—even longer this time, and then Val Lampman suddenly said: "All right, then. You shall have your little show. It won't make much difference to my plans."

"Thank you, Val. I knew you'd come round to my way of thinking. You always do. Now shall we go upstairs and join the others? They'll be getting impatient."

I heard the sound of their footsteps going up the stairs. I'd give it a few more seconds, I thought, just to be certain they were gone.

But before I could move, someone stepped out from the shadows into the middle of the corridor.

Bun Keats!

She had not seen me. Her back was turned, and she

was peeking round the corner into the foyer. It was evident that she'd been eavesdropping on the conversation I'd just happened to overhear.

If she turned round, she'd be almost face-to-face with me.

I held my breath.

After what seemed like an eternity, she walked slowly through into the foyer and vanished from sight.

Again I waited until I heard her footsteps fade away.

"It's a pity, isn't it," a voice said almost at my shoulder, "when people don't get along?"

I nearly jumped out of my skin.

I spun round and there was Marion Trodd, with a quizzical—or was it a rueful—half-smile on her face. In spite of her smart tailored suit, her dark horn-rimmed glasses gave her the look of a tribal princess who had rubbed ashes round her empty black eyes in preparation for a jungle sacrifice.

She'd been there all along. And to think that I hadn't heard or seen her!

The two of us stood motionless, staring at each other in the dim corridor, not knowing quite what to say.

"Excuse me," I said. "I've just remembered something."

It was true. What I'd remembered was this: While I was not in the least afraid of the dead, there were those among the living who gave me the creeping hooly-goolies, and Marion Trodd was one of them.

I turned and walked quickly away, before something horrid could rise up out of the carpet and suck me down into the weave.

·SEVEN·

FATHER WAS SITTING AT the kitchen table listening to Aunt Felicity. This, more than anything, brought home to me how much—and how rapidly—our little world had been shrunk.

I slipped silently, or so I thought, into the pantry and helped myself to a piece of Christmas cake.

"This has gone on long enough, Haviland. It's been ten years now, and I've looked on in silence as your situation declined, hoping that you'd one day come to your senses . . ."

This was laughably untrue. Aunt Felicity never missed an opportunity to dig in a critical oar.

". . . but all in vain. It's unhealthy for the children to go on living under such barbaric conditions."

Children? Did she think of us as children?

"The time has come, Haviland," she went on, "to stop this incessant moping about and find yourself a wife—and preferably a rich one. It is positively indecent for a tribe of girls to be raised by a man. They become savages. It's a well-known fact that they don't develop properly."

"Lissy . . ."

"Flavia, you may step out," Aunt Felicity called, and I shuffled into the kitchen, a little shamefaced at having been caught snooping.

"See what I mean?" she said, darkly, pointing at me with a finger whose nail was the red of exhausted blood.

"I was getting Dogger a piece of Christmas cake," I said, hoping to make her feel dreadful. "He's been working so hard . . . and he often doesn't take enough to eat."

I took one of Dogger's black jackets from behind the door and threw it over my shoulders.

"And now if you'll excuse me . . ." I said, and went out the kitchen door.

The cold air nipped at my cheeks and knees and knuckles as I trotted through the falling flakes. The narrow path that someone had shovelled was already beginning to fill in.

Dogger, in overalls, was in the greenhouse, trimming sprigs of holly and mistletoe.

"Brrrrr!" I said. "It's cold."

Since he wasn't in the habit of responding to chitchat, he said nothing.

The Christmas tree Dogger had promised was nowhere in sight, but I fought down my disappointment. He probably hadn't had time.

"I've brought you some cake," I said, breaking off half and handing it to him.

"Thank you, Miss Flavia. The kettle is just coming to the boil. Will you join me for tea?"

Sure enough: On a potting bench at the back of the greenhouse, a battered tin kettle on a hot plate was shooting out excited jets of steam from lid and spout.

"Let's rouse Gladys," I said, and as Dogger filled two refreshingly grubby teacups, I lifted my trusty bicycle from the corner where she had been stowed, and carefully unwound the protective sacking in which, after a thorough oiling, Dogger had wrapped her for the winter.

"You're looking quite *fit*," I told her, making a little joke. Gladys was a BSA Keep-Fit that had once belonged to Harriet.

"*Quite* fit," Dogger said. "In spite of her hibernation."

I propped up Gladys on her kickstand beside us and gave her bell a couple of jangles. It was good to hear her cheery voice in winter.

We sat in companionable silence for a while, and then I said, "She's quite beautiful, isn't she—for her age?"

"Gladys? . . . Or Miss Wyvern?"

"Well, both, but I meant Miss Wyvern," I said, happy that Dogger had made the leap with me. "Do you think Father will marry her?"

Dogger took a sip of tea, put down his cup, and picked

up a sprig of mistletoe. He held it up by the stem as if weighing it, then put it down again.

"Not if he doesn't want to."

"I thought we weren't having decorations," I said. "The director didn't want the trouble of removing them when they begin filming."

"Miss Wyvern has decided otherwise. She's asked me to provide a suitably sized Christmas tree in the foyer for her performance on Saturday night."

I felt my eyes widening.

"To remind her of the trees she had in childhood. She said that her parents always put up a tree."

"And she asked you for holly? And mistletoe?"

"Yes, sir, yes, sir, three bags full, sir." Dogger smiled.

I hugged myself, and not just from the cold. Even the smallest of jokes on Dogger's lips warmed my heart— perhaps made me too bold.

"Did *your* parents?" I asked. "Used to put up a tree, I mean? The holly and the ivy and the mistletoe, and all that?"

Dogger did not answer straight away. The faintest of shadows seemed to drift across his face.

"In that part of India in which I was a child," he said at last, "mistletoe and holly were not easily to be had. I believe I remember decorating a mango tree for Christmas."

"A mango tree! India! I didn't know you lived in India!"

Dogger was silent for a long time.

"But that was long ago," he said at last, as if returning

from a dream. "As you know, Miss Flavia, my memory is not what it once was."

"Never mind, Dogger," I said, patting his hand. "Neither is mine. Why, just yesterday I had a thimbleful of arsenic in my hand, and I put it down somewhere. I can't for the life of me think what I could have done with it."

"I found it in the butter dish," Dogger said. "I took the liberty of setting it out for the mice in the coach house."

"Butter and all?" I asked.

"Butter and all."

"But not the dish."

"But not the dish," said Dogger.

Why aren't there more people like Dogger in the world?

Remembering Father's orders to keep out from underfoot, I spent what remained of the day in my laboratory making last-minute adjustments to the consistency of my powerful birdlime. The addition of just the right amount of oil of petroleum would keep it from freezing.

Christmas Eve was now just forty-eight hours away, and I needed to be ready for it. There would be no margin for error. I would have just one chance to capture Father Christmas—if, in fact, he existed.

Why was I so mistrustful of my sisters' tales of myth and folklore? Was it because experience had taught me that both of them were liars? Or was it because I really wanted—perhaps even *needed*—to believe?

Well, Father Christmas or no, I would soon be writing

up the Great Experiment in my notebook: Aim, Hypothesis, Method, Results, Discussion, Conclusion.

One way or another, it was bound to be a classic.

Scribbled in the margin of one of Uncle Tar's notebooks, I had found a quotation from Sir Francis Bacon: "We must not then add wings, but rather lead and ballast to the understanding, to prevent its jumping or flying."

Precisely what I had in mind for Saint Nicholas! A dose of the old tanglefoot! Later, in bed, my head filled with visions of reindeer stuck fast to the chimney pots like giant bluebottles to flypaper, I realized I was grinning madly in the dark. Sleep came at last, to what might have been the sounds of a distant gramophone.

·EIGHT·

I PAUSED AT THE top of the stairs.

"It's not right," a voice was grumbling. "They've no right to lumber us with all this."

"Better keep it down, Latshaw," said another voice. "You know what Lampman told us."

"Yes, I know what His Eminence said. Same as he did on the last shoot, and the shoot before that. I've heard that beef speech of his enough times I can recite it in my sleep. 'If you've got a beef, tell it to me,' and so on and so forth. Might as well tell it to the man in the moon for all the good it does."

"McNulty used to—"

"McNulty be damned! I'm in charge now, and what I say goes. And all I'm saying is this: They've got no right to lumber us with all this extra, just so that Her Royal Highness can give the local bumpkins something to gape at."

I backed slowly away from the staircase, then re-approached it more noisily.

"Shhh! Someone's coming."

"Good morning!" I said brightly, rubbing my eyes and going into my best village idiot impersonation. If there'd been time, I'd have blacked out one of my front teeth with pulverized carbon.

"Good morning, miss," said the one, and I knew by his voice that the other was Latshaw.

"Snowy old morning, eh what?"

I knew this was laying it on with a trowel, but with some people it doesn't matter. I had learned by personal experience that grumblers are deaf to any voices but their own.

"Oh, how pretty," I exclaimed as I reached the bottom of the stairs, clasping my hands together like a spinster who has just been given an engagement ring by a red-faced squire on bended knee.

The south side of the foyer had been transformed overnight into an Italian courtyard in evening. Stone walls painted onto canvas had been set up in front of the wood panelling, and the landing on the south staircase had become a balcony in Verona.

A few artificial trees spotted here and there in pots skillfully disguised as little benches added greatly to the effect. The whole thing was so well done I could almost feel the warmth of the Italian sun.

It was here, I knew, that in just a few hours, Phyllis Wyvern and Desmond Duncan would be re-creating the scene from *Romeo and Juliet*: a production that had once kept the West End of London awake until the small hours with curtain call after curtain call.

I had read about it in the musty film and theatre magazines that were piled everywhere in Buckshaw's library, or at least *had* been until they were cleared away for purposes of filming.

"Best scamper, miss. The paint's still wet. You don't want to go getting it all over yourself, do you?"

"Not if it's lead-based," I shot back as I wandered casually away, recalling with a little shiver of pleasure the case of the American artist Whistler, who, while painting his famous *The White Girl,* because of the high content of lead white in the pigment in his prime colour, had contracted what artists called "painter's colic."

Would lead poisoning by any other name taste as sweet? I knew that rats had been known to gnaw through lead pipes because they had acquired a taste for the sweetness of the stuff. In fact, I had begun compiling notes for a pamphlet to be called *Peculiarities of Plumbism*, and had turned to thinking pleasantly on that topic when the telephone rang.

I went for it at once before it could ring a second time. If Father heard it, we were in for a day of wrath.

"Blast!" I said, as I picked the thing up.

"Hello . . . Flavia? Have I caught you at an inopportune time?"

"Oh, hello, Vicar," I said. "Sorry—I just banged my knee on the door frame."

From Flavia's Book of Golden Rules: When caught swearing, go for sympathy.

"Poor girl," he said. "I hope it's all right."

"It will be fine, Vicar, when the agony abates."

"Well, I'm just ringing up to let you know that everything at this end is going splendidly. Tickets nearly sold out and it's barely sunrise. Cynthia and her telephonic warriors outdid themselves last night."

"Thank you, Vicar," I said. "I'll let Father know."

"Oh, and Flavia, tell him that Dieter Schrantz, at Culverhouse Farm, has suggested, if your father's willing, of course, that we use the old sleigh from your coach house to shuttle our theatregoers from the parish hall to Buckshaw. He says he'll rig up a hitch that will allow him to tow it along behind the tractor. The ride itself should be worth the price of admission, don't you think?"

Father had agreed, with surprisingly little grumbling, but then, where the vicar was concerned, he nearly always did. There was a friendship between them of a deep and abiding power which I didn't really understand. Although they had both attended Greyminster, they had not been at the school in the same years, so that wouldn't explain it. The vicar had no more than a polite interest in postage stamps and Father had no more than a passing interest in heaven, so the bond between them remained a puzzle.

To be perfectly frank, I was a little envious of their easy chumminess, and I sometimes caught myself wishing that I were as great friends with my father as the vicar was.

It wasn't that I hadn't tried. Once, while using one of his philatelic magazines to fan the flame of a sluggish

Bunsen burner, the pages had riffled open and the words "nascent oxygen" had caught my eye. The stuff, it seemed, had been produced by adding formaldehyde to potassium permanganate, and had been used by the Post Office to fumigate mailbags in the Mediterranean in the days when cholera was a constant threat.

Now here was a fact about stamp collecting that was actually interesting! A bridge—however precarious it might seem—between my father's world and mine.

"If you ever need any of your stamps disinfected," I had burst out, "I'd be happy to do them for you. I could whip up some nascent oxygen in a jiff. It would be no trouble at all."

Like a time traveller who had just awakened to find himself in a strange household in an unexpected century, Father had looked up at me from his albums.

"Thank you, Flavia," he had said after an unnerving pause. "I shall keep it in mind."

Daffy, as always, was draped over a chair in the library, with *Bleak House* open on her knees.

"Don't you ever get tired of that book?" I asked.

"Certainly not!" she snapped. "It's so like my own dismal life that I can't tell the difference between reading and not reading."

"Then why bother?" I asked.

"Bug off," she said. "Go and haunt someone else."

I decided to try a different approach.

"You've got black bags under your eyes," I said. "Were you reading late last night, or does your conscience keep you awake over the despicable way you treat your little sister?"

"Despicable" was a word I'd been dying to use in a sentence ever since I'd heard Cynthia Richardson, the vicar's wife, fling it at Miss Cool, the village postmistress, in reference to the Royal Mail.

"Sucks to you," Daffy said. "Who could sleep with all that caterwauling going on?"

"I didn't hear any caterwauling."

"That's because your so-called super-sensitive hearing has blown a fuse. You're probably beginning to display the hereditary de Luce deafness. It skips from youngest daughter to youngest daughter and generally sets in before the age of twelve."

"Piffle!" I said. "There was no caterwauling. It was all in your head."

Daffy's left earlobe began twitching as it does when she's upset. I could see that I had hit a nerve.

"It's not in my head!" she shouted, throwing down her book and jumping to her feet. "It's that damned Wyvern woman. She runs old films all night—over and over until you could scream. If I have to listen to that voice of hers saying 'I shall never forget Hawkhover Castle' one more time as that cheesy music swells up, I'm going to vomit swamp water."

"I thought you liked her—those magazines . . ."

Curses! I'd almost given myself away. I wasn't supposed to know about what was in Daffy's bottom drawer.

But I needn't have worried. She was too agitated to spot my slipup.

"I like her on paper, but not in person. She stares at me as if I'm some kind of freak."

"Perhaps you are," I offered helpfully.

"Get stuffed," she said. "Since you're such great pals with Lady Phyllis, you can tell her next time you see her to keep the noise down. Tell her Buckshaw's not some slimy cinema in Slough, or wherever it is she comes from."

"I'll do that," I said, turning on my heel and walking out of the room. For some odd reason I was beginning to feel sorry for Phyllis Wyvern.

In the foyer, Dogger was atop a tall orchard ladder, hanging a branch of holly from one of the archways.

"Mind the ilicin," I called up to him. "Don't lick your fingers."

It was a joke, of course. There was once thought to be enough of the glycoside in a couple of handfuls of the red berries to be fatal, but handling the leaves was actually as safe as houses.

Dogger raised an elbow and looked down at me through the crook of his arm.

"Thank you, Miss Flavia," he said. "I shall be most careful."

Although it is pleasant to think about poison at any season, there is something special about Christmas, and I found myself grinning. That's what I was doing when the doorbell rang.

"I'll get it," I said.

A gust of snow blew into my face as I opened the door. I wiped my eyes, and only partly in disbelief, for there in the forecourt stood the Cottesmore bus, tendrils of steam rising ominously from its radiator cap. Its driver, Ernie, stood before me, digging at his dentures with a brass toothpick.

"Step down! Step down! Mind your feet!" he called back over his shoulder to the column of people who were climbing down from the bus's open door.

"Your actors," he said, "have arrived."

They came trooping past him and into the foyer like tourists flocking into the National Gallery at opening time—there must have been about thirty in all: coats, scarves, galoshes, hand luggage, and gaily wrapped parcels. They were going to be here, I remembered, for Christmas.

One last straggler was having difficulty with the steps. Ernie made a move to help her, but she brushed away his offered arm.

"I can *manage*," she said brusquely.

That voice!

"Nialla!" I shouted. And indeed it was.

Nialla Gilfoyle had been the assistant to Rupert Porson, the travelling puppeteer who had come to a rather grisly end in St. Tancred's parish hall. I hadn't seen her since the summer, when she had gone off from Bishop's Lacey in something of a huff.

But all of that seemed to have been forgotten. Here she was on the front steps of Buckshaw in a green coat and a joyful hat trimmed with red berries.

"Come on, then, give me a hug," she said, opening her arms wide.

"You smell like Christmas," I said, noticing for the first time the large protuberance that stood between us.

"Eight months!" she said, taking a step back and throwing open her winter coat. "Have a gander."

"A gander at Mother Goose?" I asked, and she laughed appreciatively. Nialla had played the part of Mother Goose in the late Rupert's puppet show, and I hoped my little joke would not stir up unhappy memories.

"Mother Goose no more," she said. "Just plain old Nialla Gilfoyle (Miss). Jobbing actress, comedy, tragedy, pantomime. Apply Withers Agency, London. Telegraph WITHAG."

"But the puppet show—"

"Sold up," she said, "lock, stock, and barrel to a lovely chap from Bournemouth. Fetched me enough to rent a flat, where Junior here can have a roof over his or her head as the case may be, come January, when he or she finally decides to make his or her grand entrance."

"And you're starring in this?" I asked, waving my hand to take in the theatrical hubbub in the foyer.

"Hardly starring. I've undertaken the less-than-demanding role of Anthea Flighting, pregnant daughter—in a nice way, of course—of Boaz Hazlewood—that's Desmond Duncan."

"I thought he was a bachelor. Doesn't he court Phyllis Wyvern?"

"He is, and he does—but he has a past."

"Ah," I said. "I see." Although I didn't.

"Let me look at you," she said, grasping my shoulders and retracting her head. "You've grown . . . and you've got a little colour in your cheeks."

"It's the cold," I said.

"Speaking of which," she said with a laugh, "let's go inside before the acorn on my belly button freezes and falls off."

"Miss Nialla," Dogger said as I closed the door behind us. "It's a pleasure to have you back at Buckshaw."

"Thank you, Dogger," she said, taking his hand. "I've never forgotten your kindness."

"The little one will be along soon," he said. "In January?"

"Spot on, Dogger. You've got a good eye. January twenty-fifth, according to my panel doctor. He said it wouldn't hurt me to sign on for this lark as long as I gave up the ciggies, got plenty of sleep, ate well, and kept my feet up whenever I'm not actually in front of the camera."

She gave me a wink.

"Very good advice," Dogger said. "Very good advice, indeed. I hope you were comfortable on the bus?"

"Well, it is a bit of a jolter, but it was the only transportation Ilium Films could lay on to get us from the station in Doddingsley. Thank God the thing's such a hulking old bulldog. It managed to hang on to the roads in spite of the snow."

By now, Marion Trodd had shepherded the others away to the upper levels, leaving the foyer empty except for the three of us.

"I'll show you to your room," Dogger said, and Nialla

gave me a happy twiddle of the fingers like Laurel and Hardy as he led her away.

They had barely disappeared up the staircase when the doorbell rang again.

Suffering cyanide! Was I to spend the rest of my life as a doorkeeper?

Another gust of frozen flakes and cold air.

"Dieter!"

"Hello, Flavia. I have brought some chairs from the vicar."

Dieter Schrantz, tall, blond, and handsome, as they say on the wireless, stood on the doorstep, smiling at me with his perfect teeth. Dieter's sudden appearance was a bit disconcerting: It was somewhat like having the god Thor deliver the furniture in person.

As a devotee of English literature, especially the Brontë sisters, Dieter had elected to stay in England after his release as a prisoner of war, hoping someday to teach *Wuthering Heights* and *Jane Eyre* to English students. He also had hopes, I think, of marrying my sister Feely.

Behind him, in the forecourt, the Cottesmore bus had now been replaced by a grey Ferguson tractor which stood *putt-putt*ing quietly in the snow, behind it a flat trailer piled high with folding chairs which were covered almost entirely with a tarpaulin.

"I'll hold the door for you," I offered. "Are you coming to the play tonight?"

"Of course!" Dieter grinned. "Your William Shakespeare is almost as great a writer as Emily Brontë."

"Get away with you," I said. "You're pulling my leg."

It was a phrase Mrs. Mullet used. I never thought I'd find myself borrowing it.

Load after load, five or six at a time, Dieter lugged the chairs into the house until at last they were set up in rows in the foyer, all of them facing the improvised stage.

"Come into the kitchen and have some of Mrs. Mullet's famous cocoa," I said. "She floats little islands of whipped cream in it, with rosemary sprigs slit for trees."

"Thank you, but no. I'd better get back. Gordon doesn't like it if I—"

"I'll tell Feely you're here."

A broad grin spread across Dieter's face.

"Very well, then," he said. "But just one whipped-cream island—and no more."

"Feely!" I hollered towards the drawing room. "Dieter's here!"

No point wasting precious shoe leather. Besides, Feely had legs of her own.

·NINE·

"Well, well, well," Mrs. Mullet said. "And 'ow's everythin' at Culver'ouse Farm?"

"Very quiet," Dieter told her. "It is perhaps the time of year."

"Yes," she said, although each of us knew there was more to it than that. It would be a grim old Christmas at the Inglebys' after the events of last summer.

"And Mrs. Ingleby?"

"As well as can be expected, I believe," Dieter said.

"I promised Dieter a cup of cocoa," I said. "I hope it won't be too much trouble?"

"Cocoa's my speci-*al*-ity," Mrs. Mullett said, "as you very well knows. Cocoa is never too much trouble in any 'ouse'old what's run as it ought to be."

"Better make three cups," I said. "Feely will be here in . . . six . . . five . . . four . . . three . . ."

My ears had already picked up the sound of her hurrying footsteps.

Hurrying? She was flat out at the gallop!

"Two . . . one . . ."

An instant later the kitchen door was edged open and Feely sidled casually into the room.

"Oh!" she said, widening her eyes in surprise. "Oh, Dieter . . . I didn't know you were here."

Hog's britches, she didn't! I could see through her like window glass.

But Feely's eyes were as nothing compared with Dieter's. He fairly gaped at her green silk getup.

"Ophelia!" he said. "For a moment I thought that you were—"

"Emily Brontë," she said, delighted. "Yes, I knew you would."

If she didn't know he was here, I thought, *how could she know he'd mistake her for his beloved Emily?* But Dieter, love-struck, didn't notice.

I had to admire my sister Feely. She was as slick as a greased pig.

Although I know it is scientifically impossible, it seemed as if Mrs. Mullet could boil milk faster than anyone on the planet. With the Aga already as hot as an alchemist's furnace, and by stirring constantly, she was able, in the blink of an eye, to conjure up steaming cups of cocoa, each with its own tropical island and mock palm tree.

"It's too hot in here," Feely whispered to Dieter, as if she could keep me from overhearing. "Let's go into the drawing room."

As I moved to tag along, she shot me a look that said clearly, "And if you dare follow us, you're a dead duck."

Naturally, I waddled along behind.

Quack! I thought.

"Did you celebrate Christmas in Germany?" I asked Dieter. "Before the war, I mean?"

"Of course," he said. "Father Christmas was born in Germany. Didn't you know that?"

"I did," I said. "But I must have forgotten."

"Weihnachten, we call it. Saint Nikolaus, the lighted Christmas tree . . . Saint Nikolaus brings sweets for the children on the sixth of December, and Weihnachtsmann brings gifts for everyone on Christmas Eve."

He said this looking teasingly at Feely, who was sneaking a peek at herself in the looking glass.

"Two Father Christmases?" I asked.

"Something like that."

I gave an inward sigh of relief. Even if I did manage to bring one of them down and keep him from his rounds, there was still a spare to carry out whatever was left of the long night's work. At least in Germany.

Feely had drifted to the piano and settled onto the bench like a migrating butterfly. She touched the keys tentatively without pressing down, as if playing the wrong combination would make the world explode.

"I'd better be getting back," Dieter said, draining his cup to the dregs.

"Oh, can't you stay?" Feely said. "I'd been hoping you'd

translate some of the annotations on my facsimile edition of Bach's *The Well-Tempered Clavier*."

"They should call it *The* Bad-Tempered *Clavier*, when you play it," I said. "She swears like stink when she hits a clinker," I explained to Dieter.

Feely went as red as the carpet. She didn't dare swat me in front of company.

With her flushed face and her green outfit, she reminded me of something I'd seen in a recent colour supplement. What was it, now . . . ?

Oh, yes! That was it . . .

"You look like the flag of Portugal," I said. "I'll leave you alone so that you can wave good-bye."

I knew that I would pay for my insolence later, but Dieter's hearty laugh was worth it.

The house, generally so cold and silent, had suddenly become a beehive. Carpenters hammered, painters painted, and various people looked at various parts of the foyer through makeshift frames formed by touching thumbs and extending their fingers.

An astonishing number of lights had been put into place, some hanging from clamps on skeletal scaffolding and others mounted on spindly floor stands. Black wires and cables twisted everywhere.

Wig-wagging my extended arms for balance, I navigated my way carefully across the room, pretending I was walking across a pit of sleeping snakes—poisonous snakes that could awaken at any moment and . . .

"Hoy! Flavia!"

I looked up to see the ruddy face of Gil Crawford, the village electrician, grinning down at me through the framework of a high scaffold that had been rigged to span the great front door. Gil had been of much assistance in bringing back to life some of the more Frankensteinian of the electrical devices in Uncle Tar's laboratory, and had even taken the time to drill me in the safe handling of certain of the high-voltage instruments.

"Always remember," he had taught me to recite:

"Brown wire to the live,
Blue to the neutral
Greenery-yallery to the propensity
So's you don't wake up in Eternity."

When it came to wires and eternity, Gil was said to be something of an expert.

"'E was a Commando durin' the war!" Mrs. Mullet had once whispered, while gutting a rabbit on the kitchen table. "They was taught 'ow to gavotte people with a bit o' piano wire round their necks. *Gzaaack!*"

She'd grimaced horribly, her eyes rolled up, her tongue lolling out the side of her mouth by way of illustration.

" 'Quick as a wink,' Alf says. Next minute the victim finds 'isself sittin' on a cloud with an 'arp in 'is 'and, wonderin' where in 'eaven's name the world's ever got to."

"Mr. Crawford!" I called up to Gil. "What are you doing here?"

"Keeping the old hand in," he shouted back above the din of the hammering.

I put one foot on the ladder at the scaffold's side and began, hand over hand, to haul myself up.

At the top I stepped off onto the broad planks that formed a makeshift floor.

"Used to work this film lark when I was an apprentice lad." He grinned, rather proudly. "Keep my dues up just in case. You never know, nowadays, do you?"

"How's Mrs. Crawford?" I asked.

His wife, Martha, had recently invited me for tea while she ferreted out, from a box of cast-off valves, an obsolete rectifier for a radio-frequency fluorescing tube—for which she would take not a penny. It was a debt which I had so far been unable to repay.

"Topping," he said. "Fair topping. She's minding the shop so's I can come out on this caper."

He worked as he spoke, fastening a second long-snouted spotlight to a tubular cross member with a couple of clamps.

"Busiest time of year it is, too. Sold six wireless sets and three gramophones this week alone, so she did, a four-slice toaster, and an electric egg-cosy. Fancy!"

"You must have a lovely view of things from up here," I observed.

"So I do," he said, tightening the last bolt. "Funny you should say so. It's the same thing that German fellow from Culverhouse told me as he left. 'Far from the madding crowd,' he called up to me. Talks over my head but he's a good lad for all that."

"Yes, his name is Dieter," I told him. "He meant Thomas Hardy."

Gil scratched his head.

"Hardy? Don't know him. From around here, is he?"

"He's an author."

Like any bookworm's sister, I knew the titles of a million books I hadn't read.

"Ah!" he said, as if that settled it. "You'd better scramble down now. If the chief sees you up here, both our gooses will be cooked."

"Geese," I said. "Latshaw, you mean?"

"Yes, that's right," he said quietly. "Geese," and turned his attention to a box of coloured filters.

I had nearly reached the bottom of the ladder when I became aware of a face too close for comfort. I jumped to the floor and twisted round to find myself standing almost on Latshaw's toes.

"Who told you you could go up there?" he asked, his ginger moustache bristling.

"No one," I said. "I was having a word with Mr. Crawford."

"Mr. Crawford is on time-and-a-half for a short call in the holiday season," he said. "He has no time for idle chitchat—do you, Mr. Crawford?"

This last part he called out loudly enough for everyone to hear. I stepped back and glanced up at Gil, who was fussing with his spotlight, but he must have heard.

"I'm sorry," I said, becoming aware of the sudden silence that had fallen upon the foyer.

"Take my advice, miss," Latshaw said, "and keep to your quarters. We've no time for nuisances."

In my mind, Latshaw was already writhing on the floor, his face engorged, his eyes bulging from their sockets, hanging on with both hands to his gut, begging for the antidote to cyanide poisoning.

"Help me! Just help me!" he was screaming. "I'll do anything—anything!"

"Very well, then," I was telling him, reluctantly handing over a beaker into which I had stirred carefully calibrated proportions of ferrous sulfate, caustic potash, and powdered oxide of magnesium, "but in future, you really must learn how properly to address your betters."

Perhaps Latshaw was a mind reader, perhaps not, but he turned, strode off abruptly, and began giving right old hob to a carpenter who wasn't driving a nail properly.

At that very instant a bloodcurdling shriek came echoing from somewhere in the upper regions of the house.

"No! No-o-o-o-o! Let me alone!"

I recognized it at once.

All eyes were turned upwards as I flew past the workers and up the stairs. At the landing, one of the actresses reached out to stop me but I shook her off and continued my flight to the top and along the first-floor corridors, my pounding feet the only sound in the eerie silence that had fallen suddenly upon the house.

Strangers fell back out of the way to let me pass, hands to mouths, their faces frozen with—what was it?— fear?

"No! No! Keep away! Don't touch me. Please! Don't let them touch me!"

The voice was coming from Harriet's boudoir. I threw open the door.

Dogger was crouched in a corner, one of his quivering hands clasping the wrist of the other in front of his face.

"Please," he whimpered.

"Leave him *alone*!" I shouted at his ghosts. "Get out of here and leave him *alone*!"

And then I slammed the door loudly.

I stood perfectly still and waited until I could bear it no more—about ten seconds, I think—and then I said, "It's all right, Dogger, they're gone. I've sent them away. It's all right."

Dogger trembled behind his hands, his face, the colour of ashes, looking up at me unseeing. It had been months—half a year, perhaps—since he had suffered a full-blown episode of such terror, and I knew that this time it was going to take a while.

I walked slowly to the window and stood gazing out through a wreath of frost. To the left, in the steadily falling snow, the lorries of Ilium Films were almost hidden beneath the thick white blanket as if, at the end of the darkening day, they were tucked in for a winter's sleep.

Behind me, Dogger let out a pitiful little whimper.

"It's snowing again," I said. "Fancy that."

In the stillness I could almost hear the falling flakes.

"Isn't it a wonder, with that number of snowflakes, that no one has ever thought to write a book called *The Chemistry of Snow?*"

There was silence behind me, but I did not turn round.

"Just think, Dogger, of all those atoms of hydrogen and oxygen, joining hands and dancing ring-around-a-rosy to form a six-sided snowflake. Sometimes they form around a particle of dust—it says so in the encyclopedia—and because of it the form is misshapen. Hunchbacked snowflakes. Fancy that!"

He stirred a little, and so I continued.

"Think of the billions of trillions of snowflakes, and the billions of trillions of hydrogen and oxygen molecules in every single one of them. It makes you wonder, doesn't it, who wrote the laws for the wind and the rain, the snow and the dew? I've tried to work it out, but it makes my head spin."

I could see Dogger reflected three times over in the triple looking glass on Harriet's dressing table as he struggled slowly to his feet, and stood at last with his hands dangling limply at his side.

I turned away from the window and, taking one of his hands, led him, shambling, to Harriet's canopied and ruffled bed.

"Sit down here," I said. "Just for a minute."

Surprisingly, Dogger obeyed, and dropped down heavily onto the edge of the bed. I had thought he would balk at the very idea of taking a seat in Father's shrine to Harriet, but the fact that he did not was probably due to his confusion of mind.

"Put your feet up," I told him, "while I gather my thoughts."

I piled a mound of snowy pillows at his back.

With glacially slow speed, Dogger eased himself back until at last he was reclining in what looked, at least, like a comfortable position.

"*Stiff Water,* we could call it," I said. "The book, I mean. Yes, that would probably have more appeal. *Stiff Water*—I quite like that. I expect some people would buy it thinking it was a detective novel, but that's all right. We wouldn't care, would we?"

But Dogger was already asleep, his chest rising and falling in gentle swells, and if the tiny crease at the corner of his mouth was not the seed of a smile, it was, perhaps, a lessening of his distress.

I covered him to the chin with an afghan, and returned to the window and there, for what might have been an eternity, I stood staring out into the gathering gloom, into the cold, blowing universes of hydrogen and oxygen.

·TEN·

AT FIVE-THIRTY THE PEOPLE of Bishop's Lacey began to arrive. First were the Misses Puddock, Lavinia and Aurelia, the proprietresses of the St. Nicholas Tea Room.

Incredibly, these two creaking relics had walked the mile through deep drifts of snow, and now their round faces glowed like little red furnaces.

"We didn't want to be late, so we set out early," Miss Lavinia said, looking round appreciatively at the decorated foyer. "Very, very swank, isn't it, Aurelia?"

I knew that they were sizing up the situation, sniffing out the possibilities of being asked to perform. The Misses Puddock had managed to insinuate themselves into every public performance in Bishop's Lacey since the year dot, and I knew that at this very moment, stuffed handily somewhere into the depths of Miss Lavinia's handbag would be the sheet music for "Napoleon's Last Charge,"

"Bendemeer's Stream," and "Annie Laurie" at the very least.

"It's not for an hour and a half yet," I told them. "But you're welcome to have a seat. May I take your coats?"

With Dogger out of action, I had decided to take over the duties of the doorman myself. I'd certainly had enough practice during the day! Father would be furious, of course, but I knew that he would thank me when he came to understand. Well, perhaps not thank me, but at least spare me one of his three-hour lectures.

But for now, Father was nowhere in sight. It was as if, having received payment for the use of Buckshaw, he had no further obligation. Or could it be, perhaps, that he was ashamed to show his face?

The film crew were putting the finishing touches to the improvised stage, adjusting the lights and moving tall basketwork trumpets of fresh flowers into position at each side of the make-believe courtyard, when the doorbell rang.

Bunching my sweater tightly round my shoulders, I opened the door to find myself nearly nose-to-nose with a complete stranger. He was wrapped in a khaki greatcoat with no insignia that I was quite sure must have been issued by some army or another.

He was short, with freckles, and was chewing gum the way a horse chews an apple.

"This Buckshaw?" he asked.

I admitted that it was.

"I'm Carl," he announced. "You can tell your big sister I'm here."

Carl? Big sister?

Of course! This was Carl from St. Louis, Missouri—Carl, the American, who had given Feely the chewing gum I had pilfered from her lingerie drawer—Carl who had told her she was the spitting image of Elizabeth Taylor in *National Velvet*—Carl who had taught her how to spell Mississippi.

There had been Americans, I recalled, who had shared the airfield with a Spitfire squadron at Leathcote, a few of whom, like Dieter, had chosen to remain in England at the end of the war, and Carl must be one of them.

He was holding a small package, almost completely hidden inside a thicket of green ribbon hung all over with red-and-white candy-cane decorations.

"Camel?" he asked, producing a packet of cigarettes at his fingertips and cleverly flipping it open at the same time with his thumb, like a conjuror's trick.

"No, thank you," I said. "Father doesn't allow smoking in the house."

"He doesn't, eh? Well, then, I reckon I'll hold my fire for a spell. Tell Ophelia Carl Pendracka is here and he's ready to boogie-woogie!"

Good lord!

Carl sauntered past me into the foyer.

"Say," he said. "Swell place you got here. Looks like they're making a movie, am I right? Do you know what? I saw Clark Gable once in St. Louis. In Spiegel's. Spiegel's is where *this* came from . . ."

He gave the gift a shake.

"My mom picked 'em up for me. Stuck 'em in with the

Camels. Clark Gable looked right at me that time in Spiegel's. What do you say to that?"

"I'll tell my sister you're here," I said.

"Feely," I said, at the door of the drawing room, "Carl Pendracka is here, and he's ready to boogie-woogie."

Father looked up from the pages of his *London Philatelist*.

"Show him in," he said.

The imp inside me grinned and hugged itself in anticipation.

I went only as far as the end of the corridor and beckoned Carl with a forefinger curled and uncurled.

He came obediently.

"Nice place you've got here," he said, touching the dark panelling appreciatively.

I held open the study door, doing my best to mimic Dogger in his valet role: a look on my face and a particular posture that indicated keen interest and at the same time keen disinterest.

"Carl Pendracka," I announced, a trifle facetiously.

Feely looked up from her own to Carl's reflection in the looking glass as Carl walked briskly to where Father sat, seized his hand, and gave it a jolly good wringing.

Although he didn't show it, I could tell that Father was taken aback. Even Daffy glanced up from her book at the breach of manners.

"Carl's family might be related to the King Arthur Pendragons," Feely said in that brittle and snotty voice she uses for genealogical discussion.

To his credit, Father did not look terrifically impressed.

"Merry Christmas, Miss Ophelia de Luce," Carl said, handing her his gift. I could tell that Feely was torn between centuries of good breeding and the urge to rip into the gift like a lion into a Christian.

"Go ahead, open it," Carl urged. "It's for you."

Father subsided quickly into his stamp journal while Daffy, pretending to have reached a particularly gripping passage in *Bleak House*, was secretly peering out from beneath her furrowed brows.

Feely picked at the bows and ribbons as slowly and as fussily as a naturalist dissecting a butterfly under a microscope with tweezers.

"Tear it off!" I wanted to shout. "That's what wrapping's for!"

"I don't want to spoil this beautiful paper," she simpered.

By the buttons of the Holy Ghost! I could have strangled her with the ribbon!

Carl obviously felt the same way.

"Here," he said, taking the package away from Feely and poking his thumbs through the folded paper at the ends. "All the way from St. Louis, Mo.—the Show Me State."

A candy cane clattered to the hearth.

"Oh!" said Feely as the wrapping fell away. "Nylons! How lovely! Wherever did you find them?"

Even Daffy gasped. Nylons were as scarce as unicorn droppings: the Holy Grail of gift-giving.

Father shot up out of his chair as if on a spring. In a

flash he was across the room, and the nylons, which he had ripped from Feely's hands, were dangling from his wrists like adders.

"This is outrageous, young man. Positively indecent. How dare you?"

He brushed the stockings off his hands and arms and into the fireplace.

I watched as the nylons shrivelled, writhing and blackening in the flames, transformed by heat into their constituent chemicals (adipoyl chloride, I knew, and hexamethylenediamine). I felt a little shiver of pleasure as the stockings gave up the ghost in one last, delicious flickering flame. Their dying breath, a wisp of the deadly poisonous gas hydrogen cyanide, floated up the chimney and then it was gone. In just a few seconds, Carl's gift was no more than a sticky black glob bubbling on the Yule logs.

"I . . . I don't understand," Carl said.

He stood looking from Father to Feely to Daffy to me.

"You Limeys are crackers," he said. "Just plain dizzo."

"Dizzo," Carl repeated to me in the foyer, shaking his head in disbelief. Feely had fled, shaken by sobs, to her bedroom and Father, in a thundercloud of outraged dignity, had taken refuge in his study.

"Have a chair," I said and, as the doorbell rang again, I introduced Carl quickly to the Misses Puddock.

"Carl's from St. Louis, in America," I told them, and by the time I reached the door, they were already chatting away like lifelong cronies.

On the doorstep, as if for inspection, was Ned Cropper, gift in hand and brilliantine in hair. A few steps behind him stood Mary Stoker.

Aside from her ruddy complexion and a bit of a squint, Mary might have been a Madonna in the National Gallery as she stood on the doorstep, radiant in the snow.

No room at the inn, I thought uncharitably.

"Ned! Mary!" I crowed, a little too cheerfully.

Ned was the potboy at the Thirteen Drakes, Bishop's Lacey's sole hostelry, and Mary was the landlord's daughter. I knew without being told that Ned had brought the gift for Feely: another box of those flyblown prewar Milady chocolates from the window of Miss Cool's confectionery, its contents lightly frosted with a mould which could, of course, if you had a strong enough stomach, be scraped away before scoffing them.

Ned's love tributes were generally left on the kitchen doorstep in the dark of the moon to be brought in dangling distastefully between finger and thumb by Mrs. Mullet.

"Them tomcats been round again," she would mutter.

"I like your hair," I said to Mary. "Did you get it cut?"

"Cut it myself, special for Christmas," she whispered. "Do you like it, really?"

"Nobody's going to give Phyllis Wyvern a second look with you in the room," I said, giving her arm a squeeze.

"Oh, you!" she laughed, and slapped my hand a little harder than she knew.

"Find a seat," I told them. "You're early, so you can take your pick."

I knew that Ned would choose front row centre, and I

was right. He'd want to be as close to Phyllis Wyvern as was humanly possible.

A roaring motor in the forecourt announced that Dieter had arrived with the first load of audience. I threw open the door just as the Fergie jerked to a stop, its lamps making cornucopias of foggy yellow light in the falling snow. Behind the tractor, brimming over with passengers—a couple of village men perched precariously on the runners—was Harriet's sleigh.

A shadow passed in front of my heart.

How sad it was to think that somewhere, Harriet should have died in snow like this. How could such tragedy occur amid such beauty?

That was the way with ghosts, though: They appeared at the strangest of times in the most peculiar places.

I hadn't long to call my mother's face to mind; people were already piling out of the sleigh and coming towards the door, laughing and talking excitedly.

"Flavia! *Haroo, mon vieux! Joyeux Noël!*"

That was Maximilian Brock, the pint-sized concert pianist (retired) who had traded his keyboard and bench for a whole new career as the village gossip mill. It was whispered (but not by me) that he wrote up and sold as fiction to the romance magazines the thinly disguised tales of door-latch scandal he had gleaned in Bishop's Lacey.

"Lust-sheets," Daffy called them.

"Have you seen Phyllis Wyvern yet?" Max demanded. "How does she look in life? Are her wrinkles as parched gullies, or was that sheer meanness on the part of *Tittle-Tattle?*"

"Hello, Max," I said. "Yes, I've seen her, and she's never been more lovely."

"And those sisters of yours; still growing?"

"You can ask them yourself," I said, somewhat impatiently. Once Max got started, you might as well put down roots.

But before he could frame another question, Max was nudged aside by the substantial tummy of Bunny Spirling, of Nautilus Old Hall, looking so much like Mr. Pickwick that it gave me the momentary creeps.

His thumbs hooked tightly in his waistcoat pockets, Bunny patted his stomach and raised his pink nostrils into the air as if he were on the scent of food.

"Flavia," he said, not putting too much effort into it before scurrying away on curiously dainty feet.

After the sleigh had emptied, Dieter made a tight circle with the tractor and sleigh in the snowy forecourt, and with the wave of a mitt, jounced off to the village for another load.

With Dogger out of commission, I was kept busy welcoming newcomers and chatting up old acquaintances. It was evident that no one else in my family was going to put in an appearance. They had obviously decided that the evening's performance was the business of the filmmakers, and that there was no need for them to lift a finger. I was on my own.

Not long before starting time, the vicar arrived, huffing and puffing in the foyer, and stamping his feet.

"It's coming down as if all the angels and archangels are plucking chickens," he said.

Cynthia hung back, scowling at his blasphemy.

"Constable Linnet tells me that all roads in and out of Bishop's Lacey are hopelessly blocked," he went on, "and are likely to remain so until the Hinley road men clear their own turf. It's the price we pay for being outlanders, so to speak, but nevertheless, it's dashed inconvenient."

Marion Trodd came squeezing herself through the hubbub.

"Miss Wyvern is ready, Vicar," she said. "If you'd be so kind—"

"Of course, my dear. Tell her I shall preface her performance with a few remarks of my own re Roofing Fund, et cetera, and then it's all hers—oh, and Mr. Duncan's, of course. Dear me, we mustn't forget Mr. Duncan."

As the vicar made his way to the front, Father, Feely, and Daffy, led by Aunt Felicity, filed slowly into the foyer and took their seats in the front row. Since Ned was occupying the chair that should have been mine, I stayed in the back.

I twiddled my fingers at Nialla and she twiddled back, tapping her tummy and rolling her eyes comically.

"Ladies and gentlemen, friends and neighbours, and anyone else I've managed to leave out—"

There was a polite titter to reward the vicar for his sparkling wit.

"We've all of us braved the roaring elements tonight to illustrate the wise old saw that charity begins at home. If we now find ourselves warm and cosy in the ancestral home of the family de Luce, it is entirely due to the kind graces of Colonel Haviland de Luce" ("Hear! Hear!")

"that we are able to come together in such inclement weather to prop up the roof of St. Tancred's, as it were.

"Without further ado, it gives me great pleasure to introduce to you Miss Phyllis Wyvern and Mr. Desmond Duncan. Miss Wyvern, it is unnecessary to tell you, is a star of stage and screen, who has thrilled all of our hearts in such productions as *Whitehall Nellie, The Secret Summer, Love and Blood, The Glass Heart* . . ."

He paused to pull a scrap of paper from his pocket, clean his spectacles with it, and then read what was written on it.

"*The Crossing Keeper's Daughter, The Trench in the Drawing Room, The Queen of Love* . . . ahem . . . *Sadie Thompson*" (a couple of nervous titters and a distinctly wolfish whistle), "and last, but not least, *The Rector's Wife.*"

This was greeted by general cheers but marred by a single catcall.

Cynthia sat staring straight ahead, her lips pursed.

"Mr. Duncan has been seen most recently in *Articles of War*. And so without further ado, we welcome to Bishop's Lacey two great luminaries of the screen, Miss Phyllis Wyvern, ably assisted by Mr. Desmond Duncan, in their world-famous interpretation of a scene from William Shakespeare's *Romeo and Juliet.*"

There was no curtain to go up, but in its place, the lights were switched out, and for a few moments we sat in the dark.

Then a spotlight pierced the blackness, picking out a little grove of potted lemon trees. A lettered placard on a wooden tripod told us that this was Capulet's orchard.

I twisted round far enough to see that the fierce white

beam of light was coming from atop the scaffolding above the door, and that the figure hunched over one of the snouted spotlights was Gil Crawford.

Romeo, in the form of Desmond Duncan, came strolling into the grove to a smattering of applause. He was dressed in tan tights, over which was a peculiar pair of red velvet shorts which looked rather like inflated swimming trunks. He wore a white shirt of the peasant variety, all fancy ruffles of lace at the neck and sleeves, and his sporty flat hat was decorated with a pheasant's tail feather.

He extended his open hands to the audience and took a series of elaborate little bows before speaking his first word.

Come on! I thought. *Get on with it!*

"He jests at scars that never felt a wound."

Another pause, and another sprinkling of applause in recognition of that famous voice.

"But, soft! What light through yonder window breaks?"

A few sparse hand claps to show that they were familiar with the line.

"It is the east, and Juliet is the sun.
Arise, fair sun, and kill the envious moon . . ."

Again he paused, gazing up, his eyes fixed on Juliet's balcony, which remained, beyond the spotlight's beam, in utter blackness.

"Spot!" Phyllis Wyvern's voice commanded loudly from somewhere above Romeo's head.

The moment was frozen. It seemed to stretch on and on.

"*Arise, fair sun, and kill the envious moon . . .*" Desmond Duncan began again, still not quite Romeo.

You could have heard a pin drop in China.

"Spotlight, dammit!" snapped the voice of the fair Juliet from the darkness, and there came from behind me the most frightful crash, as if some metal object had fallen from the scaffold onto the tiles of the foyer.

"*. . . the envious moon,*" Desmond Duncan ploughed on,

> "*Who is already sick and pale with grief,*
> *That thou her maid art far more fair than she . . .*"

There was a sudden rustling of silks as Phyllis Wyvern came swishing down the steps from the landing, her feet appearing first at the perimeter of Romeo's spotlight, and then her dress.

Her costume was absolutely gorgeous, a fawn-coloured creation, wide at the hem, tight as blazes at the waist, and shockingly low at the neck. The precious stones that lined the collar and sleeves glittered madly as she passed through the glare of Romeo's spotlight, and a gasp went up from the audience at the unaccustomed splendour that had materialized so suddenly in their midst.

Into her braided hair was woven a chaplet of flowers—real flowers, by the look of them—and I bit my lip in admiration. How young and beautiful, and how timeless she seemed!

The *real* Juliet, if ever there was one, would have spat in envy.

Down and down she came, and at last onto the foyer floor, her pointed slippers making a menacing sound on the tiles: like a pair of snakes tiptoeing on their rib ends.

Ned Cropper shrank back a little as she swept past him towards the front door.

She's leaving! I thought. *She's walking out!*

I twisted round in my chair, fighting to remain seated, as Phyllis Wyvern, having reached the scaffolding, seized hold of the ladder, placed a delicately slippered foot on the first rung, and began to climb.

Up and up she went, her Elizabethan dress, even in the darkness, shooting off sparks of light like a comet ascending the heavens.

At the top, she stepped off onto the plank flooring and edged her way along to where Gil Crawford stood watching her approach, his mouth open.

Clinging to the scaffold's railing with one hand, Phyllis Wyvern hauled off and, with the other, slapped Gil hard across the face.

The sharp crack of it echoed back and forth across the foyer, refusing to die.

Gil's hand flew to his cheek, and even in the near darkness, I saw the flash from the whites of his terrified eyes.

She hitched up the hem of her dress and manoeuvred back to the ladder, which she managed to climb down with surprising grace.

Looking neither to the right nor the left, Phyllis Wyvern

processed—there's no other word for it; she looked as if she were walking in state up the centre aisle of Westminster Abbey—she processed across the foyer to the foot of the west staircase, which she climbed, skirt still hitched in one hand, to the landing, where she turned and struck a pose at the railing of her make-believe bedroom balcony.

After a heart-stopping pause, the second spotlight came on with an audible *clack*, catching her in its beam like some exotic moth.

She clasped her hands to her breast, took a shuddering breath, and spoke her first line:

"*Ay me!*" she said.

"*She speaks!*" said Romeo.

"*O, speak again, bright angel!*" he went on, rather hesitantly,

> "*For thou art as glorious to this night, being o'er my head,*
> *As is a wingèd messenger of heaven*
> *Unto the white-upturnèd wondering eyes of mortals that*
> *   fall back to gaze on him . . .*"

I couldn't help thinking of Gil Crawford's eyes.

"O Romeo, Romeo!" she cooed. "*Wherefore art thou Romeo?*"

And so on. The rest of the performance was just a lot of that moon-June-balloon stuff—a load of old mulch, really—and I found myself wishing they had chosen a more exciting scene from the play, one of those involving toxicology, for instance, which are the only really decent parts of *Romeo and Juliet*.

We had been made to listen to the play in its entirety on one of Father's compulsory Thursday wireless nights, during which I had formed the opinion that while Shakespeare was good with words, he knew beans about poisons.

The difference between poisons and narcotics seems to have escaped him, and he was in an utter muddle when it came to those vegetable and mineral irritants that act upon the brain and spinal cord.

In spite of all the wordy hocus-pocus about gathering herbs by moonlight, Juliet's symptoms indicated the use of nothing more mystifying than plain old hydrocyanic acid administered in drinking water.

For ever and ever, Amen.

By now, Phyllis Wyvern and Desmond Duncan were taking their bows. Joining hands like Hansel and Gretel, they took a couple of steps towards the audience, then backed away, and then advanced again, like waves lapping at the sands.

Flushed with pleasure, or something, they were both perspiring freely, their makeup, at close range, suddenly ghastly in the overhead lights.

Phyllis Wyvern was so close to Ned that his mouth gaped open like a flounder on a fishmonger's stall, so that Mary had to nudge him in the ribs.

I looked up just in time to catch a glimpse of a dark figure vanishing into the shadows at the head of the stairs, just above Juliet's makeshift balcony.

It was Dogger, and I realized with a start that he had been there all along.

·ELEVEN·

With the foyer lights switched back on, I had my first chance to have a glance round at the entire audience.

There in the back row, with a happy look on his face, sat Dieter. Beside him, chewing on a mint, was Dr. Darby, and behind him, Mrs. Mullet with her husband, Alf.

Each of them seemed caught up in a trance, blinking round in silly wonder, as if they were surprised to find themselves still in their same old bodies.

Theatre, I suppose, is a form of mass mesmerism, and if that's the case, Shakespeare, despite his chemical short-comings, was surely one of the greatest hypnotists who ever lived.

I had seen a spell woven before my eyes, broken by a slap, then woven again as easily as a granny darns a sock. It was marvellous—a blooming wonder, actually—when you came to think about it.

The actors now had gone to remove their makeup, and the ciné crew vanished to the upper reaches of the house to do whatever they do after a performance. They had not stayed to mingle with the audience, but that, perhaps, was part of the spell.

A gust of cold rushed suddenly into the foyer. Someone had opened the front door for a breath of fresh air, given a gasp, cries had gone up, and now everyone, including me, was crowding for a look outside.

A sharp wind had arisen during the performance and piled a waist-deep snowdrift at the door.

It was easy enough to see that tractor or no tractor, sleigh or no sleigh, no one was going to get home to Bishop's Lacey tonight.

Still, Dieter was brave enough to give it a try. Bundling up in his heavy coat and scaling the white mountain that had appeared so suddenly, he was soon lost in the darkness.

"Better ring up Tom McGully to bring his snow-plough," someone said.

"No use doing that," came a voice from the far corner, "as I'm already here."

A nervous laugh went up, as Tom came forward and peered out the door with the rest of us.

"It's a mort o' snow," he said, somehow making it official. "A mighty mort o' snow."

The hands of several ladies flew to their throats. The men exchanged quick glances, their faces expressionless.

Ten minutes later, Dieter was back, caked with the stuff, shaking his head.

"Tractor doesn't start," he announced. "Battery's dead."

*   *   *

The vicar, as usual, had taken charge.

"Ring up Bert Archer at the garage," he had told Cynthia. "Tell him to bring his tow truck. If you can't get through to Bert, leave a message with Nettie Runciman at the exchange."

Cynthia nodded grimly and plodded off towards the telephone.

"Mrs. Mullet . . . I saw her here somewhere . . . Mrs. Mullet, do you think it would be possible to lay on some tea, and perhaps some cocoa for the little ones?"

Mrs. Mullet made for the kitchen, happy to be one of the first enlisted. As she vanished into the passageway, Cynthia reappeared.

"The line is dead," she announced in a monotone.

"Well, then," the vicar said, "as it seems we're here for the duration, we shall just have to make do, shan't we?"

It was decided with surprisingly little fuss that preference would be given to those with children, who would be allowed, wherever room permitted, to bunk in among the ciné crew who had already been assigned digs on the first floor.

Somewhere during the process, Father had put in a brief appearance, and with a couple of pointed fingers and a few words to the vicar, had mobilized the operation as if it were a precision military exercise. He had then re-vanished into his study.

Those who could not be accommodated upstairs would bunk down in the foyer. Pillows and blankets that had not been used since Harriet was alive would be brought out of their storage presses and handed out to the make-shift refugees.

"It shall be just like old times," the vicar told them, rubbing his hands together vigorously. "Not unlike the bomb shelters during the war. We shall make a great success of it; a grand adventure. After all, it isn't as if we haven't done it before."

There was more than a trace of Winston Churchill in his voice.

The vicar organized a few games for the children: puss in the corner, blindman's buff, hide-and-seek, with prizes donated by Dr. Darby—mints, of course—to the winners.

The grown-ups gossiped and laughed quietly on the sidelines.

After a while, the more boisterous activities dwindled to guessing games.

As the evening wore on, the false jollity subsided. Yawns appeared, stifled at first but eventually becoming open and damn the niceties.

Children began to doze off, and their parents soon followed. It wasn't long before most of the displaced villagers of Bishop's Lacey were in the grips of sleep.

Later, as I lay snuggled beneath my eiderdown, alone in the vast, barnlike coldness of the east wing, I could hear, for a while, the muted buzz of conversation, like the hum of a distant hive.

After a time, this, too, died down, and my ears detected only an occasional cough.

It had been a long, long day, but in spite of it, I couldn't sleep. In my mind, I saw the bundled bodies scattered helter-skelter in the foyer: sleeping mounds beneath their blankets like so many tussocks in a country churchyard.

I tossed and turned for what seemed like hours, but it was no use. Surely everyone was asleep by now, and nobody would be disturbed if I crept to the top of the stairs and took a peek. With the very real threat of Father losing his battle with the taxman, I was now consciously saving up images for a time when I was an old lady—a time when I would rummage through my recollections of Buckshaw as one might turn the pages of a dusty photograph album.

"Ah, yes," I would quaver in my old woman's voice, "I mind the time we were snowed in on Christmas Eve. The winter night that Bishop's Lacey came to Buckshaw."

I climbed out of bed and into my refrigerated clothing.

Down the corridor I crept, stopping now and then to listen.

Nothing.

I stood at the top of the stairs, looking down upon the makeshift shelter.

Perhaps because it was so close to Christmas, there was something oddly touching about those huddled forms, as if I were an aviator, or an angel, or God, even, looking down from above upon all of these helpless, sleeping humans.

From somewhere far away, in the west wing, came the sound of distant music, and of unreal recorded voices.

So profound was the silence in the house that I was even able to make out the words:

"I shall never forget Hawkhover Castle."

Phyllis Wyvern was watching herself on film again.

The music swelled, and then died.

Downstairs, someone rolled over and began to snore. From where I stood, I could see Dieter, bundled against the railing on the landing. Smart enough to choose a higher sleeping place, I thought, where the air is slightly warmer, and the flooring not so cold as the tiles of the foyer.

In the hall below, Mrs. Mullet breathed heavily, her arm draped as casually over Alf as the babes in the wood.

Slowly, I descended the staircase, taking special care to tiptoe past the sleeping Dieter.

Over there, against the wall, was Cynthia Richardson, in sleep as relaxed as an archangel on a Christmas card; her face like Flora in the Botticelli painting. I wished I'd had a camera so that I could preserve that unexpected glimpse of her forever.

At her side the vicar slept, his brow deeply furrowed.

"Hannah, please! No!" he whispered, and for a moment, I thought that he had awakened.

Who was Hannah, I wondered, and why was she tormenting him in his sleep?

Upstairs, a door closed softly.

Phyllis Wyvern, I thought. *She's finished for the night with her viewing.*

A marvellous idea floated into my mind.

Why not see if she wanted to talk? Perhaps, like me, she was sleepless.

Or what if she was lonely? We could have a nice chat about grisly murders. Being so famous probably meant that all her friends were in it for the money—or the glory: for being able to say they were chummy with Phyllis Wyvern.

She'd have no one to talk to about the things that really counted.

Besides, it would probably be a once-in-a-lifetime opportunity to have a world-famous movie star all to myself—even if only for a few minutes.

But wait! What if she was tired? What if she still hadn't got over that fierce outburst when she'd slapped Gil Crawford's face? Would she do the same to me? I could almost feel the sting of her hand on my cheek.

Still, if I told Feely I'd spent an hour or so idly chit-chatting with Phyllis Wyvern, she'd be sick jealous!

That settled it.

From the bottom of the stairs, I set out on tiptoe across the foyer, picking a precarious and winding path between the sleeping bodies.

While I was still in the midst of the encampment and halfway to the west staircase, a water closet flushed.

I froze.

It was an unpleasant fact of life at Buckshaw that the rickety maze of pipes that passed for plumbing had seen far, far better days. They were, in fact, past their prime when Queen Victoria was on the throne, if one may be permitted to say such a thing.

A flush here or a tap activated there transmitted vast shudders and groans to the farthest corners of the house like some bizarre hydraulic signalling system from another age.

To put it plainly, no one at Buckshaw had any secrets—not, at least, in the plumbing department.

I stopped breathing until the shudder of pipes subsided in a far distant clatter. Ned, who was propped up against a wall with his feet splayed out like a cast-off doll, gave a groan, and Mary, whose head was on his knees, turned over in her sleep.

I counted to a hundred, just to be sure, and again began picking my way between the sleeping bodies.

Up the west staircase I went, one step at a time, counting them as I climbed: ten to the landing, another ten to the top corridor.

I knew that the thirteenth tread from the bottom groaned alarmingly, and I took a giant step to climb over it in silence, hauling myself up by gripping the banister.

Past the top of the stairs, the corridor was in darkness, and I had to feel my way along by sense of touch. The baize door to the north front swung open without a sound.

This was the part of the house that had been assigned as billets, the dusty sheets that usually covered the furniture having been removed, and the multitude of bedrooms made ready for the visiting film crew.

I had no idea which bedroom had ultimately been allocated to Phyllis Wyvern, but common sense told me that it would have been the largest: the Blue Bedroom—the one usually occupied by Aunt Felicity on her ceremonial visits.

A crack of light at the bottom of the door told me that I was right.

Inside, something mechanical was running: a whirring, a whine, hardly louder than a whisper.

Slap! Slap! Slap! Slap! Slap!

What on earth could it be?

I tapped lightly on the door with one of my fingernails. There was no reply.

Inside the room, the noise went on.

Slap! Slap! Slap! Slap! Slap!

Perhaps she hadn't heard me.

I knocked again, this time with my knuckles.

"Miss Wyvern," I whispered at the door. "Are you awake? It's me, Flavia."

Still no response.

I knelt down and tried to peer through the keyhole, but something was blocking my view. Almost certainly the key.

As I got to my feet, I stumbled in the darkness and fell against the door, which, in awful silence, swung inward.

On the far side of the room stood the great canopied bed, made up and turned down, but unoccupied.

To the left, on a tubular stand in the shadows, a ciné projector ground on and on, its steady white beam illuminating the surface of a tripod screen on the far side of the room.

Although the film had run completely through the machine, its loose end, like a black bullwhip, was still flapping round and round: *Slap! Slap! Slap! Slap! Slap!*

Phyllis Wyvern was slumped in a wing-back chair, her

sightless eyes staring intently at the glare of the blank screen.

Around her throat, like a necklace of death, was a length of ciné film, tied tightly, but neatly, in an elaborate black bow.

She was dead, of course.

·TWELVE·

IN MY ELEVEN YEARS of life I've seen a number of corpses. Each of them was interesting in a different way, and this one was no exception.

Because the others had been men, Phyllis Wyvern was the first dead female I had ever seen and as such, she was, I thought, deserving of particular attention.

I noticed at once the way the illuminated ciné screen was reflected in her eyeballs, giving the illusion for a moment that she was still alive, her eyes sparkling. But even though the eyes had not yet begun to cloud over—*she's not been dead for long*, I thought—something had already begun to soften her features, as if her face were being sanded down for repainting.

The skin was already on its way to taking on the colour of putty, and there was a very faint but distinct leaden tinge to the inside of her lips, which were open slightly, revealing the tips of her perfect teeth. A few drops of foamy saliva were trapped in each corner of her mouth.

She was no longer wearing her Juliet costume, but was dressed rather in an elaborately stitched Eastern European peasant blouse with a shawl and a voluminous skirt.

"Miss Wyvern," I whispered, even though I knew it was pointless.

Still, there's always that feeling that a dead person is playing a practical joke, and is going to leap up at any moment and shout "Boo!" and frighten you out of your wits, and my nerves, although strong, are not quite ready for that.

From what I had read and heard, I knew that in cases of sudden death, the authorities, either police or medical, were to be summoned at once. Cynthia Richardson had reported that the telephone was out of order, so the police, at least for the time being, were out of the picture, and Dr. Darby was in a deep sleep downstairs; I had seen him during my passage across the foyer.

There was no question that Phyllis Wyvern was past medical help, so my decision was an easy one: I would call Dogger.

Closing the bedroom door quietly behind me, I retraced my steps through the house—on tiptoe across the foyer once again—to Dogger's little room at the top of the kitchen stairs.

I gave three quick taps at the door, and then a pause . . . two more taps . . . another pause . . . and then two slow ones.

I had scarcely finished when the door swung open on silent hinges, and Dogger stood there in his dressing gown.

"Are you all right?" I asked.

"Quite all right," Dogger said after a barely perceptible pause. "Thank you for asking."

"Something horrid has happened to Phyllis Wyvern," I told him. "In the Blue Bedroom."

"I see." Dogger nodded and vanished for a moment into the shadows of his room, and when he returned, he was wearing a pair of spectacles. I must have gaped a little, since I had never known him to use them before.

The two of us, Dogger and I, made our way silently back upstairs by the quickest route, the foyer, which involved yet another trek among the sleeping bodies. If the moment hadn't been so serious, I'd have laughed at Dogger's long legs picking their way like a wading heron between Bunny Spirling's distended stomach and the outflung arm of Miss Aurelia Puddock.

Back in the Blue Bedroom, I closed the door behind us. Since my fingerprints were on the handle anyway, it wouldn't make any difference.

The projector was still making its unnerving *flap-flapping* noise as Dogger walked slowly round Phyllis Wyvern's body, squatting to look into each of her ears and each of her eyes. It was obvious that he was saving the bow of ciné film around her neck for last.

"What do you think?" I asked finally, in a whisper.

"Strangulation," he said. "Look here."

He produced a cotton handkerchief from his pocket

and used it to pull down one of her lower eyelids, revealing a number of red spots on the inner surface.

"Petechiae," he said. "Tardieu's spots. Asphyxia through rapid strangulation. Definitely."

Now he turned his attention to the black bow of film that ringed the throat, and a frown crossed his face.

"What is it, Dogger?"

"One would expect more bruising," he said. "It does not occur invariably, but in this case one would definitely expect more bruising."

I leaned in for a closer look and saw that Dogger was right. There was remarkably little discolouration. The film itself was black against Phyllis Wyvern's pale neck, the image on many of its frames clearly visible: a close-up shot of the actress herself in ruffled peasant blouse against a dramatic mackerel sky.

The realization hit me like a hammer.

"Dogger," I whispered. "This blouse, shawl, and skirt—it's the same costume she's wearing in the film!"

Dogger, who was looking reflectively at the body, his hand to his chin, nodded.

For a few moments, there was a strange quiet between us. Until now, it had been as if we were friends, but suddenly, at this particular moment, it felt as if we had become colleagues—perhaps even partners.

Possibly I was emboldened by the night, although it might have been a sense of something more. A strange feeling of timelessness hung in the room.

"You've done this before, haven't you," I asked suddenly.

"Yes, Miss Flavia," Dogger said. "Many times."

*   *   *

I had always felt that Dogger was no stranger to dead bodies. He had, after all, survived more than two years in a Japanese prisoner-of-war camp, after which he had been put to work for more than a year on the notorious Death Railway in Burma, any single day of which would have given him more than a nodding acquaintance with death.

Aside from Mrs. Mullet's whispered tales in the kitchen, I knew little about Dogger's military service—or, for that matter, my father's.

Once, as I watched Dogger trim the rose bushes on the Visto, I had tried to question him.

"You and Father were in the army together, weren't you?" I asked, in so casual and offhanded a manner that I hated myself for having bungled it before I even began.

"Yes, miss," Dogger had said. "But there are things which must not be spoken of."

"Even to me?" I wanted to ask.

I wanted him to say "*Especially* to you," or something like that: something I could mull over deliciously in the midnight hours, but he did not. He simply reached among the thorns and, with a couple of precision snips, deadheaded the last of the dying roses.

Dogger was like that—his loyalty to Father could sometimes be infuriating.

"I think," he was saying, "you'd best slip down and awaken Dr. Darby . . . if you wouldn't mind, of course."

"Of course," I said, and letting myself out, made for the stairs.

To my surprise, Dr. Darby was not where I had last seen him: The spot where he had rested was empty, and he was nowhere in sight.

As I wondered what to do, the doctor appeared from beneath the stairs.

"Telephone's bust," he said, as if to himself. "Wanted to call Queenie and let her know I'm still respirating."

Queenie was Dr. Darby's wife, whose terrible arthritis had confined her to a wheelchair.

"Yes, Mrs. Richardson tried to use it last night. Don't you remember?"

"Of course I do," he said snappishly. "It's just that I'd forgotten."

"Dogger has asked if you'd mind coming upstairs," I said, taking care not to give out any details in case one of the sleepers might be listening to us with their eyes closed. "He'd like your advice."

"Lead on, then," Dr. Darby said, with surprisingly little reluctance.

" '. . . amid the encircling gloom,' " he added, extracting his first mint of the day from his waistcoat pocket.

I led the way upstairs to the Blue Bedroom, where Dogger was still crouched beside the corpse.

"Ah, Arthur," Dr. Darby said. "Again I find you on the scene."

Dogger looked from one of us to the other with something like a smile, and then he was gone.

"We'd better be having the police," Dr. Darby said,

after making the same examination of Phyllis Wyvern's eyes that Dogger had already done.

He felt one of the limp wrists and applied his thumb to the angle of the jaw.

"Is life extinct, Doctor?" I asked. I had heard the phrase on a wireless program about Philip Odell, the private eye, and thought it sounded much more professional than "Is she dead?"

I knew that she was, of course, but I liked to have my own observations confirmed by a professional.

"Yes," Dr. Darby said, "she's dead. You'd better roust out that German chap—Dieter, is it? He looks as if he'd be good with skis."

Fifteen minutes later I was in the coach house with Dieter, helping him strap the skis to his boots.

"Did these belong to your mother?" he asked.

"I don't know," I said. "I suppose so."

"They are very good skis," he said. "Madshus. In Norway, they were made. Someone has looked after them."

It must have been Father, I thought. He came here sometimes to sit in Harriet's old Rolls-Royce, as if it were a glass chapel in a fairy tale.

"Well, then," Dieter said at last. "Off we go."

I followed him as far as the Visto, climbing in my rubber boots from drift to drift. As we passed the wall of the kitchen garden, I caught a glimpse of a face at the driver's window of one of the lorries. It was Latshaw.

I waved, but he did not return my greeting.

When the snow was too deep to follow, I stopped and watched until Dieter was no more than a tiny black speck in the snowy wastes.

Only when I could no longer see him did I go back into the coach house.

I needed to think.

I climbed up into the backseat of Harriet's old Rolls-Royce and wrapped myself in a motoring rug. Words like "warm" and "snug" swam into my mind.

When I awoke, the clock of the Phantom II was indicating a silent five forty-five A.M.

"What on earth—" Mrs. Mullet said, obviously surprised to see me coming in through the kitchen door. "You'll freeze to death!"

I shrugged in my cardigan.

"I don't care," I said, hoping for a little sympathy and perhaps an advance on the Christmas pudding, which was one of the few dishes that she cooked to my satisfaction.

Mrs. Mullet ignored me. She was bustling busily about the kitchen, boiling a huge dented kettle for tea and slicing loaves of freshly baked bread for toast. It was obvious that Phyllis Wyvern's murder had not yet been announced to the household.

"Good job I laid in so much for Christmas, isn't it, Alf? Got an army to feed, I 'ave. Lyin' in this mornin' like so many lords and ladies, the lot of 'em—'ard floors or no.

That's the way of it with snow—couple of inches and they goes all 'elpless, like."

Alf was sitting in the corner spreading jam on an Eccles cake.

"'Elpless," he said. "As you say.

"What's Father Christmas bringin' you this year?" he asked me suddenly. "A nice dolly, then, p'raps, with different outfits, an' that?"

A nice dolly indeed! What did he take me for?

"Actually, I was hoping for a Riggs generator and a set of graduated Erlenmeyer flasks," I said. "One can never have too much scientific glassware."

"Arrr," he said, whatever that meant.

Alf's mention of Father Christmas, though, had reminded me that it was now Sunday—that tonight would be Christmas Eve.

Before I slept another night I would be scaling Buckshaw's roof and chimneys to set in motion my chemical experiment.

"*You'd better watch out . . .*" I sang as I strolled out of the kitchen.

Beyond the kitchen door, the place was a madhouse. The foyer, in particular, was like the lobby of a West End theatre at the interval—scores of people pretending to have a jolly old chin-wag and everyone talking at the same time.

The noise level, for someone with my sensitive hearing, was nearly intolerable. I needed to get away. The police would probably not be here for hours. There was still plenty of time to put the finishing touches to my plans for Christmas Eve.

I had first thought of the fireworks long before Father had signed his agreement with Ilium Films. My original plan had been to set them off on the roof of Buckshaw, a display of fire and lights that could clearly be seen a mile away in Bishop's Lacey: my Christmas gift to the village, so to speak—a gift that would be talked about long after Saint Nicholas had flown home to the frozen north.

I would send up showers of fire that would shame the northern lights: elaborate parasols of hot and cold fire of every colour known to man. Chemistry would see to that!

That plan had expanded slowly over the months to include a scheme to capture the bearded old elf himself, to put to rest for once and for all the cruel taunts of my stupid sisters.

Now, as I prepared the chemical ingredients, I was suddenly subdued. It had only just occurred to me that it might be disrespectful to set off such a terrific celebration with a corpse in the house. Even though, in all likelihood, the remains of Phyllis Wyvern would be removed by the time Father Christmas came to call, I wouldn't want to be accused of being insensitive.

"Eureka!" I said, as I set out in neat rows the flowerpots I had borrowed from the greenhouse. "I have it!"

I would manufacture a giant Rocket of Honour in Phyllis Wyvern's memory! Yes, that was it—a dazzling and earsplitting finale to end the show.

I had found the formula devised by the wonderfully named Mr. Bigot, in an old book in Uncle Tar's library. All that was required was to add the right amount of antimony and a handful of cast-iron filings to the basic recipe.

Twenty minutes with a file and a convenient hot-water radiator had produced the first of these ingredients—the other was in a bottle at my fingertips.

Wads of waxed paper and a hollow cardboard tube made an admirable casing, and before you could say "Ka-Boom!" the rocket was ready.

With the dessert prepared, it was now time for the main course. This was the dangerous part, and I needed to pay close attention to my every move.

Because of the risk of explosion, the potassium chlorate had to be mixed with exceedingly great care in a bowl that would not produce sparks.

Fortunately I remembered the aluminum salad set Aunt Felicity had given Feely for her last birthday.

"Dear girl," she had said, "you are now eighteen. In a few years—four or five, if you're lucky—your teeth shall begin to fall out and you shall find yourself eyeing the girdles at Harrods. The early girls get the most vigorous grooms, and don't you forget it. Don't stare at the ceiling with that vacuous look on your face, Ophelia. These aluminum bowls are manufactured from salvaged aircraft. They're lightweight, practical, and pleasing to the eye. How better to begin your trousseau?"

I had found the bowls hidden at the back of a high shelf in the pantry and seized them in the name of science.

To produce the blue explosions, I mixed six parts of potassium nitrate, two of sulphur, and one part of trisulphide of antimony.

This was the formula used for the glaring rescue rockets at sea, and I reckoned these ones would be visible from Malden Fenwick—perhaps even from Hinley and beyond.

To one or two of the portions, I added a dollop of oak charcoal to give the explosions the appearance of rain; to others a bit of lampblack to produce spurs of fire.

It was important to keep in mind the fact that winter fireworks required a different formula than those designed for summer. The basic idea was this: less sulphur and lots more gunpowder.

I had concocted the gunpowder myself from nitre, sulphur, charcoal, and a happy heart. When working with explosives, I've found that attitude is everything.

It was something I had learned at the time of that awful business with the unfortunate Miss Gurdy, our former governess—but stop! That catastrophe was no longer spoken of at Buckshaw. It was in the past and, mercifully, had almost been forgotten. At least I *hoped* it had been forgotten, since it was one of my few failures in experimenting with dualin—a substance containing sawdust, saltpetre, and nitroglycerin, and notorious for its instability.

I sighed and, banishing poor, scorched Miss Gurdy from my mind, turned it to more pleasant thoughts.

Before packing the ingredients into earthenware flowerpots I'd borrowed from the greenhouse, I had added to some of them a certain amount of arsenious oxide (AS_4O_6), sometimes known as white arsenic. Although it was pleasant to think that a deadly poison should produce the whitest of aerial explosions, that wasn't my reason for choosing it.

What appealed to me, what really warmed my heart, was the thought of suspending over our ancestral home, even if only for a few seconds, an umbrella of deadly poisonous fire that would fall—then suddenly vanish as if by magic, leaving Buckshaw safe from harm.

I didn't care if it made sense or not. It was the *idea* of the thing, and I was happy that I'd thought of it.

Each of the flowerpots now needed to be sealed, like preserves, with a lid of onionskin paper to protect the chemicals against moisture. Later tonight, just before bedtime, I would lug them, one at a time, up the narrow staircase that led from my laboratory to the roof.

And then I'd begin my work among the chimney pots.

I was halfway down the stairs, hoping I didn't smell too much of gunpowder, when the doorbell rang. Dogger appeared, as he always does, as if from nowhere, and as I reached the last step, he opened the door.

There stood Inspector Hewitt of the Hinley Constabulary.

I hadn't seen the Inspector for quite some time and our last meeting had been one I'd rather not dwell upon.

We stood staring at each other across the foyer like two wolves that have come from different directions upon a clearing full of sheep.

I was hoping Inspector Hewitt would let bygones be

bygones—that he would stride across the foyer, give me a chummy handshake, and tell me that it was nice to see me again. I had, after all, helped him out of a number of jams in the past without so much as a pat on the back or a "kiss my arsenic."

Well, that's not *quite* true: His wife, Antigone, had asked me to tea in October, but the less said of that the better.

Which is why I was now standing there in the foyer, pretending to check something that had become lodged between my teeth by examining my reflection in one of the polished newel posts at the end of the banister. Just as I decided to relent and give the Inspector a curt nod, he turned and, without a backward glance, walked away towards Dr. Darby, who had made an appearance suddenly on the west landing.

Blue curses! If I'd been thinking straight, I'd have welcomed the Inspector myself—shown him upstairs to the scene of the crime.

But it was too late. I had shut myself out of the Chamber of Death (that's what they called it on the wireless mystery programs) and it was now too late to eat humble pie.

Or was it?

"Oh, Mrs. Mullet," I said, barging into the kitchen as if I'd only just heard the news. "The most dreadful thing has happened. Miss Wyvern has met with a frightful accident, and Inspector Hewitt is here. I thought that, what with the awful weather and so forth, he'd be grateful for a cup of your famous tea."

Flattery can never be overcooked.

"If you mean she's dead," said Mrs. Mullet, "I already knewed it. Word like that gets round like beeswax. Shockin', I'm sure, but there's no 'oldin' it back, is there, Alf?"

Alf shook his head.

"I knewed it as soon as I seen Dr. Darby's face. 'E goes all-over sobersides whenever death's about. I mind the time Mrs. Tarbell was took in the bath. 'E's always been like that an' 'e always will be. Might just as well 'ave a sign plastered on 'is fore'ead sayin' 'She's Dead,' mightn't 'e, Alf."

"A signboard," Alf said. "On 'is fore'ead."

"I told Alf, I did, didn't I, Alf? 'Alf,' I said. 'Somethin's not right,' I said. 'There's *such* a face on Dr. Darby which I seen in the corridor just now an' if I didn't know better I should say as there's a corpse in the 'ouse.' That's what I said, didn't I, Alf."

"'Er exact words," said Alf.

I didn't bother knocking at the door of the Blue Bedroom. I simply strolled in as if I'd been born at Scotland Yard.

I gave the knob a twist and pushed the door open with my behind, manoeuvring the tray through the doorway in the way that Mrs. Mullet always did.

For a moment I thought I had annoyed the Inspector.

He turned slowly from Phyllis Wyvern's staring body, sparing me no more than a rapid glance.

"Thank you," he said. "You may put it on the table."

Meekly, I obeyed—dog that I am—hoping desperately he wouldn't order me to leave. In my mind, I made myself invisible.

"Thank you," the Inspector said again. "It's very kind of you. Please tell Mrs. Mullet we're most grateful."

"Bug off," was what he meant.

Dr. Darby said nothing, but noisily extracted a mint from the bottomless bag in his waistcoat pocket.

I kept as still as a snake in winter.

"*Thank* you, Flavia," the Inspector said, without turning round.

Well, at least he hadn't forgotten my name.

There was a silence that grew more uncomfortable by the second. I decided to fill it before anyone else had a chance.

"I expect you've already noticed," I blurted, "that her makeup was applied *after* she was dead."

·THIRTEEN·

To my surprise, the Inspector chuckled.

"Another of your chemical deductions?" he asked.

"Not at all," I said. "I simply observed that there was makeup on the upper surface of her lower lip. Since she has a slight overbite, she'd have licked it away in seconds if she'd been alive."

Dr. Darby bent in for a closer look at Phyllis Wyvern's lips.

"By George!" he said. "She's right."

Of course I was right. The endless hours I had spent being fitted and refitted with braces in Dr. Reekie's chamber of tortures in Farringdon Street had made me a leading authority on jaw alignment. In fact, there had been times when I'd thought of myself as the Human Nutcracker. To me, Phyllis Wyvern's mandibular displacement had been as easy to spot as a horse in a birdbath.

"And when did you make that observation?" the Inspector asked.

I had to give him credit. For an older man, he had a remarkably nimble mind.

"It was I who discovered the body," I told him. "I went for Dogger at once."

"Why would you do that?" he asked, instantly spotting the flaw in my account. "When Dr. Darby was no farther away than the foyer?"

"Dr. Darby came with Dieter in the sleigh," I said. "I saw him arrive, and I knew he hadn't brought his medical bag. He was also very tired. I noticed him dozing during the performance."

"And?" he said, raising an eyebrow.

"And . . . I was frightened. I knew that Dogger was likely the only one awake in the entire house—he sometimes doesn't sleep well, you know—and I just wanted someone to—I'm sorry. I wasn't thinking clearly."

It was a lie, but a jolly good one. Actually, I'd been thinking as clearly as a mountain stream.

I made my lower lip tremble just a trifle.

"It was easy to see that Miss Wyvern was quite dead," I added. "It wasn't a question of saving her life."

"And yet you had your wits about you sufficiently to spot the makeup where no makeup ought to be."

"Yes," I said. "I notice things like that. I can't help it.

"Please don't strike me," I wanted to add, but I knew I was already slicing the bacon a trifle on the thin side.

"I see," the Inspector said. "It's most kind of you to point it out."

I gave him my most winning smile and made a graceful exit.

I made directly for the drawing room, bursting at the seams to tell Feely and Daffy the news. I found them with their heads bent over a stack of back issues of *Behind the Screen*.

"Don't tell us," Daffy said, raising a hand as I opened my mouth. "We already know. Phyllis Wyvern's been murdered in the Blue Bedroom and the police are on the scene."

"How—?" I began.

"Perhaps, since you're their main suspect, we shouldn't even be talking to you," Feely said.

"Me?" I was flabbergasted. "Where did you ever get such a stupid idea?"

"I saw you," Feely said. "That woman and her infernal ciné projector kept Daffy and me awake again for hours. I finally decided to give her a piece of my mind, and was halfway along the corridor when guess who I spotted sneaking out of the Blue Bedroom?"

Why did I suddenly feel so guilty?

"I wasn't sneaking," I said. "I was going for help."

"There are perhaps a small handful of people in the world who would believe you, but I am not among them," Feely said.

"Tell it to the marines," Daffy added.

"As it happens," I said haughtily, "I am assisting the police with their inquiries."

"Horse hockey!" Daffy said. "Feely and I were talking to Detective Sergeant Graves and he wondered why he hadn't seen you around."

At the very mention of the sergeant's name, Feely drifted towards the looking glass and touched her hair as she turned her head from side to side. Although not first on her list of suitors, the sergeant was not to be counted out—at least I hoped not.

"Sergeant Graves? Is he here? I haven't seen him."

"That's because he doesn't want to be seen," Daffy said. "You'll see him, right enough, when he claps the darbies on you."

Darbies? Daffy had obviously been paying more attention to Philip Odell than she let on.

"What about Sergeant Woolmer?" I asked. "Is he here, too?"

"Of course he is," Feely said. "Dieter helped them shovel through the drifts."

"Dieter? Is he back?"

"He's thinking of going in for a police inspector," Daffy said. "They told him they couldn't have got through to Buckshaw without him."

"What about Ned?" I asked, seized with a sudden thought. "What about Carl?"

Feely had more swains than Ulysses's wife, Penelope, had suitors—I like "swains" better than "suitors" because it sounds like "swine"—all of whom, through some strange quirk of fate, had now turned up at Buckshaw at the same time.

Ned . . . Dieter . . . Carl . . . Detective Sergeant Graves.

Every one of them, God only knows why, was smitten silly with my stupid sister.

How long would it be before they began slugging it out?

"Ned and Carl have volunteered to help clear the fore-court. The vicar's organized a snow-shovelling party."

"But why?" I asked.

It didn't make sense. If all the roads were closed, what use was it clearing a way to the front door?

"Because," said Aunt Felicity's voice behind me, "it is a well-known fact that more than two men shut up to-gether in an enclosed space for more than an hour consti-tute a hazard to society. If unpleasantness is to be avoided, they must be made to go outdoors and work off their ani-mal spirits."

I smiled at the thought of Bunny Spirling and the vicar taking up snow shovels to work off their animal spirits, but I kept my mouth shut. I also wondered if Aunt Felic-ity had heard about Phyllis Wyvern.

"Besides," she added, "the hearse will be required to remove the remains. They can hardly drag her off by dog-sled."

Which answered my question. It also raised another.

The stairs from the laboratory were narrow and steep. No one had been up here for years, I thought, but me.

At the top, a door opened onto the roof—or, at least was *supposed* to open onto the roof. I struggled with the bolt until it suddenly shot free, pinching my fingers. But now the door itself was stuck shut, probably piled high on the other side with a drift of snow. I put my shoulder against it and pushed.

With the peculiar grunting sound that snow makes when it doesn't want to be budged, the door opened grudgingly about an inch.

I was being resisted by millions of tiny crystals, I knew, but the strength of their chemical bonds was enormous. If all of us could be like snow, I thought, how happy we should be.

Another shove—another slow inch. And then another.

After what seemed like a very long struggle, I was able to squeeze myself between the door and its frame and step out onto the roof.

I was instantly up to my knees in snow.

Shivering, I clutched my cardigan up about my chin and waded to the battlements, the back of my mind ringing with all of Mrs. Mullet's dire warnings about pneumonia and keeping one's chest warm.

"She wasn't outside more'n a minute," she had told me, wide-eyed, speaking of Mrs. Milne, the butcher's wife. "Just long enough to 'ang the baby's nappies on the line—that's all it took. By four o'clock she 'ad a cough, by seven 'er 'ead was as 'ot as the Arab desert, and by the time the sun come up she was in a box and stiff as a board. Pneumonia, it was. There's nothin' else as'll snatch you off like pneumonia. Makes you drown in your own juices."

From up here on the roof, I could look out to the east, the rolling countryside one vast unbroken blanket of snow, dazzling in its whiteness. Had there been footprints, I could have easily spotted them at once, but there were none.

In spite of the freezing wetness that was puddling in my shoes, I forced myself to clomp my way to the north front, where I stood shivering, peering down into the forecourt.

Dieter's tractor stood, like Eeyore, covered with snow—a grey form huddled beneath a white blanket. Beside it was the blue Vauxhall, which I recognized at once as Inspector Hewitt's.

In the forecourt, the vicar's crew, in coats, gloves, and galoshes, were digging bravely away at the drifts, their every breath visible on the frigid air. They had managed to clear a parking area somewhat smaller than a tennis court, and even that, with the persistence of the wind, had begun to fill in again with blown fingers of the granular drifts.

There was also a narrow passage in the middle of the drive, packed tightly on either side with layers of snow. Here and there the prints of chains were still clearly visible, and in the middle of the path, tyre tracks that led directly to the parked Vauxhall. It was easy enough to deduce that the police had commandeered a truck with a snowplough fastened to the front, to clear their way from the village.

Apart from the shadowy blue ribbon that was the ploughed path winding away to the north, all of the approaches to Buckshaw were one vast expanse of untrodden white.

With my back to the wind, the south battlement was only slightly warmer than the north. Below me, beside the kitchen garden, the snow-draped vans and lorries of Ilium Films stood huddled like a small circus in winter. Narrow trails had been trodden out between them, and I watched as a man in uniform came out of the kitchen door and picked his way precariously towards one of the smaller vans. It was Anthony, Phyllis Wyvern's chauffeur. I had forgotten all about him.

I leaned as far over the battlement as I possibly could, peering along the side of the house. Yes, there was the radiator of the black Daimler, just poking out into view. It seemed to be tucked up beside a buried flower bed. As I leaned forward another inch to see if anyone was sitting in it, I dislodged a clump of snow, which plummeted down and fell with a *whump* onto the Daimler's roof.

"Bugger!" I said under my breath.

Anthony stopped suddenly, turned, looked up, and saw me. There followed one of those peculiar moments when strangers lock eyes with each other, too far apart to speak, but too close to pretend it hadn't happened. I was wondering what would be appropriate to call out to him—condolences or Christmas wishes?—when he turned away and teetered off towards the trailer.

Those leather riding boots must be treacherous in snow, I thought.

As I made my way back towards the door, I looked up at the towering chimney pots and lightning rods of Buck-shaw, which rose up from their sturdy bases, rank upon rank, like organ pipes of brick and iron and pottery, the chimneys of the kitchen and the north and west wings sending up wind-torn tatters of smoke into the leaden sky.

I thought with a delicious shiver—half pleasure and half fear—that before the night was out I would be scaling those ragged pinnacles for a rendezvous with Saint Nicholas—an experiment whose outcome might well determine the future course of my life.

Would chemistry put paid to Christmas? Or would I, tomorrow morning, find a fat, infuriated elf caught fast and cursing among the chimney pots?

I must admit that part of me was hoping for the legend.

There were times when I felt as if I were standing astride a cold ocean—one foot in the New World and one foot in the Old. As they drifted relentlessly apart, I was in danger of being torn up the middle.

The hordes in the foyer were beginning to show their fatigue. They'd been here for the better part of twenty-four hours, and it was apparent that patience was wearing thin.

Everywhere I looked there were dark circles under tired eyes and the crowded quarters had become filled with an air of staleness.

I had noticed on other occasions that overcrowding, even in a spacious place, makes one feel like a different person. Perhaps, I thought, whenever we began to breathe the breath of others, when the spinning atoms of their bodies began to mingle with our own, we took on something of their personality, like crystals in a snowflake. Perhaps we became something more, yet something lesser than ourselves.

I would jot down this interesting observation in my notebook at the first opportunity.

Those people who had slept flat on the tiled floor were still rubbing their bones, staring balefully at the lucky souls who had staked out corners in which they could prop themselves up with their backs to the wall. Maximilian Brock had erected a wall of books around his little patch of tiled turf, and I couldn't help wondering where he had found them. He must have raided the library during the hours of darkness.

Could the good villagers of Bishop's Lacey, caged up here at Buckshaw, have so quickly become as territorial as jungle cats? If they were confined much longer, they'd soon be staking out allotments and planting vegetable gardens.

Perhaps there was something after all in what Aunt Felicity had said. Every last one of them, men and women alike, looked as if they could do with a brisk walk in the fresh air, and I was suddenly glad that I had ventured out onto the roofs, even if only for a few minutes.

But by doing so, had I breached an official order?

Although I hadn't heard it with my own ears, Inspector Hewitt must have given orders that no one was to leave the house. It was standard procedure in cases where murder was suspected, and Phyllis Wyvern's death was neither natural nor suicide—she'd been done to death with a vengeance.

But what about Anthony, the chauffeur? Hadn't he

been wandering around freely outdoors? I'd seen him from the roof. And what about the diggers in the forecourt? Wasn't the vicar, by raising a crew, flying in the face of the law? Somehow, it seemed unlikely. He must have requested permission. Perhaps the Inspector himself had asked for the forecourt to be cleared.

As I was thinking about them, the front door opened and the shovellers came stamping and blowing into the foyer. It was several minutes before I realized that someone was missing.

"Dieter," I asked, "where's the vicar?"

"Gone," he said with a frown. "He and Frau Richardson have set out on foot for the village."

Frau Richardson? Cynthia? The village?

I could scarcely believe my ears. I looked quickly round the foyer and saw that Cynthia Richardson was nowhere in sight.

"They insisted," Dieter said. "The Christmas Eve service begins in just a few hours."

"But half the congregation is here!" I said. "It makes no sense."

"But the rest are in Bishop's Lacey," Dieter said, throwing up his hands, "and one does not preach sense to a Church of England clergyman."

"The Inspector is going to do his nut," I said.

"Am I indeed?" said a voice behind me.

Needless to say it was Inspector Hewitt. Beside him was Detective Sergeant Graves.

"And what is it that will cause me to do, as you say, my nut?"

My mind made a quick jaunt round the possibilities and saw that there was no way out.

"The vicar," I said. "He and his wife have set out for St. Tancred's. It's Christmas Eve."

This was no more than the truth, and since it was hardly a state secret, I could not be blamed for blabbing.

"How long ago?" the Inspector asked.

"Not long, I think. Not more than five minutes, perhaps. Dieter can tell you."

"They must be brought back at once," the Inspector said. "Sergeant Graves?"

"Sir?"

"See if you can overtake them. They've got a bit of a head start, but you're younger and fitter, I trust."

"Yes, sir," Sergeant Graves said, his sudden dimples making him look like a bashful schoolboy.

"Tell them that while we'll do everything in our power to expedite the process, my orders must not be circumvented."

How cleverly put, I thought: compassion with a stinger in its tail.

"And now, Miss de Luce," he said, "if you don't mind, I think we'll begin with you."

"Youngest witness first?" I asked pleasantly.

"Not necessarily," Inspector Hewitt said.

·FOURTEEN·

To my surprise, the Inspector suggested that the interview be conducted in my chemical laboratory.

"Where we shall be undisturbed," he had said.

It wasn't his first visit to my *sanctum sanctorum:* He had been here at the time of the Horace Bonepenny affair, and had called the laboratory "extraordinary."

This time, with no more than a rapid glance at Yorick, the fully articulated skeleton that had been given to Uncle Tar by the naturalist Frank Buckland, the Inspector had sat himself down on a tall stool, put one foot on a rung, and pulled out his notebook.

"What time did you discover Miss Wyvern's body?" he asked, getting down to brass tacks without any pleasant preliminaries.

"I can't be sure," I said. "Midnight, perhaps, or a quarter past."

He sat with his Biro poised above the page.

"This is important," he said. "Crucial, in fact."

"How long does the balcony scene in *Romeo and Juliet* run?" I asked.

He seemed a little taken aback.

"Capulet's orchard? I don't really know. Not more than ten minutes, I should say."

"It took longer than that," I told him. "They were late getting started, and then—"

"Yes?"

"Well, there was that business with Gil Crawford."

I supposed that someone would have informed him about it by now, but I could tell by the way he gripped his Biro that they had not.

"Tell it to me in your own words," he said, and I did: the failure of the spotlight to pick out Phyllis Wyvern at her first appearance . . . her coming down from the make-shift balcony . . . her walk up the aisle to the scaffolding . . . her climb up into the darkness . . . the stinging swat across Gil Crawford's face.

It all came pouring out, and I was surprised by the outrage I had been bottling up. By the time I finished I was on the verge of tears.

"Most upsetting," the Inspector said. "What was your reaction—at the time?"

My answer shocked me.

"I wanted to kill her," I said.

We sat there in silence for what seemed like an eternity, but was, in fact, probably no longer than ten seconds.

"Are you going to put that in your notebook?" I asked at last.

"No," he said, in another, softer voice. "It was more of a personal question."

This was too good an opportunity to miss. Here, at last, was a chance to ease the ache that had been in my conscience since that dreadful day in October.

"I'm sorry!" I blurted. "I didn't mean to . . . Antigone . . . your wife."

He closed his notebook.

"Flavia . . ." he said.

"It was horrid of me," I told him. "I didn't think before I spoke. Antigone—Mrs. Hewitt, I mean, must have been so disappointed with me."

I could hear my own voice ringing in my ears.

"Why don't you and Inspector Hewitt have any children? Surely you can afford it on an Inspector's salary?"

It had been meant lightly—almost a joke.

My spirits had been elevated by her presence, her beauty, and perhaps by the chemistry of too much sugar from too many pieces of cake. I had been a glutton.

I'd sat there glaring at her gleefully like some London toff who has just made a capital joke and is waiting for everyone else in the room to get it.

"Surely you can afford it on an Inspector's salary?"

I'd almost said it again.

"We've lost three," Antigone Hewitt had said with infinite heartbreak in her voice, taking her husband's hand.

"I should like to go home now," I'd announced abruptly,

as if the power to utter every other word in the English language had been denied me.

The Inspector had driven me back to Buckshaw in a silence of my own choosing, and I had leapt out of his car without so much as a word of thanks.

"Not so much disappointed as sad," he said, bringing me back to the present. "We haven't been as successful as some in getting to grips with it."

"She must hate me."

"No. Hate is for haters."

I saw what he meant, although I couldn't have explained it.

"Like whoever it was that killed Phyllis Wyvern," I suggested.

"Exactly," he said, and after a pause, "Now, where were we?"

"Gil Crawford," I reminded him. "And then she went on with the play as if nothing had happened."

"That would have been about seven twenty-five?"

"Yes."

The Inspector scratched his ear.

"Seems odd, doesn't it, to gather a village in such inclement weather for a ten-minute performance."

"Phyllis Wyvern was only the drawing card," I said. "I think the vicar may have been planning more. It was in aid of the Roof Fund, you see. He was probably planning to ask the Puddock sisters to perform, and then end the show with one of his own recitations, such as 'Albert and the Lion.' He might have let her go on first because it would have been disrespectful to make her wait for amateurs. That's just my guess, though. You'll have to ask the vicar when he returns."

"I shall," the Inspector said. "You may well be right."

He pushed back his cuff with a forefinger and glanced at his wristwatch.

"Just a few questions more," he said, "and then I should like you to help me with an experiment."

Oh, joy! To be recognized at last as an equal—or something like it. Father Christmas himself could have devised no better gift. (I remembered with a twinge of pleasure that that old gentleman and I had business to attend to in the hours ahead. Perhaps I could thank him personally.)

"I think I can manage, Inspector," I replied, "although I do have rather a lot to do."

Stop it, Flavia! I thought. *Stop it at once, before I bite off your tongue from the inside and spit it out on the carpet!*

"Right, then," he said. "Why did you go to the Blue Bedroom?"

"I wanted to talk to Miss Wyvern."

"About what?"

"About anything."

"Why choose that particular time? Wasn't it rather late?"

"I heard the soundtrack of her film come to an end. I knew she must still be awake."

Even as I spoke, I felt the cold horror of my words. Why hadn't I realized it before? Phyllis Wyvern might already have been dead.

"But perhaps," I added, "perhaps—"

The Inspector's eyes were locked with mine, willing me to say more.

"A reel of sixteen-millimetre film runs for forty-five minutes," I said. "Two reels for a feature."

This was a fact I was sure of. I had sat through enough clunkers at the parish hall cinema series to know to the second the likely duration of my torture. Besides, I had once checked with Mr. Mitchell.

"The film ended just before I reached the Blue Bedroom," I went on. "I heard the line 'I shall never forget Hawkhover Castle' just before I started downstairs from my bedroom. By the time I found Miss Wyvern's body, the end of the film was slapping round the reel. But—"

"Yes?" The Inspector's eyes were as keen as a ferret's.

"But what if she was already dead when the film began? What if it was her killer who started the projector?"

In my mind, the pieces fell rapidly into place. An earlier time of death would explain why Phyllis Wyvern's body was already showing discolouration when I found her. I did not tell the Inspector this. He needed to work at least some of it out on his own.

"An excellent surmise," the Inspector said. "Besides the slapping of the film end, did you hear anything else?"

"Yes. A door closed as I was crossing the foyer. And a toilet flushed."

"Before or after the sound of the door?"

"After. The door closed when I was partway down the stairs. The toilet flushed when I was halfway across the foyer."

"As soon as that?"

"Yes."

"How odd," Inspector Hewitt said.

It wasn't until later that I realized what he meant.

"Of the people sleeping in the foyer, whom do you distinctly remember seeing?"

"The vicar," I said. "He cried out in his sleep."

"Cried out? What?"

Why did I feel as if I were betraying a confidence? Why did I feel like such a telltale?

"He said, 'Hannah, please! No!' Very quietly."

"Nothing else?"

"No."

The Inspector wrote something in his notebook.

"Go on," he said. "Who else was sleeping in the foyer?"

"Cynthia Richardson, the vicar's wife . . ."

I began ticking them off on my fingers.

"Mrs. Mullet . . . and Alf, her husband . . . Dr. Darby . . . Ned Cropper . . . Mary Stoker . . . Bunny Spirling . . . Max—I mean Maximilian Brock, our neighbour. Max had built a little wall of books around himself."

"Anyone else?"

"Those are the ones I noticed. Oh, and Dieter, of course. He was bedded down on the landing. I had to tiptoe past him."

"Did you see or hear anyone or anything else on your way up to the Blue Bedroom?"

"No. Nothing."

"Thank you," the Inspector said, closing his notebook. "You've been of great assistance."

Had he forgiven me, I wondered, or was he simply being polite?

"Now, then," he said. "As I said, I'd like your assistance in a little experiment, but I won't have time until later."

I nodded in understanding.

"Do you have a copy of *Romeo and Juliet* in your library? I should be surprised if you didn't."

"There's a copy of his collected works that Daffy picks up when she wants to look studious. Will that do?"

This was true, but I hadn't the faintest idea where to find it. I didn't fancy sifting through a billion books on Christmas Eve. I had, as they say, bigger fish to catch.

"I'm sure it will. See if you can dig it out, there's a good girl."

If anyone but Inspector Hewitt had made that remark, I'd have gone for their throat, but here I was, like a spaniel waiting for its master to throw the slipper.

"Righty ho!" I almost shouted at his back as he went out the door.

Feely was holding court in the drawing room, and it pains me to admit that she had never looked more beautiful. I could tell by her lightning glances at the looking glass that she was of the same opinion. Her face was as radiant as if she'd had a lightbulb installed in her skull, and she batted her eyelashes prettily at Carl, Dieter, and Ned, who stood gathered round her in an adoring circle, as if she were the Virgin Mary and they the Three Wise Men, Caspar, Melchior, and Balthasar.

Actually, not a bad comparison, I thought, since two of them that I knew of, Ned and Carl, had come bearing gifts. Carl's, of course, had been consigned to the flames by Father, but that seemed not to have affected the giver, who stood slouched smiling against the chimneypiece, his hands in his pockets, gnashing happily away at his gum with a clockwork jaw.

Ned's prehistoric chocolates were nowhere in sight, having more than likely been laid to rest with their predecessors in Feely's lingerie drawer.

Detective Sergeant Graves, who had obviously just finished questioning Feely's other happy slaves, sat in a corner copying notes, but I could tell by the furtive way he kept glancing up from his work that he was keeping an eye on his romantic rivals.

Only Dieter, I thought, had been sensible enough to skip the frankincense and myrrh.

At least that's what I was thinking when he reached into his pocket and pulled put a tiny hard-shell box.

He handed it to Feely without a word.

Cheeses! I thought. *He's going to propose!*

Feely, of course, made the most of it. She examined the box from all six sides, as if each of its faces had a secret inscribed upon it in golden ink by angels.

"Why, Dieter!" she breathed. "How lovely!"

It's just a box, you stupid porpoise! Get on with it!

Feely opened the box with agonizing slowness.

"Oh!" she said. "A ring!"

Ned and Carl exchanged openmouthed looks.

"A friendship ring," she added, although whether in disappointment, I could not tell.

She plucked it out between thumb and forefinger, holding it up to the light. It was wide and gold, and was cut out with figures in what I believe is called filigree work—a crown on top of a heart was as much as I could see of it before she twisted away.

"What does it mean?" she asked, lifting her eyes to Dieter's.

"It means," Dieter told her, "whatever you want it to mean."

Flustered, Feely flushed and shoved the box into her pocket.

"You shouldn't have," she managed, before turning and walking to our old Broadwood piano, which stood in front of the window.

She smoothed her skirt and sat down at the keyboard.

I recognized the melody before the first three notes had floated from the piano. It was "Für Elise," by Beethoven— Larry B, as I liked to call him, just to get Feely's goat.

Elise, I knew, was the name of Dieter's mother, who lived in far-off Berlin. He had sometimes spoken of her in a special voice, a voice of expectant delight, as if she were in the next room, waiting to leap out and surprise him.

This piano piece, I knew at once, was a private message to Dieter: one that would not be intercepted by other ears than mine and perhaps Daffy's.

It was not an appropriate time to let out a war whoop,

or to do a series of cartwheels across the drawing room, so I contented myself with giving Dieter's hand a shake.

"Merry Weihnachten," I said.

"Merry Weihnachten," he replied, with a grin as broad as the English Channel.

As Feely played, I noticed that Carl's jaw was milling in time to the music and Ned was tapping one of his heels energetically on the carpet.

It was as happy a little domestic scene as I've ever known at Buckshaw, and I drank it in eagerly with my eyes, my ears, and even my nose.

The logs crackled and smoked in the fireplace as "Für Elise" cast its inevitable spell.

Merry Christmas, Flavia, I thought, storing up a memory of the moment for future comfort. *You deserve it.*

Daffy was alone in the library, jackknifed sideways into a chair.

"How's everything at *Bleak House?*" I asked.

She looked up from the novel as if I were an inept cat burglar who had just fallen in through the window.

"Dieter gave Feely a ring," I said.

"And did she answer it?"

"Come on, Daffy. You know what I mean. A ring you wear on your finger."

"All the more pickled pig's trotters for you and me. And now, if you wouldn't mind—"

"Too bad about Phyllis Wyvern, wasn't it?"

"Flavia—"

"I think I could really grow to love Shakespeare," I said, baiting my hook. "Do you know which part of *Romeo and Juliet* I liked best? The part where Romeo talks about Juliet's eyes swapping places with two of the brightest stars in all the heavens."

"Fairest," Daffy said.

"Fairest," I agreed. "Anyway, the way Shakespeare described it, I could just see it in my mind—those two stars shining out of Juliet's face, and Juliet's eyes hanging up in the sky . . ."

I put my forefinger and little finger on my lower eyelids and pulled them down into bloody bags, at the same time pushing up the end of my snout with the fingers of my other hand.

"Boo-oing! Must have scared the you-know-what out of the shepherds in the fields."

"There were no shepherds in the fields."

"Then why did Romeo say 'Oh that I were a glove upon that hand that I might touch that sheep'?"

"He said 'cheek.' "

"He said 'sheep.' I was sitting right there, Daffy. I heard him."

Daffy sprang out of the chair and marched to one of the bookcases. She took down a heavy volume and leafed through it, the pages flying under her fingers as if blown by the wind.

"Here," she said, after a few moments. "Look, what does this say?"

I twisted my head sideways and stared at the page for as long as I dared.

" 'That I might touch that cheeke,' " I said, grudgingly. "Still, I think Desmond Duncan said 'sheep.' "

Daffy slammed the book shut with a snort, re-folded herself into her chair, and within seconds had wrapped herself in the past as easily as if it were an old blanket.

With the stealth of a library mouse, I picked up dear old Bill Shakespeare from the table, tucked him under my arm, and sidled casually out of the room.

Mission accomplished.

·FIFTEEN·

THE SCREAM CAME OUT of nowhere, echoing from the foyer's wooden panels in an avalanche of sound.

"My God!" Bunny Spirling exclaimed. "What in blue blazes was that?"

Everyone was looking round in all directions and the Misses Puddock clutched one another like the babes in the wood.

I was on the stairs and up them like a skyrocket. Whatever had happened, I wasn't going to be locked out as a late arrival.

I skidded round the corner and made for the north corridor. As I flew past, one of the doors was opened and a second shriek split the air. I shoved past one of the wardrobe women and into the room.

Nialla was half on, half off a Regency couch, her face as white as paste.

"The baby—" she groaned.

Marion Trodd, looking rather like a stunned owl in her horn-rims, came out of a seeming trance at the end of the couch and took a step towards me.

"Fetch the doctor," she snapped.

"Fetch him yourself," I said, taking Nialla's hand. "And on your way back, tell Mrs. Mullet to boil buckets of hot water."

Marion bared her teeth for an instant, as if she were going to bite me, then spun round and strode out of the room.

"Really, Flavia," Nialla said through clenched teeth, "you're incorrigible."

I shrugged. "Thank you," I said.

The fetching of water at a birth was, I had learned from the cinema and countless plays on the wireless, a ritual that might as well have been the Eleventh Commandment, though why *boiling* water was invariably specified was beyond me. It seemed hardly likely to be used to baste the mother without risk of serious burns, and it was simply beyond belief that a newborn would be immersed in a liquid having a temperature of 212 degrees on the Fahrenheit scale—unless, of course, that was the reason for newly delivered babies having that lobsterish colour I'd seen in the cinema.

It seemed unthinkable, though. Thoroughly barbaric.

One thing was clear: There was much that I needed to learn about the events surrounding the birth of a baby. One needed to be able to tease out the scientific facts from the mumbo jumbo. I would make a note to look more closely into this as soon as Christmas was out of the way.

"How are you?" I asked Nialla, but it came out sounding rather phoney, as if we were two old ladies meeting at a parish tea.

"I'm *quate* well, theng-kyew," she replied through gritted teeth in a put-on toffish voice. "And you?"

"Spiffing," I said. "Simply spiffing."

I squeezed her hand and she smiled.

"Hmmm," Dr. Darby said behind me, and as I spun round he had already stripped off his jacket and was rolling up his sleeves.

"Close the door on your way out," he said.

I admire a man who can take command when a woman really needs him.

Marion Trodd was standing in the corridor looking daggers at me.

"Sorry if I seemed rude," I said. "Nialla is an old friend, and—"

"Oh, well, then. Think nothing of it," she snapped. "You're forgiven, I'm sure. After all, I'm quite accustomed to being trampled underfoot."

She spun round and walked off.

Hag! I thought.

"Don't mind Marion," someone said, stepping into my view as if from the shadows. "She's a little overwrought."

It was Bun Keats.

"Overwrought? Over-*rotten* is more like it," I wanted to say, but I kept the witticism to myself.

"I'm sorry about Miss Wyvern," I said. "It must be terrible for you."

Although I had not planned it, I was aware, even as I spoke, that this was precisely the right thing to say.

"You have no idea," Bun said, and I knew she was speaking the truth. I *did* have no idea, but I intended to find out.

"Would you like some tea?" I was asking her when the bedroom door opened and Dr. Darby's head appeared.

"Tell Dogger to come at once," he said. "Tell him 'transverse dorsolateral.' Tell him 'shoulder presentation.' "

"Right-o," I said, and walked away—a model of unflustered efficiency.

"Run!" Dr. Darby roared behind me, and I took to my heels.

"Transverse dorsolateral," I repeated in a whisper as I raced along the corridor. "Transverse dorsolateral. Shoulder presentation."

But where to find Dogger? He could be in his room . . . or in the kitchen. He might even be in the greenhouse . . . or the coach house.

I needn't have worried. As I came flapping like a demented bat down the west staircase, there was Dogger in the foyer helping Cynthia and the vicar to remove their coats. They looked like survivors of a failed Antarctic expedition, as did Sergeant Graves, who stood behind them.

"Blizzard now," the vicar was croaking through ice-rimed lips. "We should have frozen to death if the sergeant hadn't come upon us."

Cynthia stood quaking in an apparent daze.

Rude or not, I whispered into Dogger's ear: "Dr. Darby needs you in the Tennyson bedroom. Transverse dorso-lateral. Shoulder presentation."

I had planned on dashing up the stairs ahead of him to lead the way, but Dogger beat me to it. He took the steps as if he had suddenly been granted wings, and I was left to tumble along behind in his wake as best I could.

Dogger paused at the door just long enough to say, "Thank you, Miss Flavia. These particular cases can sometimes come on quite quickly. When I need you I'll call."

I dropped myself into a chair outside the bedroom and whiled away the time by chewing my nails. After what seemed like a string of eternities, but was probably no more than a few minutes, I heard Nialla cry out three times sharply, followed by something that sounded like a startled bleat.

What were they doing in there? Why wasn't I allowed to watch?

Daffy had once told me how a baby was born, but her story was so ridiculous as to be beyond belief. I'd made a mental note to ask Dogger, but had somehow never got round to it. This could be my golden opportunity.

Time dragged on and I was drawing concentric circles with the toes of my shoes when the door opened and Dogger crooked a finger at me.

"Just a peek," he said. "Miss Nialla is quite tired."

I stepped cautiously into the room, looking this way

and that, as if something was going to leap out and bite me, and there was Nialla propped up with pillows in the bed holding something in her arms that seemed at first to be a large water rat.

I edged closer and as I watched, its mouth opened and it gave out a squeak like a rubber toy.

It's hard to describe how I felt at that moment. A mixture, I suppose, of profound happiness and quite crushing sadness. The happiness, I understood; the sadness, I did not.

It had something to do with the fact that suddenly, I was no longer the last baby who had cried at Buckshaw, and I felt as if one of my most secret possessions had been stolen from me.

"How was it?" I asked, not knowing what else to say.

"Oh, kid," she said, "you have no idea."

How odd. Weren't those the words Bun Keats had used when I'd extended my sympathy on Phyllis Wyvern's death?

"It's a beautiful baby," I said untruthfully. "It looks just like you."

Nialla looked down at the bundle in her arms and began to sob.

"Ohhh," she said.

Then Dogger's hand was on my shoulder and I was being steered gently but firmly towards the door.

I walked slowly back to the chair in the corridor and sat down. My mind was overflowing.

Over there, behind a closed door, was Nialla, with her

newborn baby. And there, just along the corridor, behind her own closed door, was the newly dead—relatively speaking—Phyllis Wyvern.

Was there any meaning in this or was it just another stupid fact? Did living bodies come into being from dead bodies or was that just another old wives' tale?

Daffy had told me about the girl in India who claimed to be the reincarnation of an old woman who had died in the next village, but was it true? Dr. Gandhi had certainly thought so.

Was there even the remotest possibility, then, that the soggy creature in Nialla's arms contained the soul of Phyllis Wyvern?

I shuddered at the thought.

Still, I'd have to admit that, of the two, to my mind, the dead Phyllis Wyvern was more interesting.

To be perfectly honest, *far* more interesting.

There had been a time, not long after Nialla's last visit to Buckshaw, that I had begun to worry about my fascination with the dead.

After a number of sleepless nights and a patchwork of dreams involving crypts and walking corpses, I had decided to talk it over with Dogger, who had listened in silence as he always does, nodding only occasionally as he polished Father's boots.

"Is it wrong," I finished up, "to find enjoyment in the dead?"

Dogger had dredged with the corner of his cloth into the tin of blacking.

"I believe a man named Aristotle once said that we delight to contemplate things such as dead bodies, which in themselves would give us pain, because in them, we experience a pleasure of learning which outweighs the pain."

"Did he really?" I asked, hugging myself. This Aristotle, whoever he may be, was a man after my own heart, and I made a mental note to look him up sometime.

"As best I recall," Dogger said, and a shadow had passed across his face.

I was thinking about this when, along the corridor, the door of the Blue Bedroom opened and the mountainous Detective Sergeant Woolmer began lifting his bulky photo kit out of Phyllis Wyvern's late bedroom.

He seemed as surprised to see me as I was to see him.

"Got the dabs, and so forth?" I asked pleasantly. "Scene-of-the-crime photos?"

The sergeant stared at me for a few moments, and then a smile spread across his usually stony face.

"Well, well," he said. "If it isn't Miss de Luce. Hot on the trail, are you?"

"You know me, Sergeant," I said, with what I hoped was a mysterious grin. I began sauntering towards him, hoping for at least a glance over his shoulder at the deceased Miss Wyvern.

He quickly closed the door, gave the key a twist, and dropped it into his pocket.

"Uh-uh-uh," he said, cutting me off in mid-thought. "And don't you even go thinking about Mrs. Mullet's key chain, miss. I know as well as you do that old houses like this have spare keys by the bagful. If you lay so much as a fingerprint on this door, I'll have you up on charges."

Coming from a fingerprint expert, this was a serious threat.

"What did you use for your camera settings?" I asked, trying to distract him. "A hundred-and-twenty-fifth of a second at f eleven?"

The sergeant scratched his head—almost in pleasure, I thought.

"It's no good, miss," he said. "We've already been warned about you."

And with that, he walked away.

Warned about me? What the deuce did he mean by that?

I could think of only one thing: Inspector Hewitt, the traitor, had lectured his men against me on their way to Buckshaw. He had specifically cautioned them against my ingenuity, which must have grated upon them in the past like a fingernail on slate.

Did he think he could outwit me?

We shall see, my dear Inspector Hewitt, I thought. *We shall see.*

I had become aware, as I chatted with Sergeant Woolmer, of quiet conversation in the adjacent room—two women talking, by the sound of it.

I knocked firmly at the door and waited.

The voices fell silent, and a moment later the door opened no more than a crack.

"Sorry to bother you," I said to the single slightly bloodshot eye that appeared, "but Mr. Lampman wants to see you."

The door swung inwards and I saw the rest of the woman's face. She was one of the bit players in the film.

"Wants to see me?" she asked in a surprisingly brassy voice. "Wants to see *me*, or wants to see both of us?"

"Mr. Lampman wants to see us, Flo," she called over her shoulder, without waiting for an answer.

Flo wiped her mouth and put down a bowl from which she had been eating.

"Both of you," I said, trying to put a touch of grimness into my voice. "I think he's outside in one of the lorries," I added, "so you'd better bundle up."

I waited patiently, leaning on the door frame until they hustled off towards the staircase, still shrugging themselves into their heavy winter coats.

I felt more than a little sorry for them. Goodness knows what fantasies were running through their heads. Each of them, most likely, was praying that she had been chosen to replace Phyllis Wyvern in the leading role.

I'd better get to work. They'd be back soon enough— and angry at my deception.

I stepped into their room and turned the key, which, like most keys at Buckshaw, was left in the room side of the lock.

Across the room, on the inside wall between the window and the dresser, was a hanging curtain—a leftover from the days when guest bedrooms were decorated like Turkish harems. It pictured a hunting party with elephants, and a tiger, unseen among the jungle trees, preparing to spring.

I jerked the tapestry aside, sneezing at the cloud of grey dust that flew up into the room, revealing a small, wood-panelled door. I inserted the key and, to my immense satisfaction, felt the bolt slide back with a welcome *click.*

I took hold of the knob and gave it a good twist. Again there were promising sounds but the door was stuck fast.

I muttered something that was half a prayer and half a curse. Even a fraction of a second's inspection would have shown me that it was painted shut.

Given five minutes in my laboratory, I could have produced a solvent that would strip a battleship while you were saying "Rumpelstiltskin," but there wasn't the time.

A quick look round the room revealed a lady's hand-bag tossed carelessly on the bed, and I fell upon it like the tiger upon the Maharajahs.

Handkerchief . . . scent bottle . . . aspirins . . . cigarettes (bad girl!), and a small purse which, guessing by its weight and feel, contained no more than six shillings, sixpence.

Ah! Here it was—just what I was looking for. A nail file. Sheffield steel. Perfect!

My prayer had evidently been heard and my curse forgotten.

Inserting the blade of the file between the frame and the door, and working my way round it like a Girl Guide opening rather a large tin of campfire beans, I soon had a satisfactory pile of paint chips on the floor at my feet.

Now for it. One more twist of the knob and a kick at the bottom panel, and the door jerked open with a groan.

Taking a deep breath, I stepped into the Chamber of Death.

·SIXTEEN·

THIS BEDROOM, TOO, HAD a dusty drapery covering the unused door, and I was forced to fight my way out from behind it before proceeding.

Phyllis Wyvern's body was still slumped in the chair as I had first found it, but was now covered with a sheet, as if it were a statue whose sculptor had wandered off to lunch.

The police would have finished their inspection by now, and were probably awaiting the arrival of a suitable vehicle in which to carry off the body.

No great harm, then, in having a dekko of my own.

I lifted the sheet slowly, taking care not to disturb her hair, still laced with Juliet's posies, which seemed to me the only vanity she had left.

Even in death, though, there was something exotic about Phyllis Wyvern, although after twenty-four hours, the body had begun its inevitable chemical dissolution, and had now taken on a grey and waxy appearance.

The awful pallor of her flesh—aside from her made-up face—gave her the appearance of a star from the days of the silent cinema, and for a moment I had the same awful feeling I'd had before: that she was playing the game of Statues, as I used to do with Feely and Daffy before they began to hate me—that in a moment she'd sneeze, or suck in a giant, gasping breath.

But no such thing happened, of course. Phyllis Wyvern was as dead as a door knocker.

I began my examination from the ground up. I lifted the hem of her heavy woollen skirt and saw at once that her ankles were swollen, ballooning out, as it were, above a pair of heavy black work boots.

Work boots? They couldn't possibly be hers!

Using my handkerchief to guard against fingerprints, I slipped one of the boots off her foot . . . slowly and carefully, taking special note of the way the thick white stocking was bunched in a knot beneath her instep.

As I had suspected, the boot had been shoved onto her foot after she was dead.

With great care I rolled down the knee-length stocking and removed it. Her foot was puffy, dark, and bruised with the settling blood. Her painted toenails were ghastly.

I replaced the stocking, which slid on easily over her cold flesh.

Getting the boot back on, though, was not as easy as taking it off; the stiffened toes simply refused to slide all the way back into the boot. Could this be rigor mortis?

I pulled it off again and stuck my fingers into the opening. There was something pushed down into the toe—paper, by the feel of it.

Would someone as wealthy and famous as Phyllis Wyvern buy footwear so oversized that she had to stuff paper into the toes to make it fit?

It seemed unlikely. I fished out the wad with my finger and uncrumpled it.

It was a piece of stationery printed at the top with the name: *Cora Hotel, Upper Woburn Place, London, WC1.*

Scrawled across the page in red ink were the words:

Must I tell D?

Blast her handwriting (if it was hers). Was it "Must I tell T?"?

The paper was torn from the edge diagonally across the initial—the final letter could have been anything.

D for Desmond? D for Duncan? V for Val? Or was it a B for Bun?

No time to speculate, or even to crow over finding something the police had missed. I shoved the paper into the pocket of my cardigan for later analysis.

I struggled again to replace the boot, but because of the swelling in the legs, it was like trying to squeeze an elephant's foot into a ballet slipper.

Remembering Flo, or Maeve, or whatever her name was, I dashed back into the adjacent room.

Yes! Just as I thought—the actress had left half a bowl

of fruit pieces uneaten on the night table. I helped myself to the dessert spoon and returned to Miss Wyvern.

Using the bowl of the spoon as a shoehorn, I managed to lever the boot back onto her dead foot.

Better check the other one, something told me, and I quickly pried it off. Could there possibly be more of the message in the other toe?

No such luck. To my disappointment the second boot was empty, and I quickly levered it back onto her foot.

So much for the lower extremities.

Next step was to give her a jolly good sniffing. I had learned by experience that poison could underlie all seeming causes of death, and I was taking no chances.

I sniffed her lips (the upper one, I noticed, painted larger than it actually was with scarlet lipstick, perhaps to mask the faint moustache that was visible only at extremely close range), followed by her ears, her nose, her cleavage, her hands, and as much as I could manage of her armpits without actually shifting the body.

Nothing. Except for being dead, Phyllis Wyvern smelled exactly like someone who had, just hours ago, stepped out of a bath of scented salts.

She must have come straight from her performance to her room, removed her Juliet costume (it was still laid out flat on the bed), taken a bath, and then . . . what?

I used my handkerchief again to collect from the nape of her neck a small sample of the stage makeup I had noted earlier. Smeared onto the white linen, the greasepaint had the appearance of finely ground red brick.

I gave special attention to her fingernails, which had

been coated with a shiny scarlet polish to match the lipstick. The cuticles formed stark half-moons of greyish
white where the colour had not been applied. Feely did
her nails in that way, too, and I had a sudden but momentary attack of gooseflesh.

Steady on, old girl, I thought. *It's only death.*

Phyllis Wyvern certainly hadn't been wearing these
gaudily lacquered nails on stage. Quite the contrary—
except for the slap, her interpretation of Juliet had been
notable for its village-pump simplicity. The real-life
Juliet, after all, had been no more than twelve or thirteen
years old, or so Daffy liked to claim.

"If it weren't for you lot," she had once said mysteri-
ously, "I could have Dirk Bogarde scaling my balcony
even as we speak."

Phyllis Wyvern, by contrast, was fifty-nine. She had
told me so herself. How she managed to shed forty-five
years under the lights was nothing short of a miracle.

Perhaps it was her size. She was really not that much
bigger than me.

I'd better get on with it, I thought. The actresses could
return at any moment from their wild-goose chase, and
be hammering at the locked door.

But something was niggling away at the back of my
brain—something that was not quite right. What could
it be?

I stepped back from the body for a more general look.

In her peasant blouse and skirt, Phyllis Wyvern looked
as if she had just dropped into the chair to catch her
breath before setting out to a masquerade.

Was it possible she had simply had a heart attack, perhaps, or suffered a sudden fatal stroke?

Of course not! There was no blotting out the sight of that dark decorative bow of ciné film twisted fancily around her throat. And besides, Dogger had pointed out the petechiae. The woman had been strangled. That much was clear. Part of my mind must still be milling away trying to reduce the horror of what must have been a violent scene.

From her hair to her—

Her hair! That was it!

Like little coloured stars twinkling in the winter sky, Juliet's crown of flowers was still woven into her long, golden hair. They could hardly be real, I thought. If they had been, they'd have wilted by now, and yet they looked as fresh as if they had been picked just moments before I came into the room.

I reached out and pinched a particularly dewy-looking primrose.

Hard to tell by touch. I gave the thing a jerk and—good lord!—Phyllis Wyvern's hair, posies and all, went tumbling off her head and onto the floor with the sickening *whump* of a shot bird falling dead from the sky.

It was a wig, of course, and without it, she was as bald as a boiled egg.

A boiled egg mottled with even more of the petechiae, or Tardieu's spots, as Dogger had called them.

I stared, aghast. What kind of nightmare had I stumbled into?

I retrieved the wig from the carpet and replaced it on her head, but no matter how much I twisted it this way and that, it still looked ludicrous.

Perhaps it was the knowledge of what lay beneath.

Well, I couldn't spend all day fiddling with her coiffure. I finally had to give it up and turn my attention to the dresser, which I found to be littered with a various assortment of bottles and tins: theatrical cold creams, glycerine and rose water, rank upon rank of skin cleansers and assorted toiletries by Harriet Hubbard Ayer. Although the dresser top was a veritable apothecary's shop, a few things were obviously missing: one was red theatrical makeup; the others included scarlet lipstick and nail polish.

I had a quick rummage through her handbag, but aside from a handful of paper tissues, a wallet containing six hundred and twenty-five pounds, and a handful of loose change, there was little of real interest: a tortoiseshell comb, a pocket mirror, and a tin of breath mints (of which I helped myself to one and pocketed a couple of extras for quick energy, should I need it later).

I was about to close the clasp when I spotted the zip, barely visible against the lining, a careful camouflage by the bag's maker.

Hullo! I thought. *What's this? A secret compartment!*

Disappointingly, there wasn't much in it—a set of keys and a small but official-looking booklet consisting of two grey pages with the same information repeated on each of them.

COUNTY OF LONDON
Licence to drive a Motor Car or Motor Cycle
Phyllida Lampman
"Tenebrae"
3 Collier's Walk, S.E.

It had been issued on the thirteenth day of May, 1929.

Phyllida? Lampman?

Could this be Phyllis Wyvern's real name? It seemed beyond belief that she would keep a stranger's driving licence in her handbag.

But assuming that Phyllida was Phyllis or the other way around, what was I to make of the rest of it? Was she Val Lampman's wife? Sister? Sister-in-law? Cousin?

"Cousin" and "wife" were distinctly possible. In fact, she could be both. Harriet, for instance, had been a de Luce before she married Father, and because of it had been spared having to give up her maiden name.

If Phyllis Wyvern hadn't lied to me about her age—and why would she?—she must have been . . . let me see . . . 1929 had been twenty-one years ago . . . thirty-eight years old when this driving licence was issued.

How old was Val Lampman? It was hard to tell. He was one of those gnomish creatures with tight shiny skin and pale hair who, with a silk scarf at his neck to hide the wrinkles, could pass for ageless.

What was it Daffy had said? That not since something or another—which I was too young to understand—had Phyllis Wyvern worked with any other director.

What could that something be? It was becoming

plainer by the minute that, by fair means or foul, I needed to pry open my sister's clammy shell.

I was having a second look at Phyllis Wyvern's fingernails when the doorknob turned!

I almost had an accident!

Fortunately the door was locked.

I crammed the driving licence back into the bag and pulled the zip shut. I picked up the sheet from the floor and, trying not to make a rustling noise, hurriedly re-draped the body.

That done, I fumbled my way behind the curtain, which gave off another cloud of choking dust.

I grabbed the bridge of my nose and squeezed just in time to reduce a major sneeze to a tiny, but rather rude, exclamation point of sound.

"Pee-phwup."

Bless me!

I had to be careful about the paint-swollen door. I couldn't close it as tightly behind me as I wished, but had to settle instead for a couple of careful, but almost silent, tugs. The curtains in each room would not only muffle the sound, but perhaps even keep all but the most determined observer from noticing the door's very existence.

Happily, the mess of paint chips I had dislodged was on my side of the door and I couldn't help congratulating myself on leaving the Blue Bedroom without a trace.

Taking Flo's—or Maeve's—hairbrush from the dresser (after replacing their dessert spoon carefully in its bowl of fruit) and forming a makeshift dustpan of the *Cinema Weekly* that was lying on the bed, I swept up the paint chips and tipped them carefully into the pocket of my cardigan.

I'd dispose of them later. No point in leaving confusing evidence to distract the police.

I opened the door a crack and peeked out. No one in sight as far as I could see.

As I stepped into the corridor, a familiar voice behind me said, "Hold on."

I had nearly stepped on Inspector Hewitt's toes.

"Oh, hello, Inspector," I said. "I was just looking for, uh, Flo."

I could tell at once that he didn't believe me.

"Were you, indeed?" he asked. "Why?"

Damn the man! His questions were always so to the point.

"That's not quite true," I confessed. "Actually, I was snooping in her room."

No need to drag in my fib about the summons from Val Lampman.

"Why?" the Inspector persisted.

Sometimes there's nothing for it but to tell the truth.

"Well," I said, scrambling madly for words, "actually it's a hobby of mine. I sometimes snoop on Daffy and Feely quite frightfully."

He stared at me with what somebody once called "that awful eye."

"I thought the bedrooms of cinema people were bound to be more interesting . . ."

"Including Miss Wyvern's?"

I made my eyes go wide with innocence.

"I heard you sneeze, Flavia," he said.

Bugger!

"Empty your pockets, please," the Inspector said, and I had no choice but to obey.

Remembering Father's tales of his exploits as a boy conjurer, I tried to "palm," as I believe it is called, by folding it under my thumb and pressing it into my handkerchief, the crumpled ball of paper I had found in Phyllis Wyvern's boot.

"Thank you," the Inspector said, holding out his hand, and I was, as the vicar says while playing cribbage, skunked.

I gave him the paper.

"Other pocket, please."

"It's nothing but rubbish," I told him. "Just a lot of—"

"I'll be the judge of that," he interrupted. "Turn it out."

I locked eyes with him as I turned the pocket inside out and a small Vesuvius of paint chips erupted and fluttered in horrid silence to the floor.

"Why do you do it, Flavia?" the Inspector asked in a suddenly different voice, his eyes on the mess I had made of the carpet. I don't think I had ever seen him look so pained.

"Do what?"

I couldn't help myself.

"Lie," he said. "Why do you fabricate these outlandish stories?"

I had often thought about this myself, and although I had a ready answer, I did not feel obliged to give it to him.

"Well," I wanted to say, "there are those of us who create because all around us, things visible and invisible are crumbling. We are like the stonemasons of Babylon, forever working, as it says in Jeremiah, to shore up the city walls."

I didn't say that, of course. What I *did* say was:

"I don't know."

"How can I impress upon you—" he began, at the same time uncrinkling the paper and giving it a single glance. "Where did you get this?"

"In Phyllis Wyvern's shoe," I said, remembering not to call attention that it was, in fact, a boot. "The right foot. You must have overlooked it."

I could see his dilemma: He could hardly tell his men—or his superiors—that he had found it himself.

"There's a connecting door, you see," I said helpfully. "I knew you'd already taken your photos and so forth, so I just slipped in for a quick look round."

"Did you touch anything else?"

"No," I said, standing there in plain view with my soiled handkerchief crumpled in my hand.

Please, God, and Saint Genesius, patron saint of actors and those who have been tortured, don't let him tell me to hand it over.

And it worked! All praises to you both!

I would send up a burnt offering later in my lab—a little pyramid of ammonium dichromate, perhaps—a shower of joyful sparks . . .

"Are you quite sure?" the Inspector was asking.

"Well," I said, lowering my voice and glancing along the corridor in both directions to see that we were not being overheard, "I *did* have a quick peek into her bag. You spotted the Phyllida Lampman driving licence, of course?"

I thought the Inspector was going to have an egg.

"That will be all," he said abruptly, and walked away.

·SEVENTEEN·

"I REQUIRE YOUR PERSONAL advice," I said to Daffy. This was a tactic that never failed to work.

As always, she was curled up in the library like a prawn, still deep in her Dickens.

"Supposing you wanted to look someone up," I asked. "Where would you begin?"

"Somerset House," she said.

My sister was being facetious. I knew, as well as everyone else in the kingdom, that Somerset House, in London, was where the records of all births, deaths, and marriages were kept, along with deeds, wills, and other public documents. Father had once pointed it out to us rather glumly from a taxicab.

"Besides that, I mean."

"I should hire a detective," Daffy said sourly. "Now please go away. Can't you see I'm busy?"

"Please, Daff. It's important."

She continued to ignore me.

"I'll give you half of whatever's in my Post Office savings account."

I had no intention of doing so, but it was worth a try. Money, to Daffy, meant books, and even though Buckshaw contained more books than the Bishop's Lacey Free Library, to my sister, it was not enough.

"Books are like oxygen to a deep-sea diver," she had once said. "Take them away and you might as well begin counting the bubbles."

I could tell by the twitch at the corner of her lips that she was interested in my offer.

"All right—two thirds," I said. One can always up the ante safely on bad intentions.

"If they were *someone*," she said, without looking up from her book, "*Burke's Peerage*."

"And what if they weren't someone? What if they were merely famous?"

"*Who's Who*," she said, her finger pointing to the bookcases. "That will be three pounds, ten and six, if you please. As soon as the roads are cleared, I'll personally walk you to the Post Office to see that you don't welsh on your promise."

"Thanks, Daff," I said. "You're a corker."

But it was too late. She had already begun her descent into the deeps of Dickens.

I ambled casually over to the bookcases. *Who's Who* had rung a bell. Although I had never opened one of them, the shelf of fat red volumes, their dates stretching well back into another century, were part of Buckshaw's library landscape.

But even as I approached, my heart began to sink. A wide gap at the right of the second shelf showed that a number of volumes were missing.

"Where have the 1930s and '40s gone?" I asked.

Daffy's silence provided the answer.

"Come on, Daff. It's important."

"How important?" she said without looking up.

"All of it," I said.

"All of what?"

"My Post Office savings account."

"All of it?"

"All of it. One hundred percent." (See note above re bad intentions.)

"Promise?"

"Cross my heart and hope to die."

I crossed my heart elaborately and prayed with all my might that I would live as long as old Tom Parr, whose grave we had once seen in Westminster Abbey, and who had lived to a ripe one hundred and fifty-two.

Daffy pointed, languidly.

"Under the chesterfield," she said.

I dropped to my knees and reached beneath the flowered flounce.

Aha! When my hand reappeared it was gripping the 1946 edition of *Who's Who*.

I bore the book off to a corner and opened it on my knees.

The L's didn't begin until after nearly six hundred

pages, halfway through the book: *La Brash, Ladbroke, La-marsh, Lambton* . . . yes, here it was—*Lampman, Lorenzo Angenieux, b.1866, m. Phyllida Grome, 1909, one d. Phyllida Veronica, b.1910, one s. Waldemar Anton, b.1911.*

I quickly worked out the system of abbreviations: *b.* was "born," *m.* stood for "married"—*s.* and *d.* must mean "son" and "daughter."

There was much more. It rambled on and on about Lorenzo Lampman's education (Bishop Laud), his military service (Royal Welch Fusiliers), his clubs (Boodles, Carrington's, Garrick, White's, Xenophobe), and his awards (D.S.C., M.M.). He had published a memoir, *With Bow and Rifle to the Kalahari,* and had died in the sinking of the *Titanic* in 1912, just a year after the birth of his son, Waldemar Anton.

Young Waldemar could only be Val Lampman, which meant that that imp, despite his leprechaun looks, was no more than thirty-nine.

He and Phyllis Wyvern were brother and sister—and she was forty, not fifty-nine!

I'd thought there was something fishy about her age.

I turned quickly to the back of the book—to the W's—even though Daffy had warned me that *Who's Who* wasn't keen on actors.

No Wyverns listed here except for a Sir Peregrine, the last of his line, who had died in a duel with his hatter in 1772.

I glanced rapidly through some of the other volumes, but they were much the same. In the world of the upper crust, time, it seemed, moved more slowly. When you got right down to it, *Who's Who* was not much more than a catalogue of the same dry old sticks harrumphing their way, year after year, towards the grave.

"Daff," I said, taken by a sudden idea. "How did you know I was going to ask about *Who's Who*?"

There was a silence that grew longer by the moment.

"*Pax vobiscum,*" she said suddenly and unexpectedly.

Pax vobiscum? It was the ancient signal of truce among the de Luce sisters—a formula that was usually spoken by me. All I had to do was to give the correct response, "*Et cum spiritu tuo,*" and for five minutes precisely by the nearest clock, we would be bound by blood to let bygones be bygones. No exceptions; no ands, ifs, or buts; no crossing of fib-fingers behind one's back. It was a solemn contract.

"*Et cum spiritu tuo,*" I said.

Daffy closed *Bleak House* and pulled herself out of her chair. She walked to the fireplace and stood staring down into the warm ashes, her fingertips lightly resting on the mantelpiece.

"I've been thinking . . ." she said, and I was bound by the rules of the truce not to shoot back, "Did it hurt?"

"I've been thinking," she went on, "that since it's Christmas, it would be nice, just for once, to . . ."

"Yes, Daff?"

There was something about her posture—something about the way she held herself. For the duration of a lightning flash, and no more, she was Father and then, just as quickly, she was Daffy again. Or had she, for a millionth of a second in between, been the Harriet I had glimpsed in so many old photographs?

It was uncanny. No, more than that—it was unnerving.

As Daffy and I stood there not looking at each other, and before she could speak, there was a light tap at the door. Like an arrow shot from a bow, Daffy flew in an instant back into her overstuffed chair so that when the door slowly opened a moment later, she was already carefully arranged, apparently immersed again in *Bleak House*.

"May we come in?" Inspector Hewitt asked, his face appearing round the door.

"Of course," I said, rather pointlessly, since he was already in the room, followed closely by Desmond Duncan.

"Mr. Duncan has kindly agreed to help us establish a fairly precise running time for the balcony scene. Now, then, Flavia, I believe you told me there's a copy of Shakespeare's collected works here in the library?"

"There was, but she took it," Daphne said sourly, without looking up from Dickens.

There was a momentary sinking feeling in my abdomen, partly because Daffy, in spite of my best efforts, had spotted me pinching the book, and partly because I had no recollection of what I had done with the blasted thing. What with all the uproar over Nialla and her baby, I must have put it down somewhere without thinking.

"I'll go and fetch it," I said, giving myself a mental kick in the backside. Being out of the room for even a few minutes meant that I would miss an important part of

Inspector Hewitt's investigation, of which every moment, from my viewpoint, was precious.

Flavia, you chump! I thought.

"Never mind," Daffy said, bailing out of her chair and making for the bookcases. "We've probably accumulated more than our fair share of Shakespeare over the years. There's bound to be another copy."

She ran her forefinger over the spines of the books in the familiar way that book lovers everywhere do.

"Yes, here we are. A single-volume edition of *Romeo and Juliet*. Rather tatty, but it will have to do."

She held it out to the Inspector but he shook his head.

"Hand it to Mr. Desmond, please," he told her.

Ha! I thought. *Fingerprints! He's collecting Daffy's and Desmond Duncan's all in one go. How very cunning of you, Inspector!*

Desmond Duncan took the book from Daffy and riffled through it, looking for the correct page.

"Rather distinctive print," he said, "and an old-fashioned typeface."

He fished a pair of horn-rimmed spectacles from an inner pocket and, with a theatrical flourish, settled them onto his famous nose.

"Not that I am unaccustomed to handling such texts," he went on, turning back to the front of the book. "It's just that one doesn't expect to find them in such an out-of-the-way place. Indeed, if I didn't know better . . ."

Famous cinema star or not, I angled round behind him for a better look as he studied the title page.

This is what I read:

An
EXCELLENT
conceited Tragedie
OF *Romeo and Iuliet* (it said)
As it hath been often (with great applaufe)
plaid publiquely, by the
Right Ho-
nourable the L. Hunſdon
his seruants
LONDON,
Printed by Iohn Danter.
1597

At the top of the page, in red ink horizontally and black ink vertically, was inscribed the monogram:

H
H d L
L

I held my breath as I recognized it at once: Father's and Harriet's initials intertwined—and in their own handwriting!

Time seemed to stand still.

I glanced at the clock on the mantel and saw that the five-minute truce had expired. In spite of it, I put my arm round Daffy's shoulders and gave her a sharp, quick hug.

"I'm afraid, Inspector," Desmond Duncan said at last, "that this particular edition is not sufficient to our purposes. It's a somewhat different text from that with which

I am accustomed to perform. We shall have to rely on my memory."

And with that, he slipped the book unobtrusively into his jacket pocket.

"Yes, well, then," Inspector Hewitt said, as if relieved to be over an awkward moment, "perhaps we can work with Mr. Duncan's undoubtedly perfect recollection of the scene. We'll check it later against your everyday copy of the book. Agreed?"

We looked at each other and nodded our heads.

"Daphne, I wonder if you'd mind acting as our timer?" the Inspector asked, removing his wristwatch and handing it to her.

I thought she was going to faint from importance. Without a word she took the watch from his hands, climbed up onto the armchair, and perched on its back, letting the watch dangle from her fingers at arm's length.

"Ready?" the Inspector asked.

Daffy and Desmond Duncan nodded curtly, their faces made serious, prepared for action.

"Begin," he said.

And Desmond Duncan spoke:

"He jests at scars that never felt a wound.
But, soft! What light through yonder window breaks?
It is the east, and Juliet is the sun.
Arise, fair sun, and kill the envious moon . . .
Who is already sick and pale with grief,
That thou her maid art far more fair than she . . ."

The words came pouring out of that golden throat, seeming to tumble over one another in their eagerness and yet, each one of crystal clarity.

"*Ay me,*" Daffy moaned suddenly, from atop her perch.

"*She speaks!*" said Romeo, with a look of genuine amazement on his face.

"*O, speak again, bright angel!*" he urged her,
"*For thou art as glorious to this night, being o'er my head,*
As is a wingèd messenger of heaven . . ."

Daffy's face had suddenly become as radiant as an angel in a painting by van Eyck, and Desmond Duncan, as Romeo, seemed to have been transported by it to another realm.

"*See how she leans her cheek upon her hand!*" Romeo went on, his eyes in eager communion with hers.

"*O, that I were a glove upon that hand,*
That I might touch that cheek!"

Was it just me, or was the room becoming warmer?

"*O Romeo, Romeo!*" Daffy whispered in a new and husky voice. "*Wherefore art thou Romeo?*"

Something had sprung to life between them; something had been created from nothing; something that had not been there before.

The world went blurry around the edges. A shiver shook my shoulders. I was seeing and hearing magic.

Daffy was thirteen. A perfect Juliet.

And Romeo responded.

I hardly dared breathe as their endearments poured like old and familiar honey. It was like snooping on a pair of village lovers.

Inspector Hewitt, too, had fallen under their spell, and I couldn't help wondering if he was thinking of his own Antigone.

Daffy had all the lines by heart, as if for a thousand and one nights on a West End stage she had delivered them before an enraptured audience. Could this fair creature be my mousy sister?

"Good night, good night!" she breathed at last,
"Parting is such sweet sorrow
That I shall say good night till it be morrow."

And Romeo replied:

"Sleep dwell upon thine eyes, peace in thy breast!
Would I were sleep and peace, so sweet to rest!"

"Time," Daffy announced abruptly, breaking the spell. She held the wristwatch up for a close inspection. "Ten minutes, thirty-eight seconds. Not bad."

Desmond Duncan was now regarding her fixedly, not openly staring, but not far from it. He opened his mouth as if to say something, and then at the last second, his mouth had decided to say something else.

"Not bad at all, young lady," were the words that came out. "In fact, bloody remarkable."

Daffy slipped heavily down into the seat of the chair and flung her legs over the arm. She turned to an imaginary bookmark in *Bleak House* and resumed reading.

"Thank you all," Inspector Hewitt said, jotting the timing into his notebook. "That will do for now."

It was just as well. Something was weighing heavily on my mind.

·EIGHTEEN·

I KNOCKED LIGHTLY AT Aunt Felicity's door and, without waiting for an answer, let myself in.

The window was propped open the regulation inch, and Aunt Felicity was lying on her back, tucked to the chin with an afghan, with little more than the cup hook of her nose exposed to the room's cold air.

I leaned over slowly to examine her. As I did so, one of her ancient turtle eyes came open, and then the other.

"God sakes, girl!" she said, dragging herself up by the elbows into a half-sitting position. "What is it? What's the matter?"

"Nothing, Aunt Felicity," I said. "I just wanted to ask you something."

"Was my mouth open?" she mumbled, swimming rapidly back to the surface of reality. "Was I talking in my sleep?"

"No. You were sleeping the sleep of the dead."

I didn't realize what I was saying until it was too late.

"Phyllis Wyvern!" she said, and I nodded.

"Well, what is it, girl?" she asked sourly, changing the subject. "You've caught me slumbering. An old woman's rhythmic oxygen needs to be renewed at precise twelve-hour intervals, physical culture enthusiasts be damned. It's a simple matter of hydrostatics."

It wasn't, but I didn't correct her.

"Aunt Felicity," I asked, taking the plunge, "do you remember that day last summer beside the ornamental lake? When you told me I must do my duty, even if it led to murder?"

We had been talking of Harriet, and the ways in which I was like her.

Aunt Felicity's face softened and her hand touched mine.

"I'm glad you've not forgotten," she said softly. "I knew you wouldn't."

"I have a confession to make," I told her.

"Go ahead," she said. "I enjoy a good blurting out of secrets as much as the next person."

"I let myself into Phyllis Wyvern's room," I said, "to have a look around."

"Yes?"

"I found a driving licence in her bag. In 1929 she was Phyllida Lampman. Phyllida, not Phyllis."

Aunt Felicity swung her legs heavily off the bed and walked stiffly to the window. For a long time she stood staring, like Father, out into the snow.

"You knew her, didn't you?" I blurted.

"Whatever makes you think that?" Aunt Felicity asked, without turning round.

"Well, when you arrived, the electrician, Ted, greeted you like an old friend. Val Lampman uses the same crew on every film he makes. And the same cast—even Phyllis Wyvern. Daffy says she'll allow no one else to direct her, ever since something-or-other happened. Everyone knows everybody else. When I asked you about Ted, you said he'd seen you somewhere during the war—during a blackout. When I pointed out that you couldn't have seen his face, you said I ought to be painted with six coats of shellac."

Aunt Felicity drew in a long breath—the sort of breath the queen must draw in before stepping out with the king onto the balcony of Buckingham Palace to face the newsreel cameras and the multitudes.

"Flavia" she said, "you must make me a promise."

"Anything," I said, surprised to find that I didn't have to put on a solemn face. It was already there.

"What I am about to tell you must not be repeated. Not ever. Not even to me."

"I promise," I said, crossing my heart.

She gripped my upper arm, hard enough to make me wince. I don't think she realized she was doing it.

"You must understand that there were those of us who, during the war, were asked to take on tasks of very great importance . . ."

"Yes?" I asked eagerly.

"I cannot tell you, without breaching the Official Secrets Act, what those tasks entailed and you mustn't ask me. In later years, one finds oneself running into old colleagues with monotonous regularity, whom one is bound, by law, not to recognize."

"But Ted called out to you."

"A shocking blunder on his part. I shall tear a strip off him when we're alone."

"And Phyllis Wyvern?"

Aunt Felicity sighed.

"Philly," she said quietly, "was one of us."

"One of—*you?*"

"You must never mention that," she said, squeezing my arm even harder, "until the day you die. If you do, I shall have to come for you in the night with a carving knife."

"But, Aunt Felicity, I *promised!*"

"Yes, so you did," she admitted, releasing her grip.

"Phyllis Wyvern was one of you," I prompted.

"And a most valuable one," she said. "Her fame opened doors that are barred to mere mortals. She was made to play a role that was more deadly than any she had undertaken on stage or screen."

"How do you know that?" I couldn't keep from asking.

"I'm sorry, dear. I can't tell you that."

"Was Val Lampman one of you, as well? He might well have been, since he was Phyllis Wyvern's brother."

Something rose up in Aunt Felicity's throat, and I thought for a moment that she was going to toss her tea cakes, but what came out was more like the braying of a donkey. Her shoulders shook and her bosoms trembled.

My dear old trout of an aunt was laughing!

"Her brother? Phyllis Wyvern's brother? Wherever did you get *that* idea?"

"Her driving licence. Lampman."

"Oh, I see," Aunt Felicity said, mopping at her eyes with the border of the afghan.

"Phyllis Wyvern's brother?" she said again, as if repeating the punch line of a joke to another person in the room. "Far from it, dear girl—very far from it indeed. She's his mother."

My mouth fell open like a corpse who's just had her jaw bandage removed.

"His *mother*? Phyllis Wyvern is Val Lampman's mother?"

"Surprising, isn't it. She gave birth to him when she was very young, no more than seventeen, I believe, and Val's age, to all outer appearances, is rather . . . indeterminate."

So that was it! Val Lampman *was* the "Waldemar" of *Who's Who*, but he was Phyllis Wyvern's son, and not her brother, as I had assumed. I had misinterpreted the entry in *Who's Who*. I wanted to blush but I was too excited.

"She'd already had a daughter a year earlier," Aunt Felicity went on. "Veronica, I believe the girl was called. Poor child. There was some great tragedy there that was never spoken of.

"Phyllida—or Phyllis, as she liked to call herself—had been married for a time to the late and not awfully-much-lamented Lorenzo, who, in spite of his blue blood and the great difference in their ages, was still active as a traveller in wines, or wigs, I've forgotten which."

"Wigs, probably," I said, "because she was wearing one."

Aunt Felicity shot me a disgusted look, as if I'd blabbed a secret.

"It fell off," I explained. "I was trying to keep the shroud the police had thrown over her from messing her hair."

There fell one of those silences so thick you could have stood a spoon up in it.

"Poor Philly," Aunt Felicity said, at last. "She suffered terribly at the hands of the Axis agents. Chemicals, I believe. Her hair was her crowning glory. They might as well have chopped out her heart."

Chemicals? Torture?

Dogger had been tortured, too, in the Far East. It seemed bizarre, the way in which these old atrocities seemed to be coming home to roost in peaceful Bishop's Lacey.

"Does Father know about these things? About Phyllida Lampman, I mean?"

"She had been directed by Malinovsky in a number of foreign films," Aunt Felicity went on, staring at her own hands as if they were those of a stranger. "Most notably, of course, in *Anna of the Steppes*, a role which led, indirectly, to her assignment, and to her later downfall. Although she escaped with her life, she underwent a total breakdown, during which she developed an irrational horror of all Eastern Europeans."

"Which is why she insisted on always working with the same British ciné crew," I said.

"Precisely."

We had seen the re-released version of *Anna of the Steppes* at the cinema in Hinley, where it was shown—with English subtitles—as *Dressed for Dying*.

Although it had seemed at first to be just another of those endless yawners about the Russian Revolution, I soon found myself swept into the story, my eyes as dazzled by the stark black-and-white images as if I had stared too long at the sun.

In fact, the unforgettable scene in which Phyllis Wyvern, as Anna, having put on her grandmother's Russian dress and heavy boots, carefully combed her hair, and applied the scent and makeup brought to her from Paris by her lover, Marcel, lies down with her year-old baby in front of the army of snarling tractors, was still causing me occasional and inexplicable nightmares.

"Miss Wyvern must have been a very brave woman," I said.

Aunt Felicity returned to the window and looked out as if World War Two were still raging somewhere in the fields to the east of Buckshaw.

"She was more than brave," she said. "She was British."

I let the silence linger until it was hanging by a thread. And then I said what I had come to say.

"You must have heard everything that happened. Being in the next room."

Aunt Felicity looked suddenly drawn, and old, and helpless.

"I should have," she said. "God knows I should have."

"You mean you didn't?"

"I'm an old woman, Flavia. I suffer from the vicissitudes of age. I had a tot of rum at bedtime, and slept with the pillow screwed into my good ear. That poor dear blasted soul ran ciné films all night. I knew why, of course, but even sympathy has its limits."

Does it? I wondered, or was Aunt Felicity simply deflecting further discussion?

"So you heard nothing," I said at last.

"I didn't say I'd heard nothing. I said I hadn't heard everything."

I walked across the room and stood beside her at the window. It had grown dark outside, and the snow was still falling as heavily as if the world were coming to a bitter end.

"I got up to use the WC. She was arguing with someone. The noise of the film, you see . . ."

"Was it a man, or a woman?"

"One couldn't be sure. Although they were keeping down the volume, it was evident that angry words were being exchanged. Even with an ear to the wall—oh, all right, don't look so shocked, I'll admit to clapping an ear to the wall—I couldn't make out what they were saying. I gave it up and went back to bed, determined to have a word with her in the morning."

"You hadn't spoken to her before that?"

"No," Aunt Felicity said. "There had been no opportunity. One had come across her unexpectedly in the corridor, but as I've told you, we were both of us too well trained in the art of seeming total strangers."

My mind was leapfrogging back and forth over the things that Aunt Felicity had told me. If, for instance, what she said was true, Phyllis Wyvern could not possibly have been arguing with someone when Auntie F got up to use the baffins, because she was already dead. I had heard the toilet flush and I'd been in the death chamber moments later. Before that, someone had had enough time to strangle Phyllis Wyvern, dress her in different clothing (for whatever bizarre reason), and make their escape through one of three doors: the one to the corri-dor, the one that connected to Flo and Maeve's bedroom, or—and here I shot a nervous glance over my shoulder— the one that opened into the very room in which I was now standing. Aunt Felicity's bedroom—the very same Aunt Felicity who had just told me that she was capable of coming for me in the dark with a butcher knife. If what she said was true—if only half of what she hinted at were the ramblings of a woman who had grown suddenly old at the end of the war—she was capable of anything. Who knew what havoc old loyalties and older jealousies could play with two women who had once been friends?

Or was it enemies?

I needed time to think—time to get away—to collect my thoughts.

"Thank you, Aunt Felicity," I said. "You must be very tired."

I could always come back to her later to fill in the blanks.

"You're such a thoughtful child," she said.

I gave her a modest smile.

*   *   *

The cupboard under the stairs was little more than a right-angled triangle equipped with a dangling lightbulb. Here, stowed safely away from the eyes of the ciné crew and their cameras, were the magazines that had been cleared away from the library and the drawing room. Back numbers of *Country Life* pressed down like geological strata upon old issues of *The Illustrated London News*. Heaped high with issues of *Behind the Screen* and *Cinema Weekly*, back numbers of *Cinema World* were piled in crooked stacks that must have dated back to the days of silent film.

I stepped inside, closed the door behind me, and, taking down the first handful of ciné magazines, began my search.

I flipped through page after page of *Ciné Tit-Bits* and *Silver Cinema*, smiling, at first, at the antics of the so-called "movie stars," most of whom I had never heard of.

Parties, galas, premieres, benefit performances: smiling faces, toothy grins, top hats and sequined dresses, arms around shoulders in exotic motorcars—what vast amounts of time these people had spent having themselves photographed!

It wasn't difficult to find Phyllis Wyvern. She was everywhere, spanning the years without apparently ageing a day. Here she was, for instance, sitting, legs crossed, in a canvas chair with her name painted on the back, studying a script, with a cardigan thrown over her shoulders and a look of intense concentration on her face. Here she was, dancing with a young airman in a dark nightclub that seemed to be located in a church crypt. And here she was again, on the set of *Anna of the Steppes*, standing with another actress, their faces turned skyward, in front of one of the behemoth tractors as their makeup is retouched by a man in a moustache and a beret.

Could it be?

For a moment I thought that the woman beside Phyllis Wyvern was Marion Trodd. A much younger Marion Trodd, to be sure, but still . . .

In spite of my excitement I was having difficulty in keeping my eyes focused on the page. The air in the cupboard was becoming stuffy; the bare bulb giving off a surprising amount of heat. That and the fact that I was bone tired was making my head swim.

How long had I been huddled in this cupboard? An hour? Perhaps two? It seemed like days.

I rubbed my eyes with my fists, forcing myself to pay attention to the tiny type in which the caption was printed.

Perhaps there was something after all in Father's insistence on having all of us outfitted with spectacles. I wore mine only when trying for sympathy, or when I needed to protect my eyes during a hazardous chemical experiment. I thought momentarily of running upstairs to get them, but decided against it.

I shook my head and read the caption again:

Phyllis Wyvern and Norma Durance freshen up between takes. Eyes front for the birdie, girls!

What a disappointment. I must have been mistaken. I

had thought for a moment that I was on to something, but the name Norma Durance meant nothing to me.

Unless . . .

Hadn't I seen that face a few issues back? Because the woman wasn't photographed with Phyllis Wyvern I had paid her no attention.

I went back a couple of issues.

Yes! Here it was in *Silver Cinema*. The actress is in a barnyard, throwing a handful of grain from her gathered-up skirt to a mob of frenzied chickens.

"*Pretty Norma Durance ably undertakes the part of Dorita in* The Little Red Hen. *We hear she's not working for chicken feed!*"

I held the magazine up to the light for a closer look. As I carefully studied the woman's features, the top edge of the cover pressed for a moment against the lightbulb. In an instant the tinder-dry paper had browned, then blackened—and before I could blink, burst into flame.

It's wonderful how the mind works in such situations. I remember distinctly that my first thought was "Here's Flavia, her hands full of fire in a cupboard jam-packed with combustibles."

It was the kind of thing of which front-page stories in the *Times* are made.

Smouldering ashes are all that remain of historic country house. Buckshaw in ruins.

And there would be a grisly photo, of course.

I threw down the burning magazine and stamped on it again and again with my feet.

But because of the waterproofing solution that Dogger

applied so conscientiously to our footwear—a witches' brew containing both linseed and castor oils, as well as copal varnish—my shoes burst immediately into flames.

I tore off my cardigan and dropped it onto my feet, stamping and bundling with my hands until the fire was out.

By now, my heart was pounding like a racing engine, and I found myself gasping for air.

Fortunately I had not burned myself. The fire had been quickly extinguished with little trace remaining other than a few black ashes and some lingering smoke.

I checked quickly to be sure that no sparks had lodged among the stacks of paper, then let myself out into the passageway, coughing as I went.

I was pulling on my singed sweater and scraping the toes of my smoking shoes on the floorboards when the kitchen door opened and Dogger appeared.

He looked at me closely without saying a word.

"Unforeseen chemical reaction," I said.

An air of weariness had fallen upon the foyer. No one paid the slightest attention to me as I passed through. Everywhere, the people of Bishop's Lacey sat staring blankly off into space, immersed in their own thoughts. In a corner, a card table with two chairs had been set up as an interrogation centre, and Sergeant Graves was murmuring away with Miss Cool, the village postmistress and confectioner.

"Dazed" was the word for the rest of them. The earlier

air of sharing in a jolly good adventure had worn off, pretense had vanished, and everyone had sagged, exhausted at last, into their real faces.

Buckshaw had been made over into a bomb shelter.

In the farthest corner from the police, the chauffeur, Anthony, sucked on a cigarette that he held concealed in a half-closed hand. He looked up and caught my eye, just as he had done when I'd dislodged the little avalanche of snow.

What was he thinking?

I sauntered casually off towards the west wing to have a look at the grandfather clock that stood in the corridor near Father's study. It must be getting late.

The hands of the ancient timepiece stood at ten-seventeen! Where could the day have gone?

Even twenty-four hours seemed an eternity when one was cooped up indoors and the days were the shortest of the year, but the death of Phyllis Wyvern under the roofs of Buckshaw had turned time topsy-turvy.

The roofs of Buckshaw! My bucket of birdlime!

Time was running out. If I was going to carry out my plan—my plans!—I'd better get a bustle on. Christmas was nearly upon us. Father Christmas himself would soon be here.

And so would the undertaker.

Poor Phyllis Wyvern. I was going to miss her.

·NINETEEN·

A QUICK JAUNT TO the jakes was all I needed. With that attended to, I could get on with my plans.

The closest convenience was at the top of the kitchen stairs, two doors along from Dogger's bedroom. When I reached it, I threw open the door and—

My heart stopped.

Naked from the waist up, Val Lampman was sitting on the toilet clumsily trying to wrap one of his muscular arms with surgical lint. They were both horribly scratched and torn. He was as surprised as I was, and as he looked up at me, startled, his eyes became suddenly those of an injured hawk.

"I'm sorry," I said. "I didn't know you were in here."

I tried not to stare at the matching anchors tattooed on each of his forearms.

Had he been a sailor?

"What are you looking at?" he demanded in a harsh voice.

"Nothing," I said. "May I help?"

"No," he said, momentarily flustered. "Thank you. I was trying to help the lads shift a flat in one of the lorries, and it fell on me. My own fault, really."

As if he expected me to believe him! Who in their right mind would be moving scenery, bare-armed and bare-chested, in the back of a freezing lorry?

"I'm sorry," I said, taking the roll of lint from his hands and unreeling a fresh length. "You've cut your chest, too. Here, lean forward a bit and I'll wrap it round."

My helpfulness allowed me to have a good look at his wounds, which were already lightly scabbed and red along the edges. Not fresh, by any means, but not old, either. They had been inflicted, at a guess, twenty-four hours ago.

And by fingernails, if I were any judge.

Even though I had been cashiered from the Girl Guides for insubordination, I had not forgotten their many useful teachings, including the mnemonic "P-A-D": Pressure, Antiseptic, Dressing.

"Pad! Pad! Pad!" we used to shout, rolling about on the floor of the parish hall, mauling one another horribly, trussing our victims and ourselves, like fat white mummies, in the endless rolls of bandaging.

"Did you put iodine on these?" I asked, knowing perfectly well that he hadn't. The telltale reddish brown stains of that tincture were nowhere in evidence.

"Yes," he lied, and I noticed for the first time, in

the bin, the blood-encrusted dressings he had just removed.

"It was very kind of you to help moving props," I said casually. "I don't expect many directors would do that."

"It's not been easy with McNulty injured," he said. "Still, one does what one can."

"Mm," I said, trying to sound sympathetic, hoping he'd tell me more.

But my mind was already racing through the corridors of Buckshaw, up the stairs, back to the Blue Bedroom, back to the body of Phyllis Wyvern, back to her fingernails—

Which had been remarkably clean. There had been no shreds of ripped flesh beneath them—no sign of blood (although her scarlet nail polish might have hidden the stains).

I became suddenly aware that Val Lampman's eyes were fixed on mine, as intently hypnotic as those of a cat on a cornered mouse. If he'd had a tail, it would have been swishing.

He was reading my thoughts. I was quite sure of it.

I tried not to think of the fact that the police might already have scraped out whatever bits of evidence were under Phyllis Wyvern's fingernails; tried not to think that whoever had murdered her had taken the time to re-dress her, to paint her nails, and in doing so, to remove, before any of us got there, any matter that may have been lodged beneath them.

I tried not to think—not to think—but it was no good.

His eyes were boring into mine. Surely he had seen something.

"I'd better be getting along," I said suddenly. "I promised the vicar I'd help with the . . ."

Although I could feel my heart pounding as it pumped blood into my face, I couldn't think of a single word to complete the lie.

". . . things," I added weakly.

I had already opened the door and put one foot in the corridor when he seized my arm.

"Wait," he said.

From the corner of my eye I caught a glimpse of Dogger entering his room.

"It's all right, Dogger," I called out. "I was just showing Mr. Lampman to the WC."

Lampman let go his grip and I stepped back.

He stood fixedly staring, the bandages on his chest rising and falling with every breath.

I closed the door in his face.

Dogger had already vanished. Good old Dogger. His sense of decorum kept him from intruding in all but the most extreme emergencies. Well, this hadn't been an emergency.

Or had it? I'd talk to Dogger later, when I'd had time to think things through. It was still too soon.

Had I unmasked Phyllis Wyvern's killer? Well, perhaps—but also perhaps not.

It seemed quite unlikely that someone as placid-seeming as Val Lampman should strangle his own mother, change her clothing, and apply stage makeup in order to have her looking her best when her body was discovered.

And those injuries on his arms and chest? Mightn't he simply have got into a tussle with Latshaw, his surly crew chief?

There was no doubt about it. I needed to talk to Dogger.

Yes, that was it—we'd sit down together later over a steaming kettle and a pair of teacups, and I'd run fleet-footed through my observations and deductions, and Dogger would marvel at my accomplishments.

But until then, I had other things to do.

It was with a cheery heart that I lugged my pot of birdlime up the narrow stairs. Good thing I'd thought to bring a clothes brush from the pantry to clear away the snow from the chimney pots, and a stiffish wallpaper brush from the little framing room in the picture gallery, to slather the stuff on with.

If the door had been a chore to open earlier, it was now a beast. I put my shoulder against it and shoved, and shoved, and shoved again until at last the creaking snow yielded grudgingly, enough to allow me to squeeze out onto the roof.

The wind struck me at once and I cringed against the cold.

I trudged my way slowly across the snowy wastes to the west wing of the house, knee deep in drifts. Father Christmas would come down the drawing room chimney, as he always had. There was no point in wasting precious body heat and birdlime in painting the others.

With the snow swept away from the collars of the three stacks, it was possible—although not by any means simple—to pull myself up, slipping and sliding, onto each of the towering brick turrets in turn, although I have to admit that I gave no more than a lick and a promise to the smaller pots that connected to the fireplaces in the upper bedrooms. Father Christmas wouldn't dare come down Father's chimney, and as for Harriet's—well, there was no longer any need, was there? Except for leaving myself a couple of narrow glue-free paths in which to manoeuvre without becoming stuck myself, the application of the stuff was quite straightforward.

When I was finished, I found myself frozen there for a moment on the roof, thinking, motionless in the bitter wind, a lightning-struck weather vane that points forever in the wrong direction.

And then, just as quickly, my spirits were restored. Wasn't I, after all, within hours of being able to write "Conclusion" to my grand experiment?

As I fought my way back across the snowy wastes, I whistled a few bars of "The Holly and the Ivy" in sly reference to the sticky mess I had just applied to the chimneys of Buckshaw. I even broke into song:

"The rising of the suh-hun and the running of the deer . . ."

It was time to turn my attention to the Rocket of Honour.

* * *

"What are you *doing?*" Feely demanded, as I descended the last few steps into my laboratory.

Her fists were clenched and her eyes, as they always are when she's angry, were several shades lighter than their normal blue.

"Who let you in?" I asked. "You're not allowed in this room without written permission from me."

"Oh, take your written permission and stick it up the flue."

Feely could be remarkably coarse when she felt like it.

Still, "stick" and "flue" were uncannily descriptive of what I'd just done on the roof. *I'd better be careful*, I thought. Perhaps Feely, like Val Lampman, had found a way of peering into my mind.

"Father sent me to fetch you," she said. "He wants everyone gathered in the foyer at once. He has something to say, and so does Val Lampman."

She turned and strode off towards the door.

"Feely . . ." I said.

She stopped and, without looking at me, turned halfway round.

"Well?"

"Daff and I made a Christmas truce. I thought perhaps—"

"Truces expire after five minutes, come hell or high water, as you jolly well know. There's no such thing as a Christmas truce. Don't try to suck me into any of your sordid little schemes."

I could feel my eyes swelling as if they were about to burst.

"Why do you hate me?" I asked suddenly. "Is it because I'm more like Harriet than you are?"

If the room had been cold before, it was now a glacial ice cave.

"Hate you, Flavia?" she said, her voice trembling. "Do you really believe I hate you? Oh, how I wish I did! It would make things so much easier."

And with that she was gone.

"I'm sorry we've all of us been trapped, as it were," Father was saying, "even though we've been trapped together."

What the dickens did he mean? Was he apologizing for the weather?

"Despite their . . . ah . . . polar expedition, the vicar and Mrs. Richardson have done yeoman work in keeping the little ones entertained."

Good lord! Was Father making a joke? It was unheard of!

Had the stress of the season and the arrival of the moviemakers finally cracked his brain? Had he forgotten that Phyllis Wyvern was lying—no, not lying, but *sitting*—dead upstairs?

His words were greeted with a polite rustle of laughter from the people of Bishop's Lacey, who sat rumpled but attentive in their chairs. Clustered in one corner, the ciné crew whispered together uneasily, their faces like masks.

"I am assured," Father was saying, with a glance at Mrs. Mullet, who stood beaming at the entrance of the kitchen passageway, "that we shall be able to muster up sufficient jam and fresh-baked bread to last until we are released from our . . . captivity."

At the word "captivity" Dogger sprang to mind. Where was he?

I swivelled round and spotted him at once. He was standing well off to one side, his dark suit making him nearly invisible against the stained wood panelling. His eyes were black pits.

I squirmed in my chair, hunched and unhunched my shoulders as if to relieve stiffness, and standing up, stretched extravagantly. I sauntered casually over to the wall and leaned against it.

"Dogger," I whispered excitedly, "they dressed her for dying."

Dogger's head turned slowly towards me, his eyes sweeping round the vast room, illuminating as they came until, as they reached mine, they were as the beam of a lighthouse fixed on a rock in the sea.

"I believe you're right, Miss Flavia," he said.

With Dogger, there was no need to prattle on. The look that went between us was beyond words. We were riding the same train of thought and—aside from the unfortunate death of Phyllis Wyvern, of course—all was well with the world.

Dogger had obviously noticed, as I had, that—

But there was no time to think. I had missed Father's concluding remarks. Val Lampman had now taken the spotlight, a tragic figure who was hanging on to a lighting fixture, with the most awful white knuckles, as if to keep from crumbling to the floor.

". . . this terrible event," he was saying in an unsteady voice. "It would be unthinkable to go on without Miss Wyvern, and I have therefore, reluctantly, made the decision to shut down production at once and return to London as soon as we are able."

A collective sigh went up from the corner in which the ciné crew was gathered, and I saw Marion Trodd lean forward and whisper something to Bun Keats.

"Because we are unable to communicate with the studio," Val Lampman went on, putting two fingers to his temple as if receiving a message from the planet Mars, "I'm sure you will appreciate that this decision must needs be mine alone. I'll see that specific instructions are handed out in the morning. In the meantime, ladies and gentlemen, I suggest that we spend whatever is left of this rather sad Christmas Eve remembering Miss Wyvern, and what she has meant to each and every one of us."

It was not Phyllis Wyvern I thought of, though, but Feely. With filming shut down, her chance of stardom was over.

Ages from now—sometime in the misty future—historians sifting through the vaults of Ilium Films would come across a spool of film with images of a letter being placed carefully, again and again, upon a tabletop. What would they make of it? I wondered.

It was pleasant, in a complicated way, to think that those out-of-focus hands, with their long perfect fingers, would be those of my sister. Feely would be all that remained of *Cry of the Raven*, the film that died before it was born.

I came back to reality with a start.

Father was summoning Dogger with a single raised eyebrow, and I took the opportunity to escape up the stairs.

I had much to do and there was little time left.

And yet there was. When I got to my bedroom, I saw that it was not yet eleven o'clock.

I had always been told by Mrs. Mullet that Father Christmas did not come either until after midnight, or until everyone in the household was asleep—I've forgotten the exact formula. One way or another, it was far too early to check my traps: With half the population of Bishop's Lacey wandering about at large in the house, the old gentleman would hardly risk coming down the drawing room chimney.

And then this thought came to mind. How could Father Christmas climb down—and back up—so many million chimneys without getting his costume dirty? Why had there never been, on Christmas morning, a filthy black trail on the carpet?

I knew perfectly well from my own experiments that the carbonic products of combustion were messy enough even in the small quantities in which they were encountered in the laboratory, but to think of a full-grown man descending a chimney encrusted with decades of soot while wearing an outfit that was little better than an oversized pipe cleaner was beyond belief. Why hadn't I thought of this before? Why had such an obviously scientific proof never occurred to me?

Unless there was some invisible elf who followed Father Christmas around with a broom and a dustpan—or a supernatural hoover—things were looking grim indeed.

Outside, a rising wind buffeted at the house, rattling the windowpanes in their ancient frames. Inside, the temperature had fallen to that of a penguin's feet, and I shivered in spite of myself.

I would tuck up in bed with my notebook and a pencil. Until it was time to venture out onto the roof I would turn my attention to murder.

I wrote at the top of a fresh page *Who Killed Phyllis Wyvern?* and drew a line under it.

SUSPECTS (ALPHABETICALLY):

Anthony, the chauffeur (I don't know his surname.)—A lurking sort of person with a hang-dog expression, who seems always to be watching me. PW seemed cold towards him, but perhaps this is the way of all film stars to their drivers. Is he resentful? Seemed vaguely familiar when he appeared on our doorstep. Eastern European? Or was it just his uniform? Surely not. Aunt F said PW had an irrational horror of Eastern Europeans and insisted upon always working with the same British film crew. Had Anthony, perhaps, appeared in one of her pictures? Or in a magazine photo? Look into—perhaps even ask him outright.

Crawford, Gil—PW humiliated him in front of the entire village by slapping his face. Although gentle as a lamb nowadays, it's important to remember that as a commando, Gil was trained to kill in silence—by strangulation with a bit of piano wire!

Duncan, Desmond—No obvious motive other than that PW overshadows him. He's acted with her for years on stage and in film. Rivalry? Jealousy? Something deeper? Further inquiry needed.

Keats, Bun—PW treats her like dog dirt on the sole of a dancing slipper. Although she should be filled with resentment, she seems not to be. Are there people who thrive on abuse? Or is there fire beneath the ashes? Must ask Dogger about this.

Lampman, Val (Waldemar)—PW's son. (Hard to believe but Aunt Felicity claims it's so.) PW threatened to tell DD about Val's "interesting adventure in Buckinghamshire." Obvious tension between them (e.g., the benefit performance of Romeo and Juliet). Does he stand to inherit his mother's estate? Did she have bags and bags of money? How can I find that out? And what about his horribly scratched forearms? The wounds didn't seem fresh. Another point to talk over with Dogger in the morning.

Latshaw, Ben—Seems something of a trouble-maker. But what would he gain by bringing the film's production to a halt? He had been promoted due to Patrick McNulty's injury. Could he have been hired by someone at Ilium Films to do in PW far from the studio? (Mere speculation on my part.)

Trodd, Marion—The horn-rimmed mystery. Hangs round in silence like the smell of a clogged drain. She bears a strong resemblance to the actress Norma Durance. But those were old photos. Should have asked Aunt Felicity about her. N.B.—do later.

I scratched my head with the pencil as I reviewed my notes. I could see at once that they were far from satisfactory.

In most criminal investigations—both on the wireless and in my own experience—there are always more suspects than you can shake a stick at, but in this case, the field seemed sparse indeed. While there had been no shortage of grudges against Phyllis Wyvern, there had been no outright hatred: nothing that would even begin to explain her brutal strangling or the bow of motion picture film tied almost gaily round her neck.

In fact, I could still see it: that band of black celluloid at her throat, each of its frames bearing a still image of the actress herself in her peasant blouse, her defiant face shining like the sun against a dramatically darkened sky.

How *could* I forget it when I had seen it so often in my dreams? It was from that shocking final scene of *Anna of the Steppes*, alias *Dressed for Dying*, in which Phyllis Wyvern, as the doomed Anna Sheristikova, lays herself down in front of the advancing tractors.

In my tired mind, I fancied I could hear the sound of their snarling engines, but it was only the wind, as it howled and battered at the house.

Wind . . . tractors . . . Dieter . . . Feely . . .

When my eyes snapped open it was eight minutes past midnight.

From somewhere in the house came the sound of singing.

> *"O little town of Bethlehem,*
> *How still we see thee lie . . ."*

I could see in my mind the reverently upturned faces of the villagers.

I knew instantly that, in spite of everything that had happened, the vicar had decided to observe Christmas. He had asked the men of the village to move our old Broadwood grand piano from the drawing room into the foyer, and Feely was now at the keyboard. I knew it was Feely and not Max Brock, because of the hesitating little sob she was able to extract from the instrument as the melody flew up—and then began to fall.

Because Phyllis Wyvern's remains were still present in the house, the vicar was allowing only the more subdued carols to be sung.

I leapt out of bed and pulled on a pair of the long, mud-coloured cotton stockings that Father insisted I wear outdoors in winter. Although I hated the scraggly things with a passion, I knew how cold it would be on the roof.

That done, I grabbed the powerful torch I had pinched from the pantry and passed as silently as I could into my laboratory, where I shoved a flint igniter into the pocket of my cardigan.

I gently took up the plump Rocket of Honour, cradling it in my arms for a couple of moments and smiling down upon it as lovingly as in a Nativity scene.

Then I made for the narrow staircase.

·TWENTY·

THE ROOF WAS A howling wilderness. A biting wind blew stinging gusts of snow from peak to peak, blasting my face with particles as hard as frozen sand. The weather had worsened since last I had been up here, and it was clear that the storm was far from over.

Now came the real work. Trip after trip I made, back and forth, up and down the stairs between roof and laboratory, lugging pot after pot until at last my fireworks were ranged in rings round the chimney stacks like so many unlit candles on a tiered cake.

Although it was difficult to see in the darkness, I was reluctant to switch on the torch until it became absolutely necessary. No need to attract unwanted attention from the ground, I thought, by creating a wandering will-o'-the-wisp among the dark chimney pots, which now loomed above me—tall, ominous shadows against the snowy sky. The dark clouds, sagging above my head like half-deflated blimps, were almost low enough to reach up and touch.

I had now completed my last trip and Phyllis Wyvern's Rocket of Honour was cradled heavily in my arms. I could not possibly lug it with me round acres of roof while I completed my preparations, nor could I dump it out here in the open, where it would quickly become wet and useless.

No, I would set the thing up on the east side of one of the chimneys, where it would be sheltered from the stormy blast, ready to launch when the time came.

I trudged my way through what seemed like miles of knee-deep snow, and gave a gasp of relief when I finally spotted my destination: the towering chimney pots of Buckshaw's west wing. With surprisingly little trouble, I set up the rocket in the midst of my flowerpot fireworks by folding down the legs of the wire tripod I had impro-vised from a couple of Feely's clothes hangers.

Just one flick of the igniter and WHOOSH! Up it would climb into the night sky like a blazing comet, be-fore exploding with a BOOM! that would awaken Saint Tancred himself, who had lain sleeping under the altar of the village church for more than five hundred years. In fact, I had added an extra cup of gunpowder to the rock-et's inner chamber to assure that the dozing Saint T would not be left out of the festivities.

The Rocket of Honour, of course, would be the finale to my show of chemical pyrotechnics. First would come the golden rains and the opening buds of red fire, giving

way gradually to the bangs and booms of the Bengali
Bombardes.

I hugged myself, partly in glee and partly from the cold.

I would begin with the Royal Salute, a genteel but impressive aerial display whose recipe I had found in one of
Uncle Tar's notebooks. It had been formulated originally
by the famous Ruggieri brothers for King George II in
1749, and designed to accompany the music that Mr.
Handel had composed especially for the Royal Fireworks
display.

Since the large wooden building constructed to house
the king's musicians had been set ablaze by the fireworks
and gone up in flames, and the sheer number of spectators
had caused one of the spans of London Bridge to collapse
under their weight into the river Thames, that first performance had not been entirely successful.

Who was to say? My re-creation of a few of those famous explosions might make up, if only a little, for what
must have been at the time something of a national em-
barrassment.

Let the show begin!

I swept away the snow from my waterproof flowerpots
and reached into my pocket for the igniter. If the wind let
up even for a few seconds, one good spark would be all
that was needed—a single spark to set off a display of fire
they would still be talking about when I was an old lady,
cackling over my chemical cauldrons.

I stepped back for one last look at my lovingly crafted
explosives.

Perhaps it was because my eyes had been squeezed half

shut against the blowing snow that I had not immediately noticed the second set of footprints stretching back towards the door.

Father Christmas! I thought at once. *He's parked his sleigh, walked across the roof, and gone into the house by the same door I've just come out.*

But why? Why wouldn't he have climbed immediately down the chimney, as he had been doing for hundreds of years?

Of course! It was suddenly as plain as a pikestaff. Father Christmas was supernatural, wasn't he? He'd have known about my glue and steered clear of it! Did supernatural beings even *leave* traces in the snow?

Why hadn't I thought of this stupidly simple point sooner and saved myself all the trouble?

But wait! Hadn't I been up here myself, earlier, to set up my pots of fireworks?

Of course! What a little fool you are, Flavia!

I was looking at my own footprints.

And yet . . . almost before that thought came to mind, I knew it could not possibly be true. It had been hours since I was last on the roof. With the blowing wind and the drifting snow, my own earlier footprints would surely have been filled in within minutes. Even my fresh-made prints were already losing their sharply defined edges.

A couple of leaps brought me to the trail of tracks, and I could see at a glance, close up, that they led *away* from the door, not towards it.

Someone besides Flavia and Father Christmas had been up here on the roof.

And quite recently, if I was not mistaken.

Furthermore, if I had read the signs correctly, they were *still* up here, hiding somewhere in the snowy wastes.

"Run for it, Flavia!" the ancient, instinctive part of my brain was shrieking, and yet I was still hovering—frozen by the moment, reluctant to move even an inch—when a dark figure stepped silently out from behind the chimney pot of Harriet's boudoir.

It was dressed in a long, old-fashioned leather aviator's coat that reached halfway down its riding boots, the high collar turned up above the ears. Its eyes were covered with the small, round green lenses of an ancient leather helmet of the sort Harriet had worn in her flying days, and its hands gloved in long, stiff leather gauntlets.

My first thought, of course, was that this spectre was my mother, and my blood froze.

Although I had longed, all of my life, to be reunited with Harriet, I did not want it to be like this. Not masked—not on a windswept roof.

I'm afraid I whimpered.

"Who are you?" I managed.

"Your past," I thought the figure whispered.

Or was it just the wind?

"Who are you?" I demanded again.

The figure took a menacing step towards me.

Then suddenly, somewhere inside my head, a voice was speaking as calmly as the BBC wireless announcer reading out the shipping forecasts for Rockall, the Shetlands, and the Orkneys.

"Keep your head," it was saying. "You know this person—you simply haven't realized it yet!"

And it was true. Although I had all the information I needed, I hadn't put together all of the pieces. This spectre was really no more than someone who had dressed themselves up from the film studio's wardrobe—someone who did not want to be recognized.

"It's no good, Mr. Lampman," I said, standing my ground. "I know you murdered your mother."

Somehow it didn't seem right to call him "Val."

"You and your accomplice did her in and rigged her up in the costume she wore in *Dressed for Dying*—the role you had promised to your—what do you call it?—your mistress."

It was almost comforting to hear the words of that old formula coming out of my mouth—the final exchange between a cold-blooded killer and the investigator who had cracked the case. It had taken a great deal of poring over the pages of *Cinema Secrets* and *Silver Screen* to dig out that final incriminating tidbit. I was proud of myself.

But not for long.

The figure made a sudden lunge, taking me by surprise, almost knocking me backwards into a snowdrift. Only by windmilling my arms and making a blind and off-balance leap backwards was I able to stay on my feet.

With my attacker blocking the way to the staircase, there was no point in making a dash for it. Better to find safety in height, like a cat.

I scrambled, slipping and sliding up onto one of the

chimney collars—one that I hadn't slathered with glue. From up here I could hold on with one arm while kicking the killer in the face, should the need arise.

It didn't take long.

With a hiss like an infuriated snake, my attacker pulled from one of its large coat pockets a stick which I believe is called by the police a truncheon, and brought the thing crashing down just inches from my feet.

Whack! it went—and *whack!* again, the blows raining down on the brick ledge of the chimney pot with a series of sharp, sickening sounds, like bones being broken.

I had to leap like a highland dancer to keep my toes from being pulverized.

Behind me, I remembered, on the drawing room chimney, were the fuses for the fireworks—perhaps no more than ten yards away. If only I could reach them . . . touch the striker to the fuse . . . summon help . . . the rest of it would be in the hands of Fate.

But now the gauntlets were grabbing at my ankles, and I was kicking back at them for all I was worth.

This time I was rewarded with the sound and the feel of shoe leather on skull, and the figure reeled back with a hoarse cry of pain, clutching at its face.

Taking advantage of the moment, I edged my way round to the far side of the chimney. From there, I could leap down unseen, I hoped, onto the roof.

I had to risk it. There was no other choice.

I landed more lightly than expected and was already halfway to the drawing room chimney when my attacker spotted me and, with a cry of rage, came charging across the roof, its boots throwing up clods of snow as it came.

Out of breath, I threw myself at the chimney, this one larger than the first, and pulled myself up to safety, my hand already digging into my pocket for the igniter.

The fuses were now just below me at shoe level. With any luck, just one click would do the trick.

I ducked down and squeezed the spring handle.

Click!

And nothing more.

Too late now. My attacker was already clawing at the ledge like a maddened animal, preparing to haul itself up beside me. If that happened I was finished.

I swung at its goggled face with the torch—and missed!

The torch slipped out of my hand and fell, as if in slow motion, tumbling end over end down onto the roof, where it lay half buried in a snowdrift, shooting a crazily angled beam up into my attacker's eyes, half blinding it.

I didn't waste a single instant. I ducked down and flicked the igniter again.

Click! . . . *Click!* . . . *Click!* . . . *Click!* . . .

Infuriating! I should have coated the fuses with candle wax, but one can't think of everything. Obviously, they had become damp.

The clutching gloves were coming uncomfortably closer. It was only a matter of time before they managed to seize my ankle and drag me down onto the roof.

With that disturbing thought in mind, I shimmied a little higher up the clay chimney pot, again working my way, as I climbed, fully round to the east side of the structure.

On the roof, my attacker followed me around, perhaps half expecting me to slip and fall. High above its horribly helmeted head, my every breath visible on the cold air, I clung like a limpet to the upper section of the chimney.

A moment passed—and then another.

I became aware of a growing warmness. Had the wind let up, or had summer suddenly come? Perhaps I was running a fever.

I thought of the thousand warnings of Mrs. Mullet.

"Sudden chills fills the 'ills," she never tired of telling me. "The 'ills meanin' them little 'ills in the churchyard, of course. Dress up warm, dear, if you want to get your 'undred years birthday letter from the king."

I clutched my cardigan closed beneath my chin.

Below me, the figure had turned abruptly and was walking off towards the battlements of the west wing. It seemed like a peculiar thing to do, but almost instantly I saw the reason.

At a point on the roof directly above the drawing room, the aerial for our wireless was stretched between a pair of slender vertical bamboo poles.

Seizing the closest pole with its gauntlets, my attacker put a boot against the socketed base and gave a sharp tug. Perhaps more than anything because of the cold, the bamboo snapped off as easily as if it had been a matchstick. It was now attached only to the copper wire. A quick twist of the wrist and that, too, had broken away, leaving my assailant holding a bamboo pole with two wickedly jagged ends. From one of these dangled a white china insulator that had somehow remained attached by a twist of wire.

Again I found myself staring straight down into the upturned face of my assailant. If only I could reach out and rip the goggles from that face—but I couldn't.

Those mad eyes stared up me through the green goggles in cold dead hatred, and a shiver shook my frame—a kind of shiver I had never known before.

Those eyes, I realized, with a sudden sickening jolt, were not ringed by their usual horn-rimmed glasses. My attacker was not Val Lampman.

"Marion Trodd is killing me!" I heard my own voice screaming, and the realization must have surprised her as much as it surprised me.

It might have been less frightening if she'd said something, but she didn't. She stood there in the silence of the drifting snow, still glaring up at me with that look of quite impersonal hatred.

And then, as if taking a bow at the end of a play, she lifted the goggles, and slowly removed the flier's helmet.

"It was you," I gasped. "You and Val Lampman."

She made a little hiss of contempt, rather like a snake. Without a word, she extended the pole and, placing it in the middle of my chest, gave a vicious shove.

I let out a cry of pain, but somehow managed to twist my body in the direction of the thrust. At the same time I dragged myself a little higher.

But I might as well have saved the effort. The end of the stick with its dangling insulator was now hovering directly in front of my face. I simply couldn't allow her to poke me in the eyes, or to catch the corner of my mouth with the wire, like a hooked fish.

Almost without thinking I seized the end of the pole and slammed it hard against the chimney. At the shock, Marion let go of the handle, and the pole fell away silently into the snow.

Now, suddenly infuriated, as if wanting to tear me apart personally with her bare hands, she launched herself directly at me, this time managing to get a firm grip on the bricks of the ledge. She had already pulled herself halfway up when she seemed to lurch, then suddenly stall in midair like a partridge hit on the wing.

A muffled curse came to my ears.

The birdlime! The birdlime! Oh, joy—the birdlime!

I had given the downwind ledge of the drawing room chimney pot an extra slathering of the stuff on the theory that Father Christmas would choose the sheltered side to climb out of his sleigh.

Marion Trodd was tugging away fiercely, trying to rip her hands free of the stuck gloves, but the more she struggled, the more she became entangled with her riding boots and long coat.

I had wondered, idly, while preparing the stuff, if my glue would be weakened by the cold, but it was obvious that it had not. If anything, it had become stronger and stickier, and it was becoming more evident by the minute that only by undressing completely could Marion hope to escape.

I seized the moment and bent to the fuse again:

Click! Click! Click!

Curses and counter-curses! The blasted thing refused to ignite.

In the ghastly silence that followed, as Marion Trodd tried in vain to free herself, her movements becoming ever more restricted, the sound of singing came floating to my ears:

"The hopes and fears of all the years
Are met in thee tonight."

I don't know why, but the words bit at my bones.

"Dogger!" I shouted, my voice hoarse and broken in the cold air. "Dogger! Help me!"

But I knew in my heart that with everyone singing about Bethlehem, they couldn't possibly have heard me. Besides, it was too far from the roof to the foyer—too many of Buckshaw's bricks and timbers lay between us.

The wind had torn the words from my mouth and whipped them uselessly out and away, across the frozen countryside.

And it was then that I realized there was nothing keeping me from escape. All I had to do was leap clear of Marion Trodd, and run for the stairs.

It was almost certain that she had left the door open. Otherwise, how could she have returned to the house after finishing me off?

She bared her teeth and grimaced as I jumped, but she could not free herself enough to make a grab at me as I sailed over her shoulder. My knees buckled as I landed in a snowdrift.

I wished I had thought of a noble, defiant taunt to hurl into her snarling face, but I did not. Fear and the bitter cold had left me little more than a crouching, shivering bundle.

And then, in an instant, I was on my feet again, running across the roof as if all the hounds of hell were at my heels.

I was in luck. As I had supposed it would be, the door to the stairs stood open. Yellow light poured out onto the snow in a warm and welcoming rectangle.

Six feet to safety, I told myself.

But suddenly a black silhouette filled the doorway, blocking the light—and my escape.

I recognized it at once as Val Lampman.

I slid to a stop and tried to reverse myself, my feet slipping and sliding as if I were on skates.

I fled back across the roof, not daring to look behind me as I reached the drawing room chimney and pulled myself back up onto the first ledge. If Val Lampman was overtaking me, I didn't want to know about it.

Perhaps I could lure him into the same trap as Marion Trodd. He didn't yet know about the glue, and I wasn't about to warn him.

As I scrambled higher up the chimney stack, I could see that he was walking unhurriedly across the roof. Methodically—yes, that was more the word.

It seemed likely that he had sent Marion Trodd to deal with me. She had followed me, slipping onto the roof during one of my up-and-down trips. But when she had not returned, he had come to do the dirty work himself.

He barely glanced at Marion, who was still entangled in the glue, writhing in its grip as ineffectively as a gnat stuck to flypaper.

"Val!" she shrieked. "Get me out of this!"

They were the first words she had spoken since she came onto the roof.

He turned his head—paused—and took an uncertain step towards her.

It was then I realized that the man was driven by Marion Trodd's need for vengeance. It was at her command that he had been made to strangle his own mother.

If this was love, I wanted nothing to do with it.

At the base of the chimney, not seeming to know which of us to attend to first, he suddenly tripped—stumbled—and fell onto his elbows in the snow!

I almost cheered!

As he got shakily to his feet, I saw that he had tripped over the bamboo pole, which had been lying unseen in a drift.

"Prod her, Val!" Marion screamed hoarsely as he picked the thing up. She had already gone from thinking of her own rescue to demanding my head on a platter.

"Prod her! Knock her down. Do it now, Val! Do it!"

He looked at me—looked at her—his head swivelling, unable to make up his mind.

Then slowly, as if in a hypnotic trance, he picked up the pole and moved to a point directly below where I was clinging tightly to the chimney.

Taking his time about it, he worked the sharp end of the bamboo slowly into the collar of my cardigan, giving it an extra twist to be sure that it was secured.

The sharp tendril of wire was quickly entangled in the wool of my sweater. I could feel it stabbing me between the shoulder blades.

"No!" I managed. "Please!"

One fierce shove and I was falling—landing face-first in the suffocating snow, the breath knocked out of me.

By the time I rolled over, he was already dragging me towards the edge of the roof. My hands clutched uselessly at the air, but there was nothing to hang on to—no possible way of saving myself.

I tried to scramble to my feet but could not get a grip. He was using the pole to keep clear of my hands, my feet, and my teeth, dragging me along through the snow like a gaffed cod.

Now he had hauled me to the very edge of the battlements, and his plan was perfectly clear. He was going to shove me over.

His feet were sliding on the slippery roof as he tried to plant them firmly for that final bit of deadly pole work.

How unfairly things had turned out, it seemed to me. It was downright rotten when you came to think of it. No one deserved to die like this.

And yet Harriet had, hadn't she?

What had been her last thoughts on that wintery mountain in Tibet? Did her life flash before her eyes, as it is said to do?

Did she have time to think of me?

"Stop it, Flavia!" a voice said inside my head, suddenly and quite distinctly.

"Stop it at once!"

I was so surprised that I obeyed.

But what was I supposed to do?

"Take stock," the voice said, rather crabbily.

Yes! That was it—take stock.

It was ridiculously easy to do. I had nothing left to lose.

Somehow, in that moment, I managed to twist round enough to free my collar and grab on to the end of the pole. Unexpectedly, it gave me the support I needed to lurch clumsily up onto my feet.

Now we were at the very edge of the precipice, Val Lampman and I, like two tightrope walkers, each of us hanging on for dear life to opposite ends of the same bamboo pole.

He gave the thing a sudden jerk, trying to topple me, but as he did so, his foot slipped on the icy stone gutter. He lost his grip on the pole and his arms flailed wildly at the air as he fought to keep his footing.

But it wasn't enough to save him.

In utter silence, he fell backwards and was swallowed by the night. The pole tumbled lazily after him, end over end.

From somewhere below came a sickening *thump*.

I was left teetering on the sloped edge, fighting desperately to keep my balance, but my feet were slipping slowly towards the edge of the battlement, now just inches away.

Desperately, I threw myself down onto my face, trying to dig my fingers into the icy stones.

It was no use.

As my feet shot out into empty space, I made one last frantic grab at a section of weather-worn lead gutter, trying to hook my fingertips onto its lip, but the stuff twisted, crumbled—almost disintegrating in my fingers—and I felt my body sliding . . . like a limp mannequin . . . over the precipice.

And then I was falling . . . endlessly . . . interminably . . . seemingly forever . . . down into darkness.

·TWENTY-ONE·

WHEN I OPENED MY eyes at last, I found myself staring straight up into the falling snow. A kaleidoscope of red and white flakes spun past, growing larger until they landed in horrid, slushy silence on the frozen mask that must have been my face.

Above me, the shadowy blur of the battlements lurched at a crazy angle, towering up into the low, scudding clouds.

There was a diffused flash, followed by a deep rumbling, as if mischievous clerks were rolling empty wine barrels in a warehouse.

Another flash—a flash that flared and faded with every pulsing beat of my heart—followed by an earsplitting *Crack!*

A silence followed—so intense that it hurt my ears. Only gradually did I become aware of the sizzle of the falling snow. And then . . .

Foom!

Something like a red candle lit up the night with a pallid and unearthly glow.

Foom! Foompf!

Now a green light and a blue joined with the red, as a comet the colour of sunflowers climbed the sky and burst high overhead in a dazzling shower amid the falling snow.

The night had suddenly become an inferno of icy fire, its colours blazing with such fierce splendour that it brought hard, glassy tears to my eyes.

Foom! Foom! Faroom!

It seemed to go on forever. I was becoming too weary to watch.

Somewhere, someone was beckoning me—a summons I couldn't resist.

"Who are you?" I wanted to shout. "Who are you?"

But I had no voice. Nothing seemed to matter anymore.

I closed my eyes upon the starry brilliance, then opened them again almost at once as a great coppery-green comet lifted itself on a tail of glittering yellow sparks and, like some celestial dragon, climbed into the sky and exploded directly overhead with an earth-shattering *boom*.

Rocket of Honour, I remember thinking, mentally ticking off ingredients on my imagined fingers: antimony . . . iron filings . . . potassium chlorate.

I thought for an instant of Phyllis Wyvern, the recipient of my tribute, and how sad it was that nothing of her remained alive but a series of shadowy images on coils of black film.

I thought, too, of Harriet.

And then I slept.

They were all of them gathered round my bed, their faces looming over me as if seen through a fish-eye lens. Carl Pendracka was offering me a stick of Sweet Sixteen chewing gum, while the Misses Puddock held out identical cups of steaming tea. Inspector Hewitt stood with his arm around the shoulders of his wife, Antigone, who wept silently into a dainty piece of lace. At the foot of the bed, Father stood motionless, flanked by my white-faced sisters, Ophelia and Daphne, all three of them looking as if they had just been vomited up from hell.

Dr. Darby was speaking in a low voice to Dogger, who shook his head and looked away. In the corner, her face buried in her husband Alf's shoulder, Mrs. Mullet trembled like an autumn leaf. Behind them, Aunt Felicity was fussing with some clinking object or another in the depths of her alligator handbag.

The vicar stepped back from my bedside and whispered something that sounded like "flowers" into the ear of his wife, Cynthia.

There were others lurking in the shadows, but I could not see them clearly. The room was hot and musty. Someone must have opened up the old fireplace and set a blaze going. The smell of soot and charcoal—and something else—was on the overheated air.

What was it? Gunpowder? Saltpetre?

Or was I back in the stifling cupboard under the stairs, inhaling the fumes of the burning paper?

I coughed painfully, and began to shiver.

Nasturtiums, I thought, after a very long time. *Someone has brought me nasturtiums.*

Daffy had once told me, in a rather condescending tone, that the name of those smelly flowers meant "nose-twister." But while I could easily have shot back that the stink was due entirely to the fact that their volatile oil consisted largely of sulphocyanide of allyl (C_4H_6NS), or mustard oil, I did not.

There are times when I am humble.

We had been looking through one of Harriet's water-colour sketchbooks that day, and had come across a grouping of the pretty flowers, their papery petals a warm rainbow of orange, yellow, red, and pink.

At the bottom of the page was lightly printed in pencil, *Nasturtiums, Toronto, 1930 Harriet de Luce.*

At the top, obliterating one of the petals, was a heavy black rubber stamp: *Miss Bodycote's Female Academy.* And in red pencil, B–.

My heart wanted to leap out of my chest and punch someone in the nose. What barbarian of a teacher had dared to award my dear dead mother a Bath bun—a beta minus?

I drew in a deep, offended breath and choked on the knot in my throat.

"Easy, dear," said a hollow, echoing voice. "It's all right now."

I opened my eyes, squinting against the fierce white light, to find Mrs. Mullet beside me. She stepped quickly to the window and lowered the blind until the sun was no longer shining directly into my eyes.

It took me a couple of moments to locate myself. I was not in my bedroom, but rather on the drawing room divan. I struggled to pull myself up.

"Lie still, dear," she said. "Dr. Darby's give you a nice mustard police."

"What?"

"A plaster, like. You 'ave to keep still."

"What time is it?" I asked, still dislocated.

"Why, it's past Christmas, ducks," she said. "You've gone and missed it."

I wrinkled my nose at the mess of clotted mustard on my chest.

"Don't touch it, dear. You've gone all chesty. Dr. Darby said to leave it on for 'alf an 'our."

"But why? I'm not sick."

"You've fell off the roof. It's the same thing. Good job they'd shovelled them drifts into such a bloomin' great 'eap, else you'd've gone straight through to China."

Roof?

It all came surging back in a tidal wave.

"Val Lampman!" I said. "Marion Trodd! They tried to—"

"Now, then," Mrs. Mullet said. "You're not to think of anythin' but gettin' better. Dr. Darby thinks you might 'ave cracked a rib, an' 'e doesn't want you squirmin' about."

She fluffed up my pillow and brushed a strand of damp hair out of my eyes.

"But I can tell you this much," she added, with a sniff. "They've took 'er away with the darbies on 'er wrists. They 'ad to cut 'er loose with tin-snips. You should of seen 'er. Reg'lar pouter, she is. Kept stickin' to everythin' she touched—even Constable Linnet, and 'im in 'is clean uniform—*and* after 'is wife 'ad just washed and ironed it, 'e told me. They'll more'n likely 'ang 'er by the neck until she's dead, but you mustn't let on I told you. You're not supposed to be gettin' all worked up."

"But what about Val Lampman?"

Mrs. Mullet arranged a serious look on her face.

"Fell, same as you. Landed square on Miss Wyvern's motorcar. Broke 'is neck. But remember, my lips is sealed."

I was silent for a long time, trying to work out in my mind how to respond to this honestly not unwelcome bit of news. It appeared that Justice had made up her own mind about how to deal with Val Lampman.

My mind was suddenly filled with a series of odd, faded images—of distorted faces swimming in and out of a hazy room in which I was lying helpless.

"Mrs. Hewitt," I said at last. "Antigone. The Inspector's wife—is she still here?"

Mrs. Mullet shot me a puzzled look.

"Never 'as been. Not that I knows of."

"Are you quite sure? She was standing right where you are, just a few minutes ago."

"Then she must 'ave been a dream, mustn't she. There's been no one in 'ere but me and Dogger since last night. And Miss Ophelia. She insisted on sittin' up with you and moppin' your face. Oh, and the Colonel, of course, when

Dogger found you in the snowbank and carried you in, but that was last night, wasn't it. 'E's not been down yet today, poor soul. Worries somethin' awful, 'e does. I expect 'e'll 'ave somethin' to say to you when you're yourself again."

"I expect he will."

Actually, I was quite looking forward to it. Father and I seemed to talk to each other only in the most desperate of circumstances.

Without my hearing it, the door had opened and Dogger was suddenly in the room.

"Now, then," Mrs. Mullet said. "'Ere's Dogger. I might as well get back to my mutton. They've eat us out of 'ouse and 'ome, that lot 'ave. It was never-endin', like the stream in that there 'ymn."

She bustled officiously out of the room, giving the doorknob a polish with her apron on the way out.

Dogger waited until the door had closed behind her.

"Are you comfortable?" he asked quietly.

I caught his eye, and for some stupid reason I was suddenly near tears.

I nodded my head, afraid to speak so much as a single word.

"Only foreigners cry," Father had once told me, and I didn't want to let down the side by blubbering.

"It was a very near thing," Dogger said. "I should have been most upset if anything had happened to you."

Blast it all! Now my eyes were leaking like taps. I reached for one of the tissues Mrs. Mullet had left beside me and pretended to blow my nose.

"I'm sorry," I managed. "I didn't mean to be any trouble. It's just that I . . . I was conducting an experiment involving Father Christmas. He didn't come, did he?"

"We shall see," Dogger said, handing me another tissue. "You may hawk into this."

I had hardly noticed that I was coughing.

"How many fingers am I holding up?" Dogger asked, his hand off to the right of my head.

"Two," I said, without looking.

"And now?"

"Four."

"What's the atomic number of arsenic?"

"Thirty-three."

"Very good. And the principal alkaloids in deadly nightshade?"

"That's easy. Hyoscine and hyoscyamine."

"Excellent," Dogger said.

"They were in it together, weren't they? Marion Trodd and Val Lampman, I mean."

Dogger nodded. "She could not have overpowered Miss Wyvern alone. Strangulation by cellulose nitrate ciné film would require exceptionally strong hands and arms. It is a most slippery weapon, but with an exceedingly high tensile strength, as you, through your chemical experiments, are undoubtedly aware. A uniquely *male* weapon, I should say. The motive, though, remains murky."

"Revenge," I said. "And inheritance. Miss Wyvern was trying to tell someone—Desmond, or Bun—maybe it was Aunt Felicity. I couldn't make it out. She knew they were planning to kill her. Since she kept up paid subscriptions to the *Police Gazette* and *True Crime*, *News of the World*, and so forth, she knew all the signs. She was writing her thoughts on a piece of paper when they interrupted her. She stuffed it into the toe of a boot, which they jammed onto her foot when they changed her costume. A bad mistake on their part."

Dogger scratched his head.

"I'll explain it later," I said. "I'm so drowsy, I can hardly keep my eyes open."

Dogger held out a hand.

"You may remove the mustard poultice," he said. "I believe you're sufficiently warmed. At least for now."

He held out a silver tray and I handed him the reeking thing.

"Mind the tarnish," I said, almost as a joke.

It was true, though. The sulphurous fumes would attack sterling silver before you could say "snap!"

"It's quite all right," Dogger said. "This one's coated electroplate."

I remembered with sudden shame that Father had sent the family silver to auction months ago, and I was instantly sorry for my thoughtless remark.

Without another word, Dogger pulled the quilt up under my chin and tucked me in, then went to the window and closed the curtains.

"Oh, and Dogger—" I said, when he was halfway out of the door. "One more small point—Phyllis Wyvern was Val Lampman's mother."

"My word!" said Dogger.

·TWENTY-TWO·

"So you see, Inspector," I said, "their idea was to do away with her in the midst of the greatest number of suspects, just as the killers did in *Love and Blood*. They must have seen the opportunity of shooting a film at Buckshaw as something of a godsend. Val Lampman picked the location himself."

"Rather like an Agatha Christie," Inspector Hewitt remarked drily.

"Exactly!"

It was now the fourth day after Christmas—December the twenty-ninth, to be precise.

After I'd spent two days and nights floating in a sweaty dream, awakening only to cough and to suck at soup fed to me on a spoon by Feely, who had insisted on keeping vigil at my bedside night and day, Dr. Darby had given grudging permission for me to be grilled by the Hinley constabulary.

"Two more days of mustard plasters, to be followed by no more than a couple of minutes with His Majesty's Hounds," he had said, as if I were a plate of perspiring roast beef—or an exhausted fox.

"I should be most grateful to hear your thoughts on the exchanging of Miss Wyvern's costume," the Inspector added. "Purely as a matter of interest, you understand."

"Oh, that was the easy part!" I told him. "They swapped her Juliet costume for the peasant outfit she'd worn in *Dressed for Dying*. They'd even brought it with them. Premeditation, I believe you call it. They dressed her up, right down to her original makeup. Marion Trodd wanted it that way. You've probably already found Miss Wyvern's makeup, lipstick, and nail polish in her bag. It was no more than revenge, really."

The Inspector looked puzzled.

"Val Lampman had originally promised Marion the leading role in *Cry of the Raven*, but he was made to take it away from her and give it to his mother. He had to, you see. Marion was not aware, of course, that Miss Wyvern *was* Val's mother, and he wasn't about to tell her. It's all there in *Who's Who* and the back numbers of *Behind the Screen* and *Ciné Tit-Bits*. There are tons of old film magazines in the cupboard under the stairs."

Only as I spoke the words did it occur to me to wonder who had bought them, all those years ago.

"Get onto it, Sergeant," the Inspector said to Detective Sergeant Woolmer, who closed his notepad, turned a little red, and lumbered off in the direction of the foyer.

"Now, then, you were suggesting that Marion Trodd was formerly an actress," he said when the sergeant had gone. "Is that it?"

"Under the name of Norma Durance, yes. Sergeant Woolmer will find it in *Silver Cinema*, for 1933. The September issue, I believe. It's a bit charred, I'm afraid, but in what's left of it, there's quite a good photo of her as Dorita in *The Little Red Hen*."

Inspector Hewitt's Biro had been fairly flying over the page, but he stopped long enough to shoot me a surprised smile.

In spite of looking like a barrage balloon in my woollen nightie and carpet-grade dressing gown, I must have positively preened.

"They were having an affair, of course," I added casually, and the Inspector's eyeballs gave an involuntary twitch. I didn't really understand all that was involved in such a relationship, and I didn't much care, actually. Once, when I had asked Dogger what was meant by the phrase, he had told me that it described two people who had become the very best of friends, and that was good enough for me.

"Of course," the Inspector said, in a surprisingly meek voice, scribbling away in his notebook. "Well done."

Well done? I tried not to simper. This was high praise from a man who had, at our first meeting, sent me off to rustle up some tea.

"You're very kind," I said, anxious to make the moment last.

"I am, indeed," he said. "I've found exasperation to be quite useless."

"So have I," I said, without knowing fully what I meant. In spite of that, it sounded like an intelligent response.

"Well, thank you, Flavia," the Inspector said, getting to his feet. "This has been most instructive."

"I'm always happy to help," I said, not at all bashfully.

"Of course . . . I had already come to the same conclusion myself," he added.

A sudden clamminess gripped me. Come to the same conclusion himself? How *could* he! How *dare* he?

"Fingerprints?" I asked coldly.

They *must* have found the fingerprints of the killers in the murder room.

"Not at all," he said. "It was the knot. She was strangled with a straightforward length of ciné film to which, after death, an additional bow was added. Two distinct layers and, we believe, by two different persons, one left-handed, the other right. The inner knot—the one that actually killed her—was rather an unusual one—a bowline—often used by sailors and seldom by others. Sergeant Graves has discovered—by noticing his tattoos—that Val Lampman had served for a time in the Royal Navy, a fact that we have since been able to confirm."

I'd spotted that myself, of course, but hadn't had the time to follow up.

"Of course!" I said. "The outer knot was purely decorative! Marion Trodd must have added it as a finishing touch after she had swapped the costumes."

The Inspector closed his notebook.

"There is a knot that is known to florists, who tie it with ribbon onto floral arrangements, as 'the durance,' " he said. "It is, as you say, purely decorative. It was also her signature. I hadn't spotted the connection until just now, when you were good enough to provide the missing link."

Maestro, a few triumphant trumpets! Something by Handel, if you please! "Music for the Royal Fireworks"? Yes, that will do nicely.

"Dressed for dying," I said with a touch of the old drama.

"Dressed for dying." Inspector Hewitt smiled.

"Do you suppose," I asked, "that before she became the actress Norma Durance, Miss Trodd might have been employed in a florist's shop?"

"I shouldn't be surprised," he said. "It seems as if, by two very different roads, we've both come to the same destination."

Was this another of his two-edged compliments? I couldn't really tell, so I responded with a stupid smile.

Flavia the Sphinx, he would be thinking. *The inscrutable Flavia de Luce.* Or something like that.

"You'd better get some rest," he said suddenly, making for the door. "I wouldn't want Dr. Darby holding me responsible for your extended convalescence."

What a dear man he was, the Inspector! "Extended convalescence," indeed. It was so like him. No wonder his wife, Antigone, shone like a searchlight when he was by her side. Which reminded me . . .

"Inspector Hewitt," I said, "before you go, I want to—"

But he cut me short.

"No need," he said, making a shooing motion with his hands. "No need at all."

Blast it all! Was I to be robbed of my apology? But before I could say another word, he went on:

"Oh, by the way, Antigone asked me to compliment you on rather a spectacular display of fireworks. Despite the fact that you appear to have broken almost every single provision of the Explosives Acts of 1875 and 1923, discussion of which we shall leave until the Chief Constable has been coaxed down off the ceiling, she tells me your little show was seen and heard in Hinley. In spite of the snow."

"In spite of the snow," Father was saying, with what sounded, incredibly, like a measure of pride in his voice. "A friend of Mrs. Mullet's reported seeing a distinct reddish glow in the southern sky at East Finching, and someone told Max Brock that the explosions were heard as far away as Malden Fenwick. By that time the snowfall was abating, of course, but still, when you stop to think of it . . . quite remarkable. A lightning bolt during a snowstorm is not completely unheard of, of course. I rang up my old friend Taffy Codling, who happens to be the Met officer at the Leathcote air base. Taffy tells me that although exceedingly rare, the phenomenon was indeed recorded in the early hours of Christmas morning, just about the time of your . . . ah . . . Flavia's . . . ah . . . mis-adventure."

I hadn't heard Father say so many words since he had confided in me at the time of Horace Bonepenny's murder. And the fact that he had used the telephone to find out about the lightning! Was the world coming off its hinges?

I had been cleaned up and arranged on the divan in the drawing room as if I were one of those Victorian heroines who are always dying of consumption in Daffy's novels.

Everyone was gathered round me in a circle like the game of Happy Families we had once dragged out of a cupboard when it had been raining for three weeks, and had played endlessly at the dining room table with grim and determined hilarity.

"They think a bolt of lightning touched off your fireworks," Daffy was saying. "So you can hardly be held responsible, can you? It left a ruddy great hole in the roof, though. Dogger had to organize a bucket brigade of villagers. What a smashing show! Too bad you missed it!"

"Daphne," Father said, giving her one of those looks he reserves for marginal language.

"Well, it's true," Daffy went on. "You should have seen the lot of us standing round, up to our duffs in drifts, gaping like a gang of adenoidal carolers!"

"Daphne . . ."

The vicar clamped his jaws shut, trying to suppress an angelically silly grin. But before Daffy could offend again, there was a light tapping at the door, and a tentative nose appeared.

"May I come in?"

"Nialla!" I said.

"We've just come to say good-bye," she whispered theatrically, coming fully into the room, a swaddling bundle cradled in her arms. "The film crew's gone, and Desmond and I are the last ones here. He was going to drive me home in his Bentley, but it seems to have frozen up. Dr. Darby happens to be running up to London for an old boys' dinner, and he's offered to drop the baby and me right at our own front door."

"But isn't it too soon?" Feely asked, speaking for the first time. "Couldn't you stay awhile? I've hardly had a chance to see the baby, what with all the goings-on."

She wrinkled her brow in my direction as she said it.

"Too kind, I'm sure," Nialla said, looking round the room from face to face. "It's been lovely seeing all of you again, and Dieter, too, but Bun's put me onto someone who's working on a new film adaptation of *A Christmas Carol*. Oh, please don't grimace at me like that, Daphne—it's work, and it will keep us fed until the real thing comes along."

Father shuffled his feet and looked cautiously out from beneath his eyebrows.

"I've told Miss Gilfoyle she is welcome to stay as long as she likes, but . . ."

". . . but she must be getting along," Nialla finished brightly, smiling down at the child in her arms and brushing an imaginary something off its chin.

"He looks a little like Rex Harrison," I said. "Especially his forehead."

Nialla blushed prettily, glancing at the vicar, as if for support.

"I hope he has his father's brains," she said, "and not mine."

There was one of those long, uncomfortable silences during which you pray in earnest that no one will make a rude noise.

"Ah, Colonel de Luce, here you are," said the world-famous voice, and Desmond Duncan made his entrance with as polished and attention-getting a stride as had ever been stridden in front of a ciné camera or a West End audience. "Dogger told me I should find you here. I've been awaiting the opportunity to convey to you some re-markably good news."

In his hand was the copy of *Romeo and Juliet* he had pocketed in the library.

" 'How beautiful are the feet of those who bring good news,' or so, at least, said the apostle Paul, quoting Isaiah, but presumably speaking of his own feet, in his letter to the Romans," the vicar remarked to no one in particular.

Everyone glanced at once at Desmond Duncan's Bond Street shoes, but when they realized their mistake, they all stared intently instead at the ceiling.

"This quite unassuming little volume, which has turned up in your library, is, if I am not mistaken, a Shake-speare First Quarto. That it is of great value is beyond question, and I should be guilty of a cruel trespass if I pretended it was not."

He scanned the cover, removed his glasses, glanced at Father, restored the glasses, and opened the book to the title page.

"John Danter," he said, in a slow, reverent whisper, holding the book out for inspection.

"I beg your pardon, sir?" Father said.

Desmond Duncan drew in a deep breath.

"Unless I miss my bet, Colonel de Luce, you are the possessor of a First Quarto of *Romeo and Juliet*. Printed in 1597 by John Danter. Pity about the modern inscription, though. You could, perhaps, have it professionally removed."

"How much?" Aunt Felicity demanded abruptly. "Must be worth a pretty penny."

"How much?" Desmond Duncan smiled. "A king's ransom, possibly. I can tell you that, without question, if brought to auction today . . . a million, perhaps.

"It's what is known as a 'Foul Quarto,'" he went on, his excitement barely under control. "The text is quite different in places from the one we are accustomed to seeing performed. It was believed to have been created from Shakespeare's players having to recall their parts from memory. Hence its inaccuracy."

As if in a trance, Daffy was creeping slowly forward, her hand extended towards the book.

"Are you saying," she asked, "that Shakespeare himself might have held this very volume in his hands?"

"It's certainly possible," Desmond Duncan said. "It needs to be assessed by an expert. Look here: There are inky chicken scratches all the way through—very old, by the look of them. Someone has certainly marked it up."

Daffy's fingers, now no more than an inch from the book, pulled back suddenly as if she had been burned.

"I can't!" she said. "I simply can't!"

Father, who had been standing motionless, now reached mechanically for the book, his face as stiff as a chapel poker.

But Desmond Duncan was not finished.

"Having been party to the discovery, or at least the identification of such a great treasure, I should like to think of myself as having something of an edge when and if you decide to . . ."

The room fell silent as Father took the book from the actor's hands and slowly turned its pages. He riffled through the Quarto, as most people do with a book, from back to front. He had now arrived at the title page, which lay open in his hand.

"As I say, this modern defacement could be removed easily by an expert," Desmond Duncan went on. "I believe the British Library employs specialists in restoration who could erase these unfortunate blots without a trace. I'm quite sure that, when all's said and done, you'll be happy with the outcome."

Although Father's face did not betray it, he was staring at the monogram—his own initials and Harriet's intertwined.

Slowly, his forefinger moved across the surface of the paper, coming to rest at last on the red and black inked initials, carefully tracing them out afresh: Harriet's, and then his own, in the form of a cross.

As if by wireless, I was able to read the thoughts that

were flying through his mind. He was remembering the day—the very moment—that these initials had been inscribed, the red ink by Harriet, the black by himself.

Had they been written, perhaps, as the two of them were seated at a sunny casement window in summer? Or after taking breathless shelter in the greenhouse, while a sudden sun shower ran in unnoticed rivers down the outside of the glass, casting weak, watery shadows onto their young and wonder-filled faces?

Twenty years flashed like cloud shadows across Father's face, invisible to everyone but me.

And now he was thinking about Buckshaw. The Shakespeare Quarto, at auction, would bring in enough to pay off his debts and, with a bit of prudent investing, keep us in modest but comfortable circumstances for as long as was needed, with—God willing—even a few odd pounds left over to treat himself to the occasional block of Plate 1B Penny Blacks.

I could read it in his face.

He closed the book and looked round at us all, one by one . . . Daffy . . . Feely . . . the vicar . . . Dogger, who had just come into the room . . . Aunt Felicity . . . Nialla . . . and me, as if he might find written on our faces instructions on how to proceed.

And then, quite quietly, he said to none of us:

"How oft when men are at the point of death
Have they been merry! which their keepers call
A lightning before death. O, how may I
Call this a lightning? O my love! my wife!

Death, that hath suck'd the honey of thy breath,
Hath had no power yet upon thy beauty."

Daffy gasped audibly. Feely was as pale as death, her
lips parted, her eyes on Father's face. I recognized the
words at once as those Romeo had spoken at the tomb of
Juliet.

"*Thou art not conquered,*" Father went on, his voice becoming ever more hushed, the Quarto clutched tightly in
his hands.

"Beauty's ensign yet
Is crimson in thy lips and in thy cheeks,
And death's pale flag is not advancèd there."

He was speaking to Harriet!
His words, now barely audible, were scarcely more
than a whisper.

"Shall I believe
That unsubstantial Death is amorous,
And that the lean abhorrèd monster keeps
Thee here in dark to be his paramour?"

As if she were in the room . . .

"For fear of that I still will stay with thee
And never from this palace of dim night
Depart again."

And then he turned, and walked slowly out of the room, as if from a graveside.

My father is not a hugger, but I wanted to hug him. I wanted to run after him and throw my arms around him and hug him until the jam ran out.

But of course, I didn't. We de Luces do not gush.

And yet, perhaps, when they come to write the final history of this island race, there will be a chapter on all those glorious scenes that were played out only in British minds, rather than in the flesh, and if they do, Father and I will be there, if not hand in hand, then marching, at least, in the same parade.

·POSTLUDE·

EVERYONE HAD QUIETLY FOLLOWED Father from the drawing room. They had melted away as casually as the extras in a film after the big dance number, leaving me alone at last to stretch luxuriously on the sofa, close my eyes for a while, and plan for the future, which, for now, seemed likely to be given over to a course of steaming mustard plasters, buckets of cod-liver oil, and forced feedings of Mrs. Mullet's revolting invalid pudding.

The very thought of the stuff made my uvula cower behind my tonsils. The uvula is that little fleshy stalactite that dangles at the back of your throat, whose name, Dogger told me, comes from the Latin word for "grape."

How did he know these things? I wondered. Although there had been numerous occasions when Dogger's knowledge of the human body had come in handy, I had thought of it until just recently as being due to his age. Surely someone who has lived as long in the world as Dogger has, someone who has endured a prisoner-of-war camp, couldn't help but to have acquired a certain amount of practical information.

And yet there was more to it than that. I knew it instinctively and realized with a sudden shiver that part of me had known it all along.

"You've done this before, haven't you?" I had asked as we'd stood together over Phyllis Wyvern's body.

"Yes," Dogger had replied.

My mind was teeming. There were so very many things that needed thinking about.

Aunt Felicity, for instance. Her account of her wartime service, however scanty, had reminded me of Uncle Tar's correspondence with Winston Churchill, much of which still lay unexamined in a desk drawer in my laboratory. All of it was too early, of course, to have a direct bearing upon the matter. Uncle Tar had been dead for more than twenty years, but I had not forgotten that Aunt Felicity and Harriet had spent happy summers with him here at Buckshaw.

It was definitely worth another look.

And then there was Father Christmas. Had he, in spite of the mob, managed to make his way secretly into the house? Had he brought me the glass retorts and test tubes I had asked for—all the lovely flasks and funnels, the beakers and pipettes, packed in straw and nestled in together, crystal cheek almost touching crystal cheek? Were they already upstairs in my laboratory, gleaming in the winter light, awaiting only the touch of my hand to bring them to bubbling life?

Or was the old saint, after all, really no more than the cruel myth Daffy and Feely had made him out to be?

I surely hoped not.

Then suddenly there sprang to my mind a particular proof that starts with the letter *P*, and it wasn't potassium.

My thoughts were interrupted by the sound of laughter in the next room, and a moment later, Feely and Daffy came in, their arms full of gaily wrapped gifts.

"Father said it was all right," Daffy told me. "You were out cold for Christmas and we're both of us dying to see what Aunt Felicity gave you."

She let fall onto my legs a package wrapped in what looked suspiciously like Easter paper.

"Go ahead—open it."

My curiously weakened fingers picked at the ribbon, tearing the paper at the corner of the package.

"Give it here," Feely said. "You're so clumsy."

I had already felt through the paper that the package contained something soft, and had written it off. Everyone knows that truly great gifts are always hard to the touch, and I could tell, even without opening it, that Aunt Felicity's was a dud.

I handed it over without a word.

"Oh, look!" Feely said, with fake enthusiasm, tossing aside the paper. "A bed jacket!"

She held the silk monstrosity up to her chest as if she were modelling it. Cross-stitched all over in a padded diamond pattern, the thing looked like a cast-off life jacket from a Chinese junk.

"The jade will go nicely with your complexion," Daffy said. "Do you want to try it on?"

I turned my face towards the back of the sofa.

"This next one is from Father," Feely said. "Shall I open it?"

I reached out and took the small packet from her hands. The label read:

To: Flavia
From: Father
Merry Christmas.

There was a picture of a little robin redbreast in the snow.

The paper came away easily enough. Inside was a small book.

"What is it?" Daffy demanded.

"*Aniline Dyes in the Printing of the British Postage Stamp: A Chemical History*," I read aloud.

Dear old Father. I wanted to laugh and I wanted to cry.

I held the book out for Daffy to see, forcing myself to remember how excited I had been when I'd first read that the great Friedrich August Kekulé, one of the fathers of organic chemistry, had originally envisioned the tetravalent carbon atom while coming home from Clapham on top of a horse-drawn omnibus. The voice of the conductor calling out "Clapham Road!" had interrupted his train of thought, and he had forgotten his revelation until four years later.

Kekulé had been associated with printing inks, hadn't he? Hadn't his friend Hugo Müller been employed by De La Rue, the printers of British postage stamps?

I put the book aside. I would deal with my jumble of feelings later—when I was alone.

"This is from me," Feely said. "Open it next. Careful you don't break it."

I peeled the paper carefully from the flat, square package, knowing as soon as I touched it that it was a phonograph record.

As indeed it was: Toccata, by Pietro Domenico Paradis, from his Sonata in A, played by the superb Eileen Joyce.

To me, it was the greatest piece of music composed since Adam and Eve were camped out in Eden, a melody that bubbled and danced and skittered about like the happy atoms of sodium or magnesium when they are dropped into a beaker of hydrochloric acid.

Feely had occasionally played the Paradis Toccata at my request, but only when she wasn't angry, so I hadn't heard it very often.

"Th-thank you," I said, almost speechless, and I could tell that Feely was pleased.

"Mine next," Daffy said. "It isn't much, but then you don't deserve much."

Again a flat thin package, tied with string and a label: *To F. from D.*

It was a steel engraving, glued to a piece of cardboard, of an alchemist at work among his flasks and flagons, his beakers and retorts.

"I cut it out of a book at Foster's," Daffy said. "They'll never miss it. The only books they ever open are the Badminton Library. Hawking, fishing, and hunting and so forth."

"It's lovely," I said. "Beautiful. I'll ask Dogger to help me frame it."

"If they find it's gone missing," Daffy went on, "I'll tell them *you* nicked it. After all, what would *I* want with a stinky old alchemist."

I stuck out my tongue at her.

Next was a package from Mrs. Mullet.

Mittens.

"She said you're going to need them for your frostbitten fingers."

"Are my fingers frostbitten?" I asked, spreading them out at arm's length for examination. "They tingle a bit, but they don't look any different."

"Oh, just you wait," Feely said. "Another twenty-four hours and they'll begin to turn black, after which they'll fall off. You'll need to have hooks fitted, won't she, Daff? Five little hooks on each hand. Dr. Darby says you're lucky. They've improved hooks by leaps and bounds in the past few years, and you might even be able to—"

"Stop it!" I shrieked. My hands were trembling before my eyes.

My sisters exchanged a look whose meaning I had once known, but now, for the life of me, couldn't remember.

"Let's leave her alone," Daffy said. "She's not fit company when she's like this."

At the door they turned back, as if hinged together at their waists.

"Merry Christmas," they said in unison, and then they were gone.

I lay for a long time in silence, staring at the ceiling.

Was my life always to be like this? I wondered. Was it going to go, forever, in an instant, from sunshine to shadow? From pandemonium to loneliness? From fierce anger to a fiercer kind of love?

Something was missing. I was sure of it. Something was missing, but I couldn't for the life of me think what it was.

After a while, I let my legs slide heavily to the floor, then raised myself to a sitting position. Tiny fireworks exploded behind my eyes, the result of spending too many days in a horizontal position. I got shakily to my feet, clutching at the back of the sofa for unaccustomed support.

I stood for a moment, waiting for the faintness to pass; then, wrapping my housecoat tightly around myself and trying desperately to be quiet, I shuffled slowly to the door. If anyone knew I was creeping round the house there were bound to be stern lectures.

But the corridors were empty. The villagers and the film crew had gone.

The foyer rang with its usual dark-varnished silence. Buckshaw had returned to normal.

Coming from somewhere above, a solitary beam of

sunshine shone down upon the black-and-white checkerboard tiles, falling precisely along the black line painted so many years ago by Antony and William de Luce to divide Buckshaw into two armed camps.

How sad, I thought. Their hatred had outlived them.

I made my way up the east staircase, one slow step at a time. At the top I stopped to rest, perching for a while on the last step like a bird on a bough.

Only here at the top of the house did I feel myself removed, in a way, from the crushing burden of being a de Luce. Up here, above it all, I was somehow myself.

Simply Flavia.

Flavia Sabina de Luce. Full stop.

After a time, I pulled myself to my feet and made my way unsteadily towards my laboratory. It had been simply ages since I'd been away for so long from my *sanctum sanctorum*.

I took a deep breath ... opened the door ... and stepped inside, and the smile that spread across my face brought tears to my disbelieving eyes.

"Yaroo!" I shouted, and I didn't give a beetle's bottom who heard me.

"Ya-rooo!"

ACKNOWLEDGMENTS

AGAIN TO MY EDITORS, Bill Massey, of Orion Books in London, and Kate Miciak, of Random House in New York City. Bill and Kate have been joint—and fearsome—Keepers-of-the-Gate while I've been away in 1950. Words can never express my gratitude.

To Kristin Cochrane and Brad Martin, of Doubleday Canada, whose faith in Flavia has never wavered. Kristin has twice stood in for me to accept awards: the kind of debt that can never be repaid.

To my agent, Denise Bukowski, for being there, always prepared, every step of the way. And to Sandra Homer, Elizabeth De Francesca, and John Greenwell of the Bukowski Agency, for scaling the mountains of paperwork, all with good humor.

To my friends John and Janet Harland, for their comments and many valuable suggestions.

To Susan Corcoran, Sharon Propson, and Sharon Klein, of Random House, my peerless publicists, those superheroes of the publishing world who do all the heavy lifting.

To Randall Klein, of Random House, who wears so many hats—all of them perfectly fitted, and to my copy editor, Connie Munro.

To Urban Hofstetter, of Random House, Germany, for his editorship and friendship; to Inge Kunzelmann, who got us on and off trains and planes throughout all of Germany without ever losing her smile; and to Sebastian Rothfuss for his valuable assistance with a most convoluted research question.

To my two charming masters of ceremonies, Margarete von Schwarzkopf in Berlin, Hanover, Frankfurt, and Cologne, and Hendrik Werner in Hanover, who translated with great style and good humor, making me sound as if I knew what I was talking about in German.

To the remarkable Anna Thalbach. It was my great privilege to sit at Anna's side night after night as she brought Flavia to life before enraptured audiences.

To Axel Schumbrutzki, of the bookshop Hugendubel, and Florian Kröckel of Heimthafen Neukölln, who arranged a memorable evening in a vintage 1930s dance hall in East Berlin. Life is made of memories like this. Thank you, Axel and Florian.

To Klaus Eberitzsch of the bookshop Leuenhagen & Paris, in Hanover, who shares a birthday with me: same day, same year: We are now officially brothers. To Dirk Eberitzsch and Ina Albert, also of Leuenhagen & Paris. Ina and Klaus became the first booksellers ever to rush out into a busy street to hug me as I was still climbing out of a taxicab. Now I know why everyone loves Hanover!

To Mike Altwicker of the bookshop Hansen & Kröger, in Cologne, who not only organized, but got us to and from, a most memorable reading at Castle Bielstein.

To Camille Poshoglian, of Orion Books, master of international scheduling; and to Mike Vella De Fremeaux and Faye Bonnici, of Miller Distributors, Malta.

And finally, as always, with love, to my wife, Shirley, who has spent so many happy hours with me at Buckshaw.

ALAN BRADLEY WAS BORN in Toronto and grew up in Cobourg, Ontario. Prior to taking early retirement to write in 1994, he was director of television engineering at the University of Saskatchewan media center for twenty-five years. His versatility has earned him awards for his children's books, radio broadcasts of his short stories, and national print for his journalism. He also co-authored Ms. *Holmes of Baker Street*, to great acclaim and much controversy, followed by a poignant memoir, *The Shoebox Bible*. His first Flavia de Luce mystery, *The Sweetness at the Bottom of the Pie*, received the Crime Writers' Association Debut Dagger Award, the first Saskatchewan Writers Guild Award for Children's Literature, the Dilys Award, the Agatha Award, and both the Macavity and Barry awards for best first novel. Bradley lives in Malta with his wife and two calculating cats, and is currently working on the next Flavia de Luce mystery.